I Love You*

* Subject to the
following terms
and conditions

I Love You*

* Subject to the following terms and conditions

———— A CONTRACT KILLERS NOVEL ————

ERIN LYON

A TOM DOHERTY ASSOCIATES BOOK
NEW YORK

I LOVE YOU SUBJECT TO THE FOLLOWING TERMS AND CONDITIONS

Copyright © 2016 by Erin Lyon

A Forge Book
Published by Tom Doherty Associates
175 Fifth Avenue
New York, NY 10010

www.tor-forge.com

Forge® is a registered trademark of Macmillan Publishing Group, LLC.

The Library of Congress Cataloging-in-Publication Data is available upon request.

ISBN 978-0-7653-8610-6 (trade paperback)
ISBN 978-0-7653-8611-3 (e-book)

Our books may be purchased in bulk for promotional, educational, or business use. Please contact your local bookseller or the Macmillan Corporate and Premium Sales Department at 1-800-221-7945, extension 5442, or by e-mail at MacmillanSpecialMarkets@macmillan.com.

First Edition: January 2017

Printed in the United States of America

10 9 8 7 6 5 4 3 2 1

This is for you, Mom. Obviously.
You were supposed to be here for this.
I miss you every single day.

ACKNOWLEDGMENTS

This is my acknowledgment page. There are many like it, but this one is mine.

You're going to want to read this. You might be in here. You don't know.

I should probably start by thanking my ridiculously amazing husband, Steve, for all of the encouragement, unending support, and dinners you cooked because I was busy writing (although, it did give you a lot of uninterrupted PlayStation time—so let's not go overboard). Thanks for resisting the urge to smother me with a pillow for the last twenty years—that couldn't have been easy. You are my best friend and the hottest nerd I know.

Thank you to my wonderful sister-in-law Penny Lyon, my

friend Katie Copeland, and my mom, Paula, for your willingness to read anything I put in front of you over the years. It's meant so much having you on this journey with me.

Thanks to my truly awesome agent, Michelle Wolfson, for picking me out of the slush, helping me make my dream a reality, and for your glorious New York accent that makes me smile whenever I hear it.

Thanks to my wonderful editor, Whitney Ross, for knowing exactly what to cut, pointing out that I say "hmm" far too often, and, most of all, for the smiley faces in the margins. ☺ Thanks for making this book the best it could be. Also, a huge thank-you to Amy Stapp and all those brilliant and creative souls at Tor/Forge who did such awesome work with the book.

Thanks to my fabulous friends (in alphabetical order because they're cool, but I'm not crazy): Tonii Alejandrez, Katie Copeland, Katie Estes, Kat Kelly, Nina Raddatz, Nadia Sbeih, Sheryl Smentek, Dani Wilt, and Sidra Zumot for being the craziest, funniest, and loveliest bunch of bitches around. It is because of all of you that I can write true friendship and funny crap so easily. But, you all know damn well that 90 percent of the shit you say is far too risqué for me to include in the book, so thanks for the other 10 percent. Love you all.

Thanks to my mom and dad, Paula and Bob Lyon, for never being surprised when I succeeded and for never telling me to shut up when I'd ramble on incessantly about book ideas, agents, publishers, and possibilities.

Lastly, thanks to Steve, Penny, and my beautiful cousin,

Jennifer Hodder, for being the glue that held me together through a year that was the epitome of the *best of times and the worst of times*. You gave me the strength to keep chasing my dreams, even without my mom by my side.

And to you—yes *you*—the special person who did that amazing thing that time which made all the difference. Thank you. (See? I told you you might be in here.)

* Subject to the following terms and conditions

CHAPTER *1*

What am I doing? Rhetorical question. I know *what* I'm doing. This just isn't where I thought I would be at thirty-four. No, not this bar. Starting over with a brand new career. I had a job (emphasis on "had"). Not a great job, but a good job. And I suddenly decided I needed law school. No one *needs* law school, by the way. Now I'm thirty-four, out of law school; I've passed the bar exam, but am unemployed. With a capital U. I'm too old for this shit.

Yes, I'm signed, thank god, but one's love life is only part of one's life, right? So after finishing law school with a bunch of snot-nosed twenty-five-year-olds (no offense), I'm starting over. Starting over sucks, FYI.

So the seeming failure of my ill-conceived master plan led me to a bar on a Wednesday night (not like it's a work night for me) to commiserate with my BFF, Logek. Yes, that is her real name.

"Seriously. It'll work out. You're brilliant. You're talented. Fuck 'em," Logek said.

And this is why I go out with Logek when I'm down. She always has the right words, in the right order. Unfortunately, her usual pick-me-up wasn't enough to get my eyes up from the bar.

"I know," I said. My voice was muffled since my head was resting on my forearms on the bar. "I know."

And she knew what was coming next.

I picked myself up from the bar. "But, I just wish I'd gotten a 'We'd love you to apply again when you have more experience' or even a 'We think you're an idiot.' That at least might have been helpful. But after months of interning there for free to just get a 'We went with a different candidate'? No explanation. Nothing."

Logek gave me a frustrated face. She's been talking me off this particular ledge for a week now. "Kate. What do you hate more than anything?"

"Hypocrites."

"Oh, right. But what do you hate almost as much?"

"People who feel sorry for themselves."

She raised her eyebrow. I let out a loud sigh and gave myself a physical shake.

"Kate," she said. "You worked your ass off for them—for free—for six months feeling sure you'd get the job. Then they say, 'Thanks but no thanks'? I'd say they weren't the right fit for you if that's how they treat their interns. Give it a couple months. You'll probably realize it was for the best."

Logek hugged me and put my drink in my hand. "To bigger and better things," she said emphatically.

I nodded, took a swig of my drink, and straightened my shoulders.

"So," Logek said, a little louder than necessary. "How's Jonathan?"

I smiled. "He's good," I said. "He's been a doll through all this, of course. 'Their loss, better things to come . . .' All support, all the time."

Logek pushed her heavy, blonde hair back over her shoulder. There must be a man around. "Some things matter more than others. Screw the idiots at the DA's office. If they aren't smart enough to want you, it only means that someone better will. And, in the meantime, you've got a gorgeous man who loves you and thinks you're brilliant." She finished with an overly bright smile, busting out her halogen-white teeth and her dimple. Yep. Definitely a man around.

Right on cue, a predictably attractive man strolled up behind Logek, pretending to order a drink. He was good-looking, but not my type of good-looking—a little too pretty. And he knows it. I hate that. But, Logek is a different animal and maybe he's just her type. Best of luck, Pretty Boy.

Logek is my best friend. We've been friends since high school. She has signed five times and never had a single one go to term. Not me. When I fall in love and sign, I mean it for the entire seven years. I'm traditional that way. Of course, she always intends it when she signs, too; it just never works out that way. I guess, like the rest of us, she's a romantic at heart. Every time she signs, she wants to believe it's the person she will re-up with for life.

Pretty Boy paid for Logek's drink and tried to charm her pants off. From the look she gave me, her pants are securely in place, but at least the drink was free. I smiled. Being with her does make me forget about my barely-on-life-support career. Which is her ultimate goal. Which is why she's the BFF.

But because she's signed five times and breached four times (one time the guy actually breached, if you can imagine that) she is perpetually low on cash and is always happy to accept a free drink. What do you expect when you are paying on four failed contracts? Moral of the story: sign well, or, at the very least, only breach when you've got nothing to lose.

"So, really?" the guy asked. I know where this is going.

"Yes, really," Logek said, with a gloriously fake smile on her face. "It's pronounced 'logic,' but it's spelled L-O-G-E-K. Mom was a little heavy on the painkillers and Dad was off getting coffee." Logek and I have told this story *thousands* of times. Her name is the ultimate icebreaker.

The guy looked appropriately dazzled. Naturally. Men are simple. All it takes is long, blonde hair and a name no one else can pronounce and they're asking you for a pen. The stereotype about women always trying to get men to sign is usually debunked around Logek. Even when she has no interest, men want to get a pen in her hand.

I watched her big, blue eyes do their damage to a guy that, let's be real, was no match for her.

So while Logek is paying off her two remaining breaches of contract, I'm about to let my contract go into automatic renewal. These seven years have flown by. Jonathan is every bit as sexy, funny, and sweet as he was when we signed. The contract is up in a couple of weeks, but, like most contracts, it has an automatic renewal clause. If neither of us contacts the attorney to notify of cancellation, it automatically renews for another seven years. So many contracts don't renew and it seems like just as many don't even go to term, so I'm a lucky girl.

With Logek and Pretty Boy engaged in conversation a couple feet away from me, I sipped my drink and casually (at least I was shooting for casually) glanced around the room in case I knew anyone here. Nope. Nice to know my luck hasn't changed that much.

From the rim of my glass, I noticed someone watching me. Why is he looking at me? I'm wearing my token. I looked down at my necklace—a gold feather quill with a diamond at the tip. He knows I'm taken—it's not as though I intentionally left it at home.

He walked over and stood in front of me with his back to Logek (which is hardly ever the case, I might add). I had to do the quick math (sad, I know)—if I'm five foot nine and I'm wearing three-inch heels and he's at least three inches taller than me . . . screw it. I can't do math sober—now it's pointless. Whatever, he's tall. He's got dark, dark hair and light eyes. We were in a bar so I couldn't vouch for the eye color—either green, gray, or hazel, though. Big eyes. Perfect lips. Holy shit. He's beautiful.

He held out his hand. Big hand, long fingers, tan. Gasp. I shook his hand, politely, because that's what you would do when any man offers to shake your hand. Regardless of his movie-star quality.

"I'm Adam," he said in a deep voice. Figures. He does kinda make you think of original sin.

"Kate Shaw," I said, trying to sound casual.

"Kate. I love that name." I'm sure you do, incredibly hot guy, who is inexplicably hitting on me.

"Thank you," I said, turning back toward the bar. Score one for Kate.

"What do you do?" he asked, seeming genuinely interested. He's good.

"I'm an out-of-work attorney," I told him, with a quick nod and an ironic smile. "You?"

"Oh . . . sorry," he said, cringing slightly, acknowledging that he just stepped in it. "I'm in marketing."

Of course he is. It's pretty much the vortex that sucks up young, attractive men, giving them no actual job definition other than "marketing." Translated as: I'm good at selling shit to people that don't need it because I'm (incredibly) good-looking. Oh, Adam. I am so onto your game.

I cocked an eyebrow at him. "Really? Just marketing? That encompasses anything from being a sign spinner to being an advertising executive."

He smiled. "I'm not a sign spinner," he said. Shit. He has a dimple. Whatever. Jonathan is six feet, gorgeous; has dark Latino skin, black hair, dark eyes. Hot. All that on top of him being the love of my life. Like this guy is going to sway me.

"Good," I said, playing with the token on my necklace. "Too much sun is bad for you."

He laughed. At my stupid joke. I narrowed my eyes at him, looking, I'm sure, bitchier than I intended.

"What?" he asked, eyebrows raised.

"Nothing," I said, looking over at Logek who, unfortunately, was engrossed in Pretty Boy. Shameful.

Adam frowned at me. "You're a beautiful girl. Why am I a dirtbag for noticing?"

Difficult question to answer. "You're not. But it's obvious that I'm signed. Maybe you should run along and find an *available* playmate."

"I'm aware that you're signed." He frowned. "Does that mean you aren't allowed to talk to a man?"

"No. I just like to be clear from the get-go. I mean, this *is* a bar. I've heard that, on occasion, single people actually try to meet in places like this."

He laughed. "I've heard that as well. But I *know* that you're not single. So can we move on?"

Hmm. "Sure."

"So, what were we talking about?"

"We were just discussing what you do for a living."

"I'm in advertising with Samson and Tule."

Oh. They're good. Even I have heard of them.

"So, Kate, what types of law are you interested in?"

"Right now, I'm interested in the kind that makes me employed. Well. Except signing law."

He chuckled. "Not interested in signing law? That certainly would be an easy meal ticket at least. Suckers sign every day. And then breach the very next day. Steady employment."

I smiled. "Most signing firms deal strictly with breaches. Spending my days with bitter, angry couples trying to deconstruct their contracts does not sound fun. Too emotional. Add in the child custody battles and the thought makes me cringe. Everything is sunshine and roses when people sign, so they aren't practical about covering themselves."

He nodded. "Yeah. People sign when everything's great. And then one year later, everything is shit and they don't understand why their contract doesn't cover it."

"Exactly."

"But that wasn't the case with you?"

"No. We did a practical contract with the typical re-up terms. No blinders there."

He nodded as though he was thinking over what I said. "I sort of bailed on a buddy over there," he said, gesturing to the other side of the bar. "I should let him know where I am in case he's looking for me," he said. "You'll still be here?" he asked, pointing at the bar in front of me.

I nodded.

He poked his long finger against the polished bar. "Still here, right?"

I couldn't help but smile. I nodded again.

I watched him walk away, broad shoulders, tall frame, and all. Good lord.

Now Logek turned back to me, ignoring the guy in front of her like she had been listening, waiting, for Adam to leave.

"Kate!" she hissed.

"Logek!" I said, sarcastically matching her level of excitement. No idea where it was coming from.

"You know who that was, right?"

"Adam?" I had a feeling there was more.

"I'm pretty sure that was Adam Lucas."

"And?"

"You've heard us talk about those guys before."

"I have?"

She gave an exaggerated sigh. "Yes. He's a *contract killer*."

Oh. I knew I should know that term. I know I'd heard it mentioned, but I couldn't recall the meaning.

"He's one of those guys that only goes after signed women."

"Really?"

"Yep. They're notorious."

"Why is that?"

"Why are they notorious or why do they only go after signed women?"

"The signed women thing."

"I don't know," she said, reaching for her cocktail that was sitting on a napkin on the bar. She picked up her glass, holding the napkin against the bottom. I was never sure why people did that. "Maybe because they're more of a challenge. Maybe because they only want women who aren't looking to sign a guy." She clearly thought the second option was the more likely possibility. It probably was.

Wow. A contract killer. After me. Insulting and exciting at the same time.

"Well, I guess that makes sense," I said, momentarily slipping back into my sour mood. "An incredibly gorgeous guy comes over to talk to *me*, not *you*. I should have figured there was a reason."

"Kate! Shit! You are beautiful! And smart! And a pain in the ass!" With that she gave a frustrated growl and turned to the guy that was still waiting for her attention to turn back to him. "Bill," she said.

"It's Ben."

"Ben, this is Kate. Is she gorgeous?"

Perfect. Thank you, Logek. This is the cherry on the top of my sundae.

Ben looked at me as though he hadn't realized I was there before and I had magically appeared. He looked into my face for a minute before smiling.

"Yes, she is."

"See," Logek said, turning to me with eyebrows raised. As though *Ben's* validation was what was going to save me from a lifetime of insecurity. I rolled my eyes and she turned to the bartender and pointed to my empty glass. The bartender nodded.

"Enough," I said. "Talk to Ben." She frowned at me and turned back to Ben who had waited most patiently.

The bartender took my empty glass and handed me another gin and tonic. I wasn't sure that I should have this fourth drink. Usually three is entirely ample to buzz my tower. But screw it. Tonight was the night for it. Jonathan was working late and, anyway, he deserved a break from me crying on his shoulder.

"Good girl," said a low voice behind me.

I spun around and sure enough, there was Adam. Back just like he said he'd be.

"Good girl?" I asked.

"You are still here."

"Do I get a dog treat? Or a scratch behind the ear or something?" I probably didn't need any more to drink.

He just looked at me with the slightest smile. He leaned down to me, since he was tall enough to need to, and got close to my face. Too close. Close enough to tighten things in me.

"Do you want a scratch behind the ear, Kate?" he said, lifting his hand to my ear, brushing it gently with his forefinger. Well, I guess it was his forefinger—I don't have eyes in the side of my head. It did, however, elicit an unexpected shudder from me.

"I'm good," I said, pushing away his hand.

He laughed. "Okay, Kate. So you're an unemployed attorney. What's the plan?"

I was tempted to tell him it was none of his business. Or that I didn't want to talk about it. But three and a half cocktails in, you bet your ass I wanted to talk about it. "I've recently been operating under the assumption that I would get a job that I, in fact, did not get." Shit. Was I slurring? "So, I'm sort of regrouping." Bullshit. "Actually, starting from scratch."

"That sucks."

"What sucks more is that I *really* wanted that job."

"Ouch."

Uh-oh. Tears. Close to the surface. I was not going to cry. Not going to. Dammit. A traitorous tear ran down my cheek. Son of a bitch.

He brushed his thumb across my cheek, wiping away the tear before I had a chance to. "I'm sorry, Kate. I get how disappointing that must be."

I shrugged and took another drink of my cocktail.

"So," he went on. "What have you been applying for?"

"Anything. Everything that is looking for a new attorney—

which, by the way, most are not. What the hell was I thinking? I'm thirty-four and a brand new attorney. Why in the world did I do this?"

"Because it was a personal goal?"

I laughed and shook my head. "I mean, I'd thought about it, but really did it because I wasn't happy where I was and couldn't find anything else."

"And where were you?"

"TV." He looked at me, assessing. I was used to this. "Not in front of the camera," I offered. "Behind. Sales, programming. Funny thing is—TV doesn't translate to other fields. So I'd basically painted myself into a corner. Career-wise."

Adam just nodded. Why was he even listening to all this? Oh, right—because I'm a signed woman and he's a contract killer. I can't even get hit on right.

"You know," he said, pulling out his cell phone. "I'm a member of the Chamber of Commerce and they just sent out something about a new job site they were launching. I didn't really look at it, but it might be useful. Here," he said, without looking up from his phone. "Give me your number and I'll text you the link."

Give him my number. That seems imprudent. But my fourth gin and tonic was assuring me that it was for a completely legitimate, nonpromiscuous reason so I rattled off my cell phone number to him and he typed away on his phone.

"There you go," he said, slipping his phone back into his pocket. "Maybe it'll have some good leads on it."

"Thanks."

He nodded, smiling seductively. Or just smiling. With this guy, who could tell?

"So." Subtlety was not in my vocab right now. "I hear you're a *contract killer*."

He laughed, but also nodded ever so slightly, clearly not denying the accusation.

"So you admit it then?"

"Why should I deny it? Although I do find the term amusing."

"Why?"

"Why do I feel no need to deny it or why am I amused by the term?"

Why does everyone do that to me? "Why *are* you?"

"Why am I what, Kate?" Why does he keep calling me Kate? Because that's your name, dumbass. It's just that people rarely call you by your name. Like that first time, sure, when you're being introduced, but after that, no. Even Jonathan—I get "baby," "sweetheart," "beautiful," but hardly ever Kate. It's sort of a thing for me when people use my name—when I hear it, it electrifies me a little, feeling oddly intimate.

"Only after taken women."

"Hmm." He leaned down close to me again. Too close again. "I don't see the need to sign a contract with a woman to be with her."

"You don't have to sign. Lots of people date and never sign."

"But women can't help it. They ultimately want that. They are raised believing that relationships involve a piece of paper. The fairy tales teach little girls that a happy ending only comes when Prince Charming asks you to sign a contract to be his and his alone. I'm not saying there aren't men with the same ingrained ideals—but I do think all women fall victim to it in one way or another."

"Not all."

"You didn't?"

Hmm. Tell the truth or not? The gin said to tell the truth. "I did. What can I say? My parents have been re-upping since I was born. What about yours?"

I wasn't sure he'd answer. So far this had been the "Kate Show" as far as sharing personal information went. "No. They were one and done."

"Do you think that changed the way you feel about it?"

"No," he said, smirking. "I think *logic* made me feel that way about it."

At the mention of her name (sort of) Logek turned around, eyebrows raised in question.

"Adam," I said, hand extended. "This is my friend, Logek."

"Oh," he said, smiling. He shook Logek's hand. "Interesting name."

"Isn't it, though?"

He smiled and nodded at her. And then turned back to me. Like she wasn't there.

"So it's illogical to want to commit to someone?" I said, falling back into our conversation.

"No. Not for some people."

"You don't really believe that, though."

"No," he said, with a secret smile. "I guess I don't. It just feels like a trap to me."

"What about children?" I was seeing the allure of the

contract killer already—I could ask these bold questions without being misconstrued. He knew I wasn't testing him out to see if he'd be white-picket-fence material.

"What about them?"

"It's kind of irresponsible to have them without being under contract."

"Is it?"

Hmm. I'd always thought so. I was wondering whether I was prepared to have this depth of conversation right now. "I think so."

"Why?"

"Because. It provides for their future. It doesn't leave their life to chance."

"Did it do that for you?"

I nodded.

He smiled. "I can't say it did that for me. I just think that there are plenty of people that will be good parents without a paper mandating it."

"I think you're the one being naïve now," I said.

He looked disconcerted. I don't think he had people challenge him often. Or maybe just women. I got the impression he wasn't used to having this much depth in his conversations, either.

"I don't mean to make you uncomfortable," I said. "I'm just saying that it's possible that because it didn't work for your parents, it shaped your views on it."

Something flickered through his eyes momentarily. Some sadness or longing. It was strange how much I could read from his subtle expressions.

He shrugged noncommittally. "I suppose anything is possible," he said, looking at me steadily. He glanced at his watch. "I've got to get going."

He leaned in again and gave me a peck on the cheek. "I'll see you again, Kate Shaw."

CHAPTER 2

Logek dropped me off and waited for me to get inside and wave her off. I went into my bedroom, doing only half of my nighttime regimen before falling into bed. I'm not gonna lie. The room was spinning a tad. It was 11:00 p.m. and Jonathan wasn't home.

I dialed his number. "Hey, baby," he said.

"Jonathan. It's late, honey. I was getting worried."

"Oh. Well, I knew you were out with Logek so I figured I'd take the time to get caught up on all this budget crap I have to get done so that I don't have to stay late at all tomorrow." He chuckled. "I didn't know you'd be home this early or I would have timed it better."

"Oh, really? Wanted to be home to catch me drunk?"

"Are you drunk?"

"Close enough."

"Well, in that case, I'll be home in ten minutes—five if I break all the speed limits."

I smiled into the phone. "See you soon, baby."

I think I fell asleep because the next thing I remember was Jonathan's warm, naked body sliding next to me in the bed. I smiled.

"Miss me?" he asked in my ear.

"Mm-hmm."

He slid his hand up to my breasts for a minute and then down between my legs. Yes, I missed him. We've been missing each other a lot lately.

I rubbed my back into his front and I heard him breathing heavy. He slipped his fingers into me and followed with the rest of him. I groaned when he was in. I felt good. I felt complete. After seven years of practice, I knew when to push, when to pull. He knew when I needed a little bit more. And he knew when I was right there.

No—I didn't fantasize about Adam at all. He didn't even cross my mind. For more than a second. Right when I came. But they say a little fantasizing is healthy for relationships, right? When it's harmless. And this definitely was.

*

The next day, Jonathan had left for work and I was sitting in my yoga pants, watching TV while on my laptop. I was checking for job postings twice a day, but there was nothing out there I hadn't already applied for. I clicked on the Chamber of

Commerce link Adam had sent me but it looked like the page hadn't gone live yet.

Jonathan and I had never been a single-income couple so it's not as though this was easy. I mean, Jonathan brought home a nice salary, but we'd always budgeted our lives on *both* our salaries. I needed a job. Now.

I felt certain that at some point I was going to have to apply for seasonal help at a department store or a waitressing job. But I had no waitressing experience. Irony. I'd managed to amass more than $100,000 in student loans and I wasn't qualified for a waitressing job. Let's hear it for higher education!

My phone chirped. I had a text from Logek: *How ya feeling, drunkie? Last night was fun—hope you're not too hungover.*

Hungover. I should be, but I'm not. I guess that's where all my luck went.

Not hungover even though I should be. Did you give Pretty Boy your number?

No he was boring. But the drinks were free :)

Thanks for taking me out

Not that it made you feel any better

It did . . . a little

Yeah yeah. What about Adam?

Adam. Shit. I probably should not have given him my cell number. Not even just so he could send me the job board link. I'm sure he won't call or text. And then, of course, since I had just thought it, I got a text from him. Oh, hell.

Kate—I enjoyed our talk last night. Can we do it again?

Shit. That's an emphatic no. I'm not the kind of woman that breaches—even a little. Maybe he'll think I gave him a wrong number. Like I should have. Instead I texted Logek.

I'm thinking of writing an article . . . inside the mind of a contract killer . . . like a serial killer, but more diabolical.

LOL. I dunno . . . I was kinda wishing I was wearing a token last night just so he'd pay attention to me. SO hot.

So cynical and damaged . . . and hot ;)

I stared at my phone and figured "What the hell?" I texted Adam back. *Busy looking for a job. Nice meeting you though.*

I can help.

How?

Suggestions?

Adam—I don't have time to mess around—I really need to find a job.

I get it—really. Let's meet for coffee and we'll work together.

Say no. Say no. But . . . a job would be good. *Ok. But JUST coffee and job hunting. NO contract killing.*

Lol. Just coffee. Peet's? On 7th? 12:30?

Yes, yes, and yes. See you then.

I may be having a slight nervous breakdown. But I need a job. At least I told him it was strictly platonic.

I went into the bathroom and looked in the mirror. Yep. The vision of perfection I'd expected. I had circles under my eyes from too much alcohol and not enough sleep. The up-side of the dark circles, however, was that my light blue eyes looked freakishly light in contrast. See? Who says I'm not a glass-half-full girl?

I did the makeup thing (extra concealer) and put some

soft curls in my shoulder-length, dark brown hair. Hmm . . . clothes. You're signed, girl—act like it. I slipped into my comfy jeans, my Converse, and, for irony, I threw on my law school sweatshirt. There. I was the epitome of not trying too hard. Score a point for Kate.

I put on my token necklace and decided to wear my token watch, too, for good measure. If I was going to meet a gorgeous, single man for coffee, I was going to look like the poster child for "off the market." All safe and harmless. I must really believe that because I only had the tiniest twinge of guilt.

I grabbed my laptop and headed out.

I got to the coffee shop with butterflies in my stomach. I stepped inside and scanned across the room. I spotted him and he was watching me, looking amused.

When I got to his table, he stood and waited for me to sit.

"Kate."

"Adam."

"How are you feeling? Hungover?"

"Not really. Guess I dodged a bullet there because I'm pretty sure I did what I could to earn one."

He smiled, but didn't say anything. Holy shit, he was pretty. I thought maybe it was the booze. Nope. And the eyes? Green. Really freaking green.

"So . . ." I said, as my brilliant lead-in.

He nodded. "So, tell me where you're at."

Okay, this works. Down to business. Guess my outfit was doing its job.

"I go onto the school job board a couple of times a day, follow the standard job sites, and go through the newspaper want ads. I apply for everything whether it sounds like something I'd want to do or not. I keep a list of all of the firms I've applied to and when so that if I get a call I can at least pretend to be interested in their kind of law." I set my pad of paper in front of him.

He scanned down the first page, then the next, and by the time he flipped to the third page, he raised his eyebrows and looked at me. "Well, it isn't for lack of trying, that's for sure."

I smiled and nodded. I'll take that as a compliment.

"Only attorney jobs?"

I nodded.

"So, I get you're frustrated, but do you *want* a job, or do you *need* one?"

"Need one," I responded with a sigh.

"Well, we have an opening at Samson and Tule if you want it. It's just administrative, but it would start right away. It won't pay a ton, but it might tide you over."

I stared at him. "You don't even know me, Adam. For all you know I could be a total moron."

"You aren't a total moron, Kate."

"And you know this how?"

He leaned in toward me. "I'm in the business of reading people."

I tried not to back away when he leaned in. I didn't want to look like he scared me. Even if he did. "You are doing the hiring?"

For the first time he actually looked smug. "I can."

I grunted or growled or some combination of the two. "What does that even mean? Is this *your* assistant? Are you in management? Would this be reporting to you?" Pause.

Breathe. "It's not that I'm not grateful for the offer—I am. It's just so out of left field. *You* are out of left field."

Smug Adam was gone and he was back to looking amused with me. Well, I guess there are worse things. He reached out and covered my hand where it rested on the table between us. "This is legitimate, Kate. I would never screw around about something important. You need a job—I just happen to be able to help. Just good timing."

I slid my hand out from under his and put it in my lap. He held his hand up and mouthed the word "sorry."

Jesus, Kate. This is so great in a really, really messed up way. "Details?"

He smiled as though he'd been following my internal dialogue. "It's in my department, but it doesn't report to me. I'm an executive, but I don't do hiring. I mentioned to my boss this morning that I met a really bright just-out-of-school lawyer who might be available to jump in and cover for us until she lands an attorney gig. He said to get you if I could. I told him I would."

And things were so promising up until the *get you if I could* double entendre. I raised an eyebrow and he chuckled. Damn. It was like that chuckle vibrated in my chest instead of his. But the job doesn't report to him. It could work.

My phone vibrated in the kangaroo pocket of my sweatshirt. I pulled it out and checked the screen. Text from Jonathan.

Hey, angel. Lunch today?

Sorry, love, can't—I'm busy working my way between a rock and a . . . oh for god's sake.

I'm at Peet's job hunting.

I can meet you there.

"Adam?"

He waited, expectantly.

"This job offer . . . what sort of strings are we talking about?"

He frowned. "No strings, Kate. Jesus. I'm not a total dickhead."

Oh. Oops. "I'm sorry."

He propped his elbows on the table and interlaced his fingers and watched me. Just watched me. He was annoyed. Playtime was over. I'd struck a nerve.

"Easy, tiger," I said. "Put away the claws."

Now he shrugged as though he didn't know what I was referring to. "I'm not upset," he said, with a lukewarm smile.

"Yes, you are. It's oozing out of every pore."

Now he looked uncertain.

"What?" I asked. "Does that usually fool people?"

"Fool people?"

"Casual Adam that never gets his feathers ruffled." Good, Kate. Let's see how uncomfortable we can make him. That's always a surefire way to land a job.

He leaned in again, getting way into my personal space. These coffee shop tables weren't much bigger than an end table, so he didn't have much in his way. "Yes, Kate. Casual Adam usually fools them. But apparently not you."

"Kate?"

Jonathan's voice. And I came out of my freaking skin. Thankfully I hadn't gotten any coffee because I jumped up so fast that the table rocked back and forth. Perfect. Let's be sure to look as guilty as possible. Nailed it.

I turned and faced Jonathan. He was grinning so we must not have looked too incriminating. Small victories. He was in khakis and a polo shirt. And he looked good. Really good. Even Adam Lucas wasn't going to make Jonathan pale in comparison, thank you very much. I gave him a tight squeeze and soft kiss, before turning back to Adam.

"Adam, this is my partner, Jonathan. Jonathan, I met Adam at de Vere's last night when I was out with Logek. He was nice enough to offer to help with the job search thing."

Adam stood and offered his hand. "Good to meet you."

"You, too," Jonathan said, all easygoing and friendly. He looked at me, taking my hand. "So how goes it?"

"Funny you should ask—I think my new friend Adam here is hooking me up with a job. A temporary one anyway."

I turned to Adam and there was something sort of intimate in the way he was looking at me—like unspoken communication that two people who just met should not have. It made me feel like he was reading my thoughts.

Adam turned to Jonathan. "I'm in advertising with Samson and Tule and we need some administrative help. They fired one of the clerks a couple of days ago and we are buried. We need someone who can proof copy, draft correspondence, stuff like that. Needless to say a law school grad looking for a job is a perfect fit for us, even if we'll only have her till she finds an attorney position."

"Wow," Jonathan said. "That's great. And you're right— Kate will be a perfect fit."

Adam nodded in agreement. "So, it's hers if she wants it. She can start Monday."

"That's great, babe." Jonathan hugged me tightly. "I'm

going to go order a sandwich. Do you want anything?" He pointed at me, then at Adam. We both shook our heads so he headed up to the counter to order.

Adam stood, staring at me. He was relaxed again—the intensity of our earlier moment had passed. "Well, Kate Shaw. It looks like I'll be seeing you Monday."

"Yes. I really appreciate this, Adam."

"Just give your name at the front desk when you get there in the morning and they'll get you where you need to go."

I nodded. "Looking forward to it," I said.

He rested his hand against my upper arm. "I have to get back to the office."

"Okay. Thanks for coming."

"Wouldn't have missed it," he said quietly.

He let his hand slide down the length of my arm as he walked past me. "Very nice to meet you, Jonathan," Adam called out, as he headed for the door.

"Likewise."

Jonathan gathered his sandwich and coffee from the counter and set them on the table before dragging me into his arms again and lifting me off the ground.

"That is so awesome, baby!"

I grinned.

"Thank god you went out and got drunk on a week-night."

I laughed. "The silver lining of depression."

"Seriously. You get to work at a good company who already knows you are only there until you find an attorney job, so you won't even have to feel bad about leaving. What an amazing find."

"I know. Right place at the right time." Right contract killer gunning for you.

Jonathan sat down and wolfed down his sandwich.

"So, that didn't bother you, right?" I asked, as he ate.

"What? You being here with a guy? Or here with a guy that looked like a taller, darker, better-looking Brad Pitt?"

"Yeah."

"It might if I didn't know you were so sprung on me." And he winked before giving me the full benefit of his uber-white smile. He's right. I am whipped. Adam may be beautiful and get me a little tingly, but Jonathan is my world.

＊

"Wait, wait, wait. Wait."

Logek was more than a little surprised by news of my new job, and she got a little loud, causing me to pull the phone away from my ear a bit.

"Samson and Tule."

"Don't be cute," she said. "It isn't the employer so much as the coworker."

"Logek," I said, using my exasperated voice. "I told you. It doesn't report to him or anything. Not to mention that I'll be some kind of clerk or something. He's an advertising executive. I suspect there won't be a ton of mingling."

"Holy shit."

"Jonathan met him."

"Met him?"

"Yeah. I met Adam at Peet's today because he offered to help with the job hunt. Then Jonathan texted asking about

meeting for lunch and I told him where I was. Like any de-
voted, well-behaved, guilt-free partner would."

Silence.

"Logek?"

"Sorry, I'm here. Just picturing this meeting. Hmm. Does
make a nice picture. Maybe you should try to wrangle a
three-way . . ."

"Way ahead of you. It's on for tonight. I'll have it on
YouTube in the morning."

She laughed. "Okay, okay. Good for you, doll. I'm glad
this will take the pressure off while you find the right job."

"Thank you."

"You really aren't worried about seeing Adam every day?
If I was signed, I'd be worried about seeing him every day."

"Come on. You know I'm madly in love with Jonathan.
You really think I could be swayed by some gorgeous guy
who only wants to screw me because he knows I'm already
signed?"

"Well, when you put it that way, never mind."

"Exactly."

"What are you going to wear?"

"I don't know. I feel like a suit might come off a little
above my station."

"Your *station*? What is this? *Pride and Prejudice*?"

"You know what I mean. I'm a clerk. I want to fit in with
the other clerks, not show up like I'm trying to remind the
other clerks that I'm actually an attorney. I thought everyone liked me at the DA's office, but I still got passed over for
the job, so they must not have liked me *that* much. I just
want them to like me here."

"They'll love you. I wonder . . ."

"What?"

"Just . . . I wonder if the women at the office will know that Adam brought you on."

I groaned. "It crossed my mind, too. It would suck to have everyone assume the moment I arrive that I'm sleeping with Adam."

"And cheating on your partner to do it."

"And probably slept with Adam to get the job."

"And that you are planning on sleeping your way to the top."

"And that I make fur coats out of puppies."

"Pariah."

"Indeed. Well, maybe it's time I embrace my villainess role."

"Amen," Logek said, laughing. "Wear something tight and fuel that rumor mill."

"I'm thinking it won't need much fuel. Let's not forget— you knew who he was by reputation. Can't wait to see what people who actually know him have to say about him."

"Hmm. I expect to hear all about it."

"Promise."

CHAPTER *3*

Samson & Tule was nestled in the prime real estate of Capitol Mall. The building was green-mirrored glass, thirty stories or so, and S & T comprised the top five floors. From the lobby, I got into the elevator with a dozen other people. The button for 25 was already illuminated.

I tried to hide in the back without looking like I was hiding in the back. I'd dressed in a pencil skirt (not too short, not too tight) and a simple blouse. Professional. Hopefully nothing that would paint a bull's-eye on my back. I was keeping my expectations low this time, operating under the assumption that they are going to hate me and start vicious rumors about me. It certainly takes the pressure off.

At the front desk, Marley, according to her nameplate, held a finger out to me as she answered the phone. She was twentysomething, pretty, with kind of wild hair that looked strategically windblown.

"Samson and Tule. How can I direct your call?" she asked in a silky voice. "One moment, please." She pushed some buttons, hung up the phone, and turned back to me, smiling.

"Kate Shaw?"

I widened my eyes and gave my best friendly, warm, nonpretentious, who-li'l-old-me? smile. Guess I lied about that low expectations thing. These assholes were going to like me if it killed me.

Marley reached over the desk and shook my hand.

"So nice to meet you," I said. "Not sure where I'm supposed to be headed."

"Don't you worry. Alice, our HR manager, is on her way down to collect you."

Just as I was taking a seat in one of the leather chairs in the lobby, Alice appeared, looking exceptionally crisp, yet vintage and, thankfully, friendly.

"Kate?"

"Yes," I said, standing and extending my hand.

She had a firm handshake, authoritative, confident. They say a person's handshake says a lot about them. I always try to make mine nondescript—not too firm, but not limp. I'd hate to tip my hand too early.

Alice chattered all the way to her office, with me trying to keep up with her quick pace. She introduced me to every person we passed. So far I remember Marley from the front desk. And Alice.

We stopped in front of a plain, fortysomething woman who seemed frazzled. Perfect. Pass me off to the woman who doesn't have time for me. That'll get me into her good graces.

"Kate, this is Marnie." Sweet. Marnie and Marley. I think I'll actually remember her name.

"Marnie is going to give you the crash course and get you started."

"Great," I said.

Marnie seemed nice enough as she gave me the tour of our floor along with more names I'd never remember. She showed me to my desk and got my computer login set up for me.

"So, basically we back up the ad execs. We proof a lot of copy, type and edit correspondence, prepare client presentations, and other general clerical stuff. Do you have experience in advertising?"

Shit. "Actually, no."

"Oh," she said with a head tilt, looking like she wanted to ask how I got the job, but didn't know if it would be rude. "So how did you end up here?" Guess rude won over.

"I happened to meet someone who worked here and I'd been looking for a job and I guess you guys were shorthanded . . ."

Please leave it at that. Please, please, please.

"Oh. Who?"

Figures. "Adam Lucas?"

"Oh, Adam," she said, grinning. I couldn't place that grin at all. There definitely seemed to be some judgment in it, but who's to say—I can be kind of paranoid sometimes.

"Well, we are shorthanded, that's for sure," she continued. Yes. Moving on.

"I really appreciate the opportunity. And I learn quickly," I said.

"Oh, I'm sure you'll catch on fast."

Two hours later I was sitting at *my* new desk with a stack of copy to proof, dictation to type, and presentations to prep. Sink or swim time.

My phone buzzed with a text from Jonathan.

Hope your first day is going great, sweetie. Knock 'em dead.

Thanks, babe. So far, so good. Everyone is nice and they're keeping me busy.

See you tonight ;)

<3

The afternoon flew by and five o'clock was here before I knew it. Well, it definitely could be worse.

"So? How was your first day?" Marnie was standing behind me.

"Great," I said sincerely. "I love staying busy and you guys have plenty to do."

"Yeah—thank goodness you're here."

Thank goodness I'm here? I like that sentiment.

"See you tomorrow," she said, and headed for the elevator.

I shut down my computer and gathered my stuff and followed the flow of people to the elevator. I got some random smiles from people I'd been introduced to whose names I'd promptly forgotten.

"So how was your first day?" a girl asked. She was young and bubbly and I think her name was something stripperish. Candy? Sadie?

---

* Subject to the following terms and conditions

"It was great, thank you. I'm sorry—I got so many names today. Tell me your name again?"

"Paris." Okay, funky, but not stripper. I wonder who the stripper was?

"Right," I said smiling. I touched my chest. "Kate."

"I remember. I only had to learn one name today."

I laughed.

I hadn't seen him standing in the back of the elevator, but Adam stepped through a few people and stood in front of me. He was in black slacks and a black crew-neck sweater that was surely cashmere. And it fit him perfectly—loose but fitted just enough to see the shape of his pecs through it. I have a thing for pecs. Down girl.

Adam just stood there, smiling at me. I was afraid to look around to the others in the elevator. Isn't this how rumors get started?

"How are you?" he asked.

"Very well. You?"

He smiled like I said something funny. "Very well. How was your first day?"

Now I did look at Paris. I knew she was standing right next to me and it felt more natural to include her in the conversation. Otherwise it felt a little too personal. And suspicious.

"It was great." My tagline for the day. Paris seemed happy to be included in the conversation and I don't think it was my imagination that she couldn't take her eyes off of Adam.

"Good. How are you, Paris?" She looked like she was blushing because he was talking to her. I wonder if she's slept with him? Oh—probably not. She's single.

"Good," she said in a high voice. "What's new on twenty-seven?"

"Nothing interesting. What's new on twenty-five? Aside from Ms. Shaw, of course."

Okay. That felt flirty. I laughed a little, wanting to deflect any attention. Didn't seem to work, though, because Paris was definitely eyeing me a little more closely.

"Just Kate," Paris said.

And thankfully the elevator ride was over. I said a hasty good-bye and headed for the door. I was out of the lobby and almost around the corner of the building, heading toward the parking garage, when I heard my name.

I stopped, because it would be rude not to, and waited for Adam to catch up with me. He did this graceful, two-stride, jog thing with his long legs and was standing in front of me again.

"Are you running away from me?" he asked, his hands tucked in his pockets. The sun was in his eyes and he was squinting a little. He even made squinting look good.

"Now why would I do that, Adam?"

"I don't know, Kate. That's why I asked."

"I really appreciate you getting me this job. But, I'm a little worried about what the others will think if they find out that you got me the job. You know—you being . . . you."

"Who cares what they think?"

"I do. I'd rather not have my coworkers think I'm a tramp that slept with you to get a job."

"But now you already have the job, so obviously when you sleep with me it won't be for that."

Holy shit. My mouth hung open. I couldn't even do a

* Subject to the following terms and conditions

sarcastic comeback, I was so shocked by that particular combination of words. So I just stared at him like a deer in headlights, waiting for impact.

He chuckled. "Breathe, Kate. I'm teasing. Sort of."

Okay. And . . . I'm back. "Adam. You own a mirror. You are well aware that you are exceptionally good-looking. You no doubt have women throwing themselves at you wherever you go. But you are also damaged and cynical and, somewhere inside, you believe that everyone has some ulterior motive and that they want something from you, so you don't trust anyone—probably because you've never felt like anyone really wanted you for you—just for what's on the outside. Which is kind of tragic." Ouch. I should have dialed it back, but I was on a roll. "And it isn't as though I could forget that you are really only interested in me because I'm signed. Not exactly a flattering little tidbit of information. So, while you are *really* beautiful, you are also a marble fortress, which, for me anyway, makes you much easier to resist. And resist you, I will. Oh, and I hate being a foregone conclusion."

His turn to look stunned. But not offended this time. More . . . intrigued.

He took a step, closing the distance between us, and bent over a little so that his face was way too close to mine. He even smells good. My heart was beating faster and I suspected there was a decent chance I'd broken out in one of those embarrassing, blotchy, red flushes on my chest.

"You are *really* beautiful," he said in a low voice, not much above a whisper. "And you are turning out to be fairly interesting, signed or not. And I do want to fuck you." Oh god. That sounded like porn. He put just enough emphasis on the word "fuck" for it to be dirty and shocking, just as he'd intended. And I was pretty sure it was having exactly the effect on me he'd intended as well.

He continued in that deep, quiet voice. "But I realize that you are not a foregone conclusion. You'd be amazed how many women are." Okay. Arrogant. But possibly true in his case. "I do want you and I have this feeling it would be kind of amazing for both of us. There is definitely . . . chemistry."

Yeah, and my chemistry was making me tingle in all sorts of places, high and low.

I had no response. There really wasn't much to say to a declaration like that. So I raised one eyebrow defiantly, making it clear that I was entirely unmoved. Or *mostly* unmoved.

He was still standing close, bent over me. Something in his face made me think he was going to try to kiss me.

"No," I said.

"No, what?"

"You know what you're thinking."

"How do *you* know what I was thinking?"

"I don't know exactly. There is something about you that hits me like déjà vu."

"I see."

"And I've been clear from the beginning. It's not happening. Good night, Adam," I said, holding out my hand for a handshake.

"Good night, Kate Shaw." And the son of a bitch grabbed my hand and pulled me against him for a second before releasing me and turning and walking away in the opposite direction, with his long, perfect effing stride.

It took the entire walk to the parking garage and into the front seat of my old BMW before my heart rate was back down to normal. Or near normal.

I've never cheated on a guy in my life whether there was a contract or not. I won't start now, but I have to admit, this is the first time since I signed with Jonathan that *anyone* but him got me flushed. But, to be fair, a corpse would probably respond to Adam. And that does make me feel better. Even though I know I'd never cross that line, just the attraction bugged me.

But I guess it also says a lot about Adam. Who would you be if you could have anything you wanted, whenever you wanted it? Sure, it seems like a nice idea, but I'd think you couldn't help but start to view people—at least women—like pets rather than people. No wonder he looked intrigued by me. I'm the equivalent of a talking house cat.

*

Naturally, I got home and my partner was being a complete doll. There were candles and flowers. And Jonathan being hot as hell. He scooped me up in his arms right when I walked through the door.

"So? How was your first day?"

"It was great." Right back to my tagline. "Everyone was really nice. Enough so that I'm thinking they might not secretly hate me."

He laughed, giving me that smile . . . those teeth . . . and I was pretty much back to "Adam who?"

He guided me over to the table and sat me down, even spreading a napkin across my lap. He'd already poured wine in our glasses. He sat across from me, looking at me. Really looking at me.

"You are beautiful."

I smiled in reply. After seven years, the flattery still made me blush.

"I can't believe we're coming to the end of seven years already," he said, as he steepled his fingers under his chin.

"And on to the next seven," I said, leaning toward him across the table with my wineglass lifted.

He looked down. Why would he look down? "Babe?"

"Kate," he said. But he said it like it was the whole sentence. Like somehow it was a complete thought. Like "Kate" should enlighten me to what was going on in his head.

"Jonathan?"

"It has been a great seven years. So great."

I'm going to throw up. Every word out of his mouth was sucking air from the room. "Why do I feel like there is a huge fucking 'but' in there somewhere?" Don't cry. Don't, don't, don't.

"I love you, Kate." Fuck. "But, I never saw myself being signed the rest of my life."

"Oh." Eloquent, Kate. Nicely done. You showed him.

"I just feel like I want to be on my own for a while. And now you have a job . . ."

Wait. "But for the contract to not automatically renew,

you had to notify the attorney at least a month before the contract expired that you weren't exercising the renewal option."

Silence. Oh my god. He's known for a while he didn't want to renew. "So you knew it was over before I had a job."

"But now you'll be fine on your own, Kate."

Tears. No more fighting it. Time for the ugly cry. Huge, sucking, wet sobs. Jonathan came to me and tried to wrap his arms around me. Screw that. Crushed as I was, I was determined to find some dignity. I shoved him away. What was I going to do? Keys. Door. Car.

As I backed out of the driveway, he came out and stared at me sadly.

"Kate. Let's talk about this," he called out.

I don't fucking think so. Every uncertainty about my future flooded me at once. Where was I going to live? When was the contract up? Two weeks? Two and a half? What provisions were in there that carried on past the expiration? I don't know that I thought much about it seven years ago. I just thought Jonathan . . . oh my god. My chest was crushing painfully against my lungs. I couldn't get enough air to sob.

The irony of the Adam situation was a bitter taste on my tongue. Of course Jonathan wasn't jealous when he saw me with Adam at the coffee shop. He knew I was on borrowed time. And I was so worried about getting into an inappropriate situation with Adam. Turns out my inappropriate situation was with Jonathan. Thinking we had a solid future. That I was on sure footing. But my footing just gave way.

I pulled up to Logek's house and sat for a minute. I didn't

call her on my way over. I was too busy doing loud, obnoxious gasps in between sobs to think I could get any words out.

I knocked on the door and stood awkwardly, still doing the ugly cry thing.

"Oh my god," she said when she opened the door and saw me.

"Jonathan . . ." I started, but couldn't say more because I apparently needed all my air for crying.

"What? Is he okay?"

"He . . . he . . ." He what? Doesn't love me? Doesn't want me anymore?

"He isn't renewing?"

Okay. How did she figure that out? I nodded and she pulled me inside. She wrapped her arms around me in a super tight hug. She always knew how hard to hug. It seemed to be instinctual for her to know how hard she needed to squeeze to hold me together. Tonight it was pretty effing hard.

I don't know how long we stood there. She was just going to keeping holding me together until I broke away. I knew that about her. If I wanted her to hug me all night, she would.

I took a step back and looked at her from my puffy eyes that felt like they were only half open about now.

"Alcohol?"

And this is why we were best friends. I nodded emphatically.

"Wine? Or is this more of a whiskey situation?"

I nodded. She could interpret that how she would.

She poured two shot glasses of whiskey. We tapped glasses and downed the shot. She turned and grabbed an open bottle of wine from the counter and a glass from the cupboard and poured a glass . . . to the rim. Bless her.

I took a long, really long, drink of wine before setting my glass down and taking slow deep breaths. Time to pull your shit together, Kate. I took another painfully deep breath and blew it out slow enough that I felt winded.

I looked at the open bottle on the counter. "How is it that you have an open bottle of wine?" Our friends have an on-going joke about open bottles of wine, as in, we never have any. When we open a bottle, we finish it.

"It was a second bottle," she said with a shrug.

I laughed, which led right back into hysterical sobs. I've never understood why that happens—like somehow laughter opens the door to tears. Logek grabbed the open bottle, an unopened bottle, another glass, and the wine key and led me over to the sofa.

We sat and drank for a while without saying much.

"He had flowers and candles. To break up with me."

"Seriously?"

"I thought it was just to congratulate me on the new job." God. I'm so sick of crying. Between losing out on the DA job and now this? I feel like this feeling of disappointment and despair was the new normal.

"He never tipped you off at all? That he might not want to re-up?"

I shook my head. Never. Well, unless it was there and I was just too blind to see it.

"Maybe this is my punishment. For being attracted to Adam."

"Kate. A nun would be attracted to Adam. And just

because you were doesn't mean there was any doubt how you felt about Jonathan. You have nothing to be punished for."

"I feel like a fool."

"You aren't."

"I don't want to be this person. God! I feel like you've been trying to pick me up off the floor for weeks!"

"You've had a string of really shitty luck, honey."

I laughed. And it turned to tears again.

My phone buzzed on the coffee table where I'd set it down. I don't think I can handle more of Jonathan *wanting to talk*. What more was there to say?

When I didn't move toward the phone, Logek picked it up and looked at the screen. She turned it toward me so that I could see.

Adam.

"Shall we read it?"

I shrugged and started crying again. Who gives a shit what he has to say?

Logek looked at the screen and frowned. She read it aloud.

"The tragic marble fortress is going to bed. See you tomorrow, yes?"

Logek just looked at me with lowered brows, waiting to see if I would explain.

I sniffed, then straightened my shoulders. Time to pull yourself up, Kate. This fragile, damaged girl is not you. I blew out a long sigh.

"Let's see. We got into it a little after work when he followed me out of the building. I sort of gave him my 'you're a broken toy and I'm not the least bit interested in a cold fish like you' speech. I guess he was wondering if it would be enough to make me quit."

Logek, god love her, dropped her head back onto the couch and started laughing. Really laughing. Which got me laughing.

"Only you, Katie-girl! I can't imagine any woman with a functional vagina reading Adam Lucas the riot act for hitting on her." And then we started giggling some more. "You're not quitting are you?"

"How can I now? Not that it matters. Single, I can't live on what I'm making at Samson and Tule, especially once my student loans go into repayment. I really need to find a job." And the moment the word "single" hit me again, the laughing was over and I fell apart all over again. Screw the employment problem, the money issues. I was losing the man I loved and right now, it feels a little like death.

My vision was pretty blurry from the tears, but I could see Logek pick up my wineglass from the coffee table. She put it in my hand and pushed it toward my mouth. I guess she knew that in order to drink it, I'd have to stop crying.

"So, I'm just going to say it," she said. "Uncle Tony."

This elicited a loud moan from me and an exaggerated eye roll. Uncle Tony is my very, very odd uncle on my mother's side. An eccentric, inappropriate signing attorney with his own firm who has been offering me a job since the day I took the law school entrance exam. But I do not want to do signing law. I have said that every way I can think of. I do *not* want to do signing law. I don't want to do it so much, I was led to wonder whether Starbucks paid above minimum wage. The thought of giving in on the signing law front is almost as depressing as the thought that I'm losing the love of my life. Almost.

"I can't think about Tony tonight," I said, the tears starting once again. She rubbed her hand down my hair a couple of times and turned on the TV and found some bad reality show for us to watch while I finished my wine.

CHAPTER 4

I woke up, disoriented, until I realized I was in Logek's bed. All the memories of last night flooded back, and I thought maybe I would just stay in bed all day. As if Logek would allow that.

"Get up. You have a job now, remember?"

In response, I snatched the pillow out from under my head and covered my face with it.

"Come on. Up. No wallowing in my house." And she wisely put a cup of coffee in my hand.

And somehow, because Logek is the most amazing friend in the world, I was in my car driving to work, showered, with fresh makeup (hers), teeth brushed (an extra toothbrush she kept on hand . . . probably not for girlfriend sleepovers), and actually *not* wearing the same clothes I wore to work yesterday. Luckily, Logek and I are roughly the same size, so I could borrow her clothes. Of course, *roughly* translates to a skirt being about two inches shorter on me and definitely a little snugger in the ass. Just in case I didn't manage to start any nasty rumors about me yesterday, I can definitely spark some today.

All of this paled in comparison to the thought that in two weeks I would no longer be signed. To Jonathan.

I kept my head low and rode the elevator to my floor. I didn't know my coworkers well enough for anyone to be able to tell that I was a little off today. Instead, I got a fresh stack of paperwork and buried myself in the mundane.

My phone buzzed. A text from Uncle Tony.

Hey, darling (not a term of endearment—he calls all women darling. It's really more of a condescending, sexist thing than anything else). *Heard your contract went to shit and you might need a job.*

What the hell? Only Logek knows. And Jonathan. Crap. I guess this isn't the sort of thing that won't spread like mad.

Just figuring out where I'm at. Thanks for checking in though, Tony.

Still got a job with your name on it.

I appreciate the offer—really—but I'm still figuring things out.

Yeah yeah yeah. You're about to be single, jobless, and buried in student loans.

I hate you, Uncle Tony. *Thanks for pointing out the obvious.*

Signing law is fun. And I'm slammed. I really need a new associate and I want it to be you, but I can't wait forever.

I see his point. Part of the reason I wasn't finding a job is because I have *no* experience in law aside from interning with the DA's office. What would be the harm of working for Tony for a year and getting the experience I needed to move on to something better? The fact that I was about to give in made me want to cry—or drink heavily. I've been pretty good at both lately.

Deep breath. Jump off the bridge. *I just started a new job. Wouldn't feel right not giving them a 2-week notice . . .*

Alright. Good to hear you're finally coming to your senses! You're gonna be great at this, darling!

What's the starting salary?

Normally I start brand-new associates at $60k, but since you've also got 10 years of experience in business from before law school, I'll start you at $70k.

Seventy thousand dollars. Wow. That's real money. It'll give me independence. But I'll be doing signing law. Suck it up, Kate. Life's not perfect—like I needed to remind myself of that.

I'll give notice today so I can start in 2 weeks, ok?

Sounds great.

Thanks, Tony.

Thank you, darling.

Oh . . . and how did you hear about my contract?

Your mother told me.

And she knew how? Jonathan. He must have called her worried last night when I took off.

Holy shit. That just happened. I got up from my desk and went to find Marnie. Since she was the senior clerk, I thought I'd give her the heads-up before I went to Alice.

She had earbuds in listening to dictation as she typed away furiously on the keyboard. She looked up at me and smiled, pulling one of the earphones out of her ear.

"Hey. How's it going?"

"Great," I said. Damn. I felt worse doing this than I thought I would. "Um, so I don't know if I mentioned it, but I recently passed the bar and I've been looking for an attorney job, but they're hard to come by. And they sort of knew when they hired me that I was just going to be temp help until I could find an attorney position—and I have."

"Oh. Well, that's great. Good for you, Kate." She said it sincerely, but was definitely disappointed. I couldn't help but be somewhat pleased that she was sad to see me go.

"I'm going to give two weeks. I know you guys are swamped and I don't want to just leave you hanging."

She sighed, smiling. "Bless you."

"Anyway, I just wanted to let you know before I went to Alice. I really appreciate the time you put into training me yesterday and I feel so bad doing this my second day on the job."

"You need to do what you need to do. I mean, if I was an attorney, I sure as hell wouldn't be doing this!"

I let her get back to work and got into the elevator to head up to Alice's office on twenty-seven. I stepped out on the twenty-seventh floor and stopped. I knew Alice was on this floor, but there wasn't a receptionist to ask up here. I headed down one hallway and it was lined with identical offices along both walls. I tried to walk past each, inconspicuously, taking a quick peek inside to see if it might be Alice's office. Most of the people didn't look up from their desks. They were on their computers or on the phone.

I peeked into the fifth office and paused. Adam. He was standing, looking out one of his large picture windows over an impressive view of the city skyline. He had his hands in the pockets of his slacks. He was wearing another thin cashmere sweater, gray this time, and he was shaking his head.

"I think that would be a mistake, John." Pause. "Because you don't want to put this kind of money into a campaign and then start cutting corners on production."

Oh. He's on the phone. I didn't notice the headset he was wearing.

He looked down, shaking his head again. If he sees me here, it'll look like I was looking for him. I started to pass his office, and, on cue, he turned and saw me. He held up a finger, indicating he wanted me to wait. Run away, Kate. But I didn't. I stood in his doorway and waited for him to finish his phone call.

"Look at the samples I sent you. That's what you want. Look at them and call me tomorrow. The decision is obviously yours, but you know I'm not going to lie to you if I think you're making a mistake." Pause. "Alright. Tomorrow. Bye."

Adam pulled the headset off and tossed it on his desk before turning to me. His office suddenly felt overly warm and I think my face was flushed. From the warmth. Of the office, of course.

He walked toward me and did a very unsubtle scan of my clothing. "Well that's an improvement over yesterday." He raised an eyebrow and smiled ever so slightly.

I looked down. Shit. I had forgotten what I was wearing. Logek's clothes—a little too short, a little too snug. "Oh. I had to borrow clothes from Logek this morning and she's a little smaller than me."

"It wasn't a criticism. I think you look great."

"Thank you," I said awkwardly. Why was I here again? "I was actually trying to find Alice's office, but this floor is kind of a maze."

He stopped smiling. "I see. And I was hoping you were coming to say 'hi.'"

I laughed. Couldn't help it. He had this little boy vibe at times when he didn't get his way. "Don't pout, Adam. It's unbecoming."

His eyes opened wide. "I am *not* pouting, Kate."

"Okay," I said, smiling. "Must be my mistake. Anyway, I may as well let you know. I'm looking for Alice because I need to put in my two-week notice."

He raised his eyebrows at me. Most people would ask "why?" He just looked at me, waiting.

"I've accepted an attorney job."

"That's great, Kate. Where?"

"Manetti, Markson, and Mann."

He stepped in close to me. His office was definitely too warm. He cocked his head to the side, scrutinizing me. "That's a signing firm, Kate. I thought that was your line in the sand."

I took a step back. "It was. But I really needed the job."

"You have a job. I thought this was supposed to tide you over until you found something you wanted."

"Circumstances have changed." Moment of truth. I wonder

how he'll react when he finds out that I'm going to be single. Will it really just flip a switch in him so that he'll go from wanting me to not being interested at all? Could his aversion to single women really be that hardwired?

"How so?"

Uh-oh. Lump in my throat. I'd kept it together pretty well today, but when I actually have to say it out loud, that Jonathan doesn't want to renew, I feel like I've got an elephant sitting on my chest.

He took a step closer again. He put two fingers under my chin and lifted my face till he could see in my eyes. He looked concerned. "Kate?"

I pulled my chin away from his hand and walked over to his windows and looked out at the city. I brushed away the couple of tears that had slipped out before turning back around. "I found out last night that Jonathan doesn't want to re-up. So when I realized that I was going to be on my own in two weeks, it was time for me to stop being choosy and to take what I could get."

Wow. It was hardwired. There was a *visible* change in him, at least to me. Something in his eyes, his posture. The undercurrent of seductiveness was gone and he was just Adam. Friendly still, even kind, and of course still gloriously beautiful. But just like that—he wasn't after me.

He walked up to me quickly, like a long-lost friend . . . or brother . . . and put his hands on my shoulders. "Shit. I'm so sorry, Kate. Man, you've really been put through it lately."

I nodded and more tears streaked down my face. He sighed and pulled me into a hug. Okay, this is, by far, the strangest part of my day. Crying on Adam Lucas's shoulder? Heartbroken as I was, the fact that my cheek was against Adam's buttery-soft sweater and just beneath that, his perfectly formed chest, was not lost on me.

I pulled back and stepped out of his arms, wiping my cheeks dry. "I don't want to get makeup on your sweater."

"I don't mind, Kate."

I sniffed, wiped my nose. "Don't suppose you have a mirror in here?"

"There's one on the inside of the door of the cabinet over there," he said, pointing.

I opened the cabinet and inside was hanging what was no doubt a very expensive overcoat beside a suit jacket. I opened the door all the way and, sure enough, there was a full-length mirror on the inside of it.

Super. My eye makeup was running and my cheeks were red and blotchy. Adam passed me a tissue. I wiped away the smeared mascara and patted my cheeks dry. I smoothed my skirt, or rather Logek's skirt, and tried to make it a fraction of an inch longer.

"You look fine, Kate. You can't even tell."

"Thanks," I said, clearly for more than the tissue.

"Come on. I'll take you to Alice's office." Yep. We had definitely flipped his switch. If I wasn't essentially single, he'd probably be chasing me around his desk right now.

"Nice office, by the way," I said, once we were walking down the hall.

"I like it. Took me a while to get it."

"I can imagine."

"Okay. Here's Alice's office." He stopped a couple feet short of her door. He put a friendly hand on my arm and smiled. "Talk to you later. Gotta get back to work."

"Of course. Thanks, Adam."

He gave my upper arm a light squeeze before turning and heading back down the hall.

I poked my head into Alice's office and she looked up from a stack of paperwork in front of her. She took one look at me and propped her elbows on the desk and put her chin on the backs of her interlaced fingers. "Damn."

"But I'm going to give you two weeks," I said hurriedly.

*

I'd been busy all day, so when I got to the parking garage and sat down in my car, I looked at my phone for the first time in hours.

Good god. Fourteen text messages. Two from Logek, four from mom, and eight from Jonathan. Part of me wanted to delete them all, unread, and not deal with anyone. But I'm way too curious for that.

Logek texted to ask where I'd be going after work—home or to her house—and again to tell me that Jonathan had texted her.

Mom was what I expected. *Why didn't you call me? Are you okay? Did Uncle Tony call you?* (She's been barking up that tree almost as long as Tony has.) And my favorite:

Do you want to stay with Dad and me for a while?

Kill me now.

And this is what Jonathan had to say . . .

Kate, I'm so sorry. I didn't mean to dump it on you like that. I blew it. I do love you. So much. I just want to be on my own for a while. Just didn't see myself re-upping for the next 40 years . . .

Please answer. I need to know you're okay.

I don't know if you're busy or ignoring me . . .

I realize I should have talked to you about this earlier. Just because we aren't signed, I still want you in my life. I can't imagine not still seeing you and spending time with you . . . Wow. Jonathan: this year's winner of the "Having Your Cake and Eating It, Too" award.

I hope you're okay. You're my best friend.

Is this really going to be it? You're just going to stop talking to me altogether? Please talk to me.

If it makes you feel any better, I'm pretty sure your parents and Logek want me dead.

And lastly, and probably my favorite . . . *I'm still in love with you. Just not in love with the contract anymore.*

What the hell is that even supposed to mean?

I replied. *I'm not giving you the silent treatment. Just not ready to talk yet. You turned my whole world upside down yesterday, Jonathan. I'm lost and confused. And unlike you, I'm still in love with you and the contract, I guess. Can't deal with this yet.*

Okay. Now. Where to go? Home? Logek's? My parents'?

*

Parents win. Might as well pull the Band-Aid off since they must be chomping at the bit to find out what happened. The joys of being an only child—oversolicitous parents. Amazing, but oversolicitous.

I pulled up in front of their beautiful two-story home with the perfectly manicured lawn and the big, weathered concrete fountain in front that doubled as a birdbath. I love this house. Unlike most people I know, I actually grew up in the same house, with the same people. My parents will be celebrating their fifth renewal in a few months. Which means I was already on the way when they decided to sign. See? I can do math.

I was just about to the door when my mom opened it and rushed toward me, wrapping me in a bear hug.

"I'm so glad you're here," she said.

"Can't breathe so good, Mom."

"Sorry, baby." And she let go, but kept hold of my hand and led me into the house.

My dad was in the kitchen, and immediately after releasing me from a tight hug, he put a glass of wine in my hand. God love them. Then they both stood there leaning against the kitchen counter, quietly watching me sip my wine, figuring I'd talk when I was ready.

"I don't really know what there is to tell you," I began. "Things between us were so wonderful. It just never occurred to me that we wouldn't renew. So it was a total sucker punch last night when he dropped it on me."

They were both still listening quietly, looking sympathetic without giving their thoughts away.

"He's been texting me today. Says he still loves me, but he's not *in love with the contract*. What the hell does that mean?"

"Honey, there are lots of people that aren't cut out to be

perpetually signed," Dad said. "I mean, you grew up watching your mom and me and we just kept renewing. Didn't you say that Jonathan's dad has been signed to six different women?"

"Yeah, he has. And I get that Jonathan was raised in very different circumstances. I just thought . . . I don't know. I guess it doesn't matter what I thought," I said, shaking my head.

"The way you grow up can really shape your view of contracts. To lots of people, as long as you don't breach in the seven years, deciding it's over at the end of the contract is seen as no harm, no foul. That said, I will kick his ass if you want me to."

I laughed and almost dribbled wine on Logek's blouse—which is expensive. I grabbed a napkin and held it against my mouth. Dad is sixty, but he is a very fit, ex-military, still-runs-marathons sixty. And Jonathan . . . well, he's perfect. Bastard.

"I will definitely back-burner that idea, Dad. Thanks."

"So, I heard you talked to Uncle Tony," Mom said. Her face was all lit up. She's been pushing for this for so long that today must be like Christmas for her.

"Yep. You can finally stop nagging me about it. I gave my two-week notice at work today and I start with Tony right after that."

"What work?" Dad asked.

"I got a job as a clerk at Samson and Tule to hold me over till I found an attorney job. After Jonathan dropped the bomb last night—well, desperate times call for desperate measures."

"Oh, stop making it sound like it's the end of the world," Mom said, waving her hand in the air. "You are going to be getting experience and I have no doubt that you'll be amazing at it."

"Thanks, Mom. I know. I need the experience."

Dad was still stuck on the S & T job thing that he didn't know about. Yeah. That's how into my life these two people are. My father was very disturbed that I started a job two days ago and he didn't know about it.

"How did you end up at Samson and Tule?" he asked.

"I met a guy. At a bar." That got the smirk from Dad that I was aiming for. "And he said, 'Hey, little girl, I think I've got a job for you.'"

Dad poked me in the rib.

"Partly true. I was out drowning my sorrows with Logek last week over the DA job and I met an ad exec from there and he said they were really shorthanded and that if I wanted a job, it was mine."

"So you started *yesterday* and quit *today*?"

"Desperate times, Dad."

"I get that. How did they take it?"

"They appreciated that I was staying for two weeks."

"So," Mom interjected, unable to control her excitement about my job with Uncle Tony any longer. "Did Tony say what the pay would be?"

I smiled. "Yes. He's going to start me at seventy thousand dollars."

"That's great!" I knew she'd be excited about that. "You are going to be just fine on your own."

And I deflated, just like that. "Yep. On my own." Not going to cry. I'm going to try not to cry. Shit. I'm going to cry.

As soon as the tears started flowing, Mom and Dad wrapped me in a joint hug and hung on until I stopped crying, which, sadly, took a while.

So after I pulled myself together (again), Dad topped off my wine and we changed the subject. Sort of.

"So, baby. Want to stay here for a while? Until you save up enough for rent and deposit and all that?" Mom asked.

Shoot me. Thirty-four years old and living with my parents? "Yeah. That'd be great," I said, swallowing my bruised pride. "Logek offered, of course, but her apartment is a one bedroom so that would give me the joy of sharing the bed with her, when it's free, or sleeping on the couch."

"Well, you know we always have your room made up for you." She was smiling like crazy. They totally did not see the downside to their adult daughter moving back home. I think they'd prefer that I never left. Cute and overbearing at the same time.

My room is still made up for me because they have three other guest rooms for guests, which I will never be. Point being, they don't need the space. This house has five bedrooms; a beautifully furnished, gourmet kitchen; a home office; a pool *with* a pool house; and only *two* people living here. Even when I did live at home, the house felt oversized.

"Well, as much as I'd love to finish off that bottle with you both right now, I've got to go home. I took off last night without packing so much as a toothbrush. Plus, I should probably talk to Jonathan. He's been blowing up my phone all day."

"Yeah," Mom said, "he called here last night looking for you and gave me the gist of what was going on."

"I figured that was how you found out. Okay. I'll probably be home late tonight by the time I get out there and back."

"You've got your key, right? Do you need any help packing up?" Dad asked.

"I'm just packing for a few days. I'll try to do the actual moving this weekend."

I put the half-full wineglass on the counter (since I was driving) and gave each of them an extra-long, extra-grateful hug. I'm a very lucky girl.

"Love you," I said, on my way out the door.

One awkward encounter down, one to go. I got in my car and headed home. Or ex-home. Whatever.

CHAPTER 5

As I suspected, Jonathan was already home when I got there. Deep breaths, Kate. Dignity. There will be no crying, whining, or punching anyone in the nose. Probably.

He was in the kitchen when I came in. He looked contrite. Apologetic. And he put a glass of wine on the counter in front of me. What is it with the people in my life? Am I at that point where alcoholism has become a viable option? A girl's got to wonder when everyone around her is always trying to subdue her with alcohol. I picked up the glass and started drinking as I headed to the bedroom.

I grabbed a small suitcase from the top of the closet and set it on the bed and started filling it.

"Baby."

"Don't call me that, Jonathan."

He gave an exaggerated sigh and came to stand between me and the suitcase.

"Please talk to me. I know this doesn't make sense, Kate—that I would choose not to renew when you are the most important person in my life. Because you are. The absolute most important person in my life."

Okay. Shelve the sarcasm. "You're right, Jonathan. It makes no sense."

I reached around him and pulled the suitcase to where I could reach it and continued throwing items in it.

"I just want some independence, some freedom. I just want life without the constraints for a while."

Constraints translated to *I can't sleep with other women when I'm under contract with you.* "Are you kidding me?" Ooh. That sounded shrill. I took a breath, roped in the hysteria. "Freedom to screw other women is what you're really saying."

"No. Not entirely."

Ouch. "Well. Wish granted. Fuck all the women you want."

He grabbed my arm and turned me around and hugged me fiercely. He pulled back and looked in my face. His black hair was messed up enough to look even more perfect than usual. His rich, brown eyes were intense and focused. His hands, which I've always had a weakness for, all big and manly, came up to the sides of my face. He rubbed one of his thumbs along my jawbone, as he leaned down and rested his forehead against mine.

Whoa. Offsides. High-sticking. Hitting below the belt. And other such sports metaphors I could think of that express my feelings that he was so not playing fair. He's dumping you. Focus. Eye on the prize. Prize? Not sure there's any prize to be had here, so let's go with the "focus" suggestion.

Before I could push away (and it would have been *indignantly*, I assure you), he grabbed my face and turned it up to his and kissed me. *Kissed* me, kissed me. His full lips were like butter on mine and his thumb still on my jaw was urging me to open my mouth. When I did (because I'm weak and under the influence of some dark magic) his tongue came into my mouth, warm and soft. Seven years together and he knew what I liked, and he was making sure to give me all of that—just enough tongue, lots of his super-soft lips, one hand to my lower back, pushing me against him. I am so screwed. That was meant figuratively. Let's hope not literally.

His mouth left mine and started trailing down my neck, over to my ear just long enough to squeeze an expletive or two out of me. His hands reached down to my waist and I knew he was going to take off my shirt.

Wake up, Kate! But Kate had left the building. Kate was already thinking about how much better things were going to feel once he got that shirt off. Hormones definitely rule this roost. When sex is involved, common sense always loses. And what if this is really, really amazing Jonathan Sex for the last time?

Last time. That is sobering. And I did sober—right as he pulled my shirt over my head. Perfect. So now I'm sad *and* half-dressed. This is always an ideal scenario because when you're feeling sad and vulnerable, the best thing is always to be topless. Awesome.

"Jonathan," I said, coming to my senses.

"Kate . . . I love you." And he was back to the kissing, making-Kate-lose-her-mind thing.

I remember his removing my shirt, but not my bra, and I'm pretty sure I had one on. But now it was off. His mouth was on me. One nipple, then the other. Drawing each one into his mouth hard, sending sparks of pleasure surging through me. My legs were giving out so he took the opportunity to lay me back on the bed. I was only vaguely aware of him heaving my suitcase, literally and symbolically, across the room.

Let's see . . . a glass of wine at my parents', one since I got home. Enough to blame the alcohol? Not if I'm honest with myself. The truth was that once I was turned on, nothing mattered. There was no self-respect, no restraint, no right or wrong. Only the orgasm. It was too late for me. I might as well enjoy myself because I knew I wasn't going to stop it.

He stripped off my skirt and undies and then buried his mouth between my legs with an enthusiasm that was purely Jonathan. He genuinely loved this part of foreplay.

And half of my body rose off the bed. Sensation, barely tolerable, shot through my entire body. I moaned and pushed against his shoulders, which, as always, only encouraged him to perform more aggressively. And aggressive was the word for it. It was like being gloriously, erotically attacked and eaten alive. He wrapped his arms around my thighs to hold me in place because he knew that if he didn't have a good grip, he would lose hold when I got there. But he had a good hold. And I exploded. My mind, my body, my heart. He kept at it with his tongue and it was more than I could stand in my aftermath. I tried to pull away but he held me tight and continued to gently rub his tongue across my most sensitive spots.

Then he stood up and stripped off his clothes. His dark skin was smooth and flawless. And he was excited. Very excited. I don't know if it was because the end was in sight, but he looked even more endowed than usual. He crawled up between my legs and entered me hard and fast, making me cry out. As he began to move, he put a hand on each side of my face and stared at me intensely. He watched my reaction with every thrust of his hips, occasionally running his thumb across my lower lip.

A combination of his size and his technique had me on the verge of another orgasm. And he could tell, so he went in deep and stopped moving, waiting for me to come back down. Oh—it was going to be one of those sessions. Drawn out, torturous, and mind-blowing. When I was no longer on the verge, he resumed his rhythm. Each time he thrust in hard, he hit sensitive spots deep inside and created little flickers of pain mixed with the pleasure. And that mix brought me right to the edge again.

"Please," I whispered, pretty sure I couldn't take much more of the torture without breaking tonight.

He responded with a punishing rhythm that made me feel like it could induce an aneurysm. I saw spots in my vision and I dug my nails into his shoulders. I came again, my whole body convulsing, my senses completely overloaded. The sensation was too much, too intense, but he wasn't finished so he kept up the pace until he came. As always, it was those minutes between my orgasm and his that nearly brought me to tears, every nerve in my body raw and screaming.

Subject to the following terms and conditions

I was relieved when he stopped his movement. The trembling throughout my body slowly subsided. He lay down on top of me for a minute before rising up and looking into my face again. He had such beautiful eyes, lined with thick, dark lashes—the kind that women always want, but men usually get. His lips were parted and he was panting.

"I love you, Kate. I always will."

Shit. I put my arm across my face, knowing tears were coming. Great sex always ends in tears, right?

Jonathan rolled off to the side of me and pulled me into his arms. I started to pull away once, but he seemed unwilling to let go, so I stayed. But I knew it was temporary. He loved me, and he was definitely the best sex of my life, but nothing changed the fact that we were still over.

Eventually I disentangled from him and, after cleaning up a bit, got dressed and went back to packing. He threw his pants back on, but remained shirtless, which was cruel. I studied him for a minute, the tight ab muscles, the curve of his chest, his broad shoulders. If only I could flip a switch like Adam and not want Jonathan anymore.

He watched me finish packing without saying another word. When I zipped up the suitcase and started for the door, he followed me, but still kept silent. I left without another word. As I walked out the door, he grabbed my hand and put his lips to my palm in a strangely intimate kiss.

I drove to my parents slowly, not eager to get there. Not really eager to be anywhere. So I hit the Jack in the Box drive-through because when you've just had amazing yet regrettable sex with the former love of your life, you deserve a friggin' milk shake, dammit. I got my chocolate milk shake (yes, *with* the thousand calories of whipped cream on top) and parked in the parking lot to drink it, rather than continuing to my parents.

My guilt-ridden solitude was interrupted by my phone buzzing. It was a text from Adam.

How's it going?

Hmm. How is it going? I just gave in and had sex with the man that's dumping me. I'm on my way to move in with my parents, which is every thirty-four-year-old woman's dream. And I'm getting random texts from a man I don't know that well, but who I would be more than willing to let screw me into forgetting about Jonathan. Oh, right—that guy's no longer interested in me.

Adam. Question. Why are you texting me now that you are no longer trying to sleep with me?

Because I like you.

But I'm about to be single.

I want to be your friend. I don't have any women friends so you can be my first.

Why no women friends?

Because they never want to keep it just friends. It gets awkward.

And me?

I got to know you before you were single so you were only interested in being friends. I like talking to you. I want to keep talking to you.

Why?

Why do I like talking to you or why do I want to keep talking to you?

Here we go again.

Never mind. What makes you think I'll be satisfied keeping it just friends?

Because you're in love with someone else.

Oh. Right. Damn. I'm sorta hoping to not be in love with him forever, you know.

Well, we'll be friends until you fall for me ;)

Wow. Arrogant. No. *We'll be friends until YOU fall for ME.*

Either way, Kate.

Where was his conceited rebuttal? What is that sensation? Butterflies?

Gotta go. Talk to you later.

Good night, Kate.

Good night, Adam.

And just for the hell of it, I hit my head against the steering wheel.

*

I got to my parents and slipped in quietly. Their room was on the other end of the house so I was pretty sure I wouldn't wake them even if I was slamming doors. I went upstairs to my room and looked around. Nothing had changed. I moved out like ten years ago and they kept this room the same. This was twenty-four-year-old Kate's room. College pics of Logek and me. College pennant on the wall. A couple of stuffed animals on the bed. Weird.

I got into some sweat shorts and a T-shirt, and went into the bathroom adjacent to my room. I stared at my reflection. About what I expected. My eyes were a little puffy. Too many spontaneous bursts of crying lately. I'd apparently cried enough today to remove most of my makeup. I looked pale. I need to get some sun. I mean, I'm always fair-skinned, but this is ridiculous. Fair skin, dark hair, ice-blue eyes. It works pretty well for me when I have the right makeup on. Right now I just looked frail. Yuck.

I brushed my teeth, washed my face, and climbed into bed. To stare at the ceiling. I looked at the clock. Midnight. My parents' house is outside the city so it'll probably take me about thirty minutes to get to work. I set the alarm for 6:00 a.m. and went back to staring at the ceiling. This sucks.

I looked at my phone. Checked Facebook and Twitter. Nothing interesting.

I texted Adam. Because I apparently wanted to make sure I squeezed in one more terrible decision for the day.

Hey. You up?

Nothing. Just when I'd decided he must be asleep, my phone buzzed.

Yes.

Can't sleep. What are you doing?

Reading. Not sleeping.

What are you reading?

Stephen King. Under the Dome. *Have you read it?*

I have. Really good. Did you read his Dark Tower series?

Yes. Some of his best stuff.

Agreed.

Where are you?

My parents'. Yes. Moving in with my parents. High-water mark in the life of Kate Shaw.

Ha-ha. Kate Shaw will land on her feet. I have no doubt.

Thank you.

So, insomniac—why'd you decide to text me?

I don't know. Thought maybe you'd be up. And you're usually entertaining ;)

Well thanks for that. Obviously "entertaining" is always my goal.

When you found out I was gonna be single, you just flipped a switch and you weren't into me anymore. Can you teach me that?

No. Sorry. It's a special talent . . . takes years of cynicism and distrust . . . things you are not cut out for.

How do you know? I can be WAY cynical. And I trust no one.

Kate. You're such a cream puff.

Did Adam Lucas really just call me a cream puff?

In the graduation newspaper in high school people voted for students as Norse gods and I was voted Goddess of Ice

I have trouble believing that.

True story. Hand to God. Although, I guess it could have been my eyes.

Doubtful. You have some of the warmest eyes I've ever seen.

Oh. Thankfully I didn't have to respond to the compliment because he immediately followed it up with another text.

So why the question about flipping the switch?

I need to flip my Jonathan switch. Desperately.

It'll get easier.

Thanks, Mom.

You're welcome, princess.

*Ok. Must try to sleep. Maybe I'll see you tomorrow.
Anything's possible. Good night, Kate.*

*

The rest of the workweek flew by. They kept me buried in
work, trying to take advantage of the help while they had it.
And the personal life had gone pretty quiet, too. Jonathan
had texted once or twice, only with practical questions—no
more professing his undying love. At least not in the last
three days. I hadn't talked to Adam at all. Never caught a
glimpse of him around the office. And after my late-night
texting, I was left feeling a little like maybe he thought I was
coming on to him or something. Maybe he'd decided I fit
into that category of other women who wanted too much
from him. Which I *totally* don't. That would be absurd.
Either way, I decided it was best to back away from that
whole thing.

Friday night I drove to Logek's straight from work. We
were going to a friend's signing party. Some people keep them
low-key, but some people turn them into formal affairs.
This was the latter. And I was so not up for it.

I knocked once on Logek's door and walked in.

"Hello?"

"In my room," she called.

Logek loved these swanky parties. I guess I usually do,
too, but I didn't feel like much of a party person at the moment.

Logek was slipping a black dress over her head when I

walked in. She smoothed it, zipped it, and turned to me with her hands on her hips.

"Wow. You look amazing," I said.

"Thank you. What are you wearing?"

"I brought a couple of things," I said, tossing a garment bag on her bed. "I'm not all that excited about either, though."

"You can always borrow something of mine."

"Logek. Five foot seven," I said, pointing at her. "Five nine," I said, pointing at me. "Combine that with the fact that I've got at least fifteen pounds on you and it adds up to me not borrowing your cocktail dresses because I wind up looking like a hooker."

"A really expensive hooker, though."

"Naturally."

"So show me what you brought."

I pulled the two dresses out of the bag. One was a simple, snug black dress that came to just below my knees. The second was a shorter, flowier, girlier dress in a print of red and purple. I only brought it because I've never worn it and I keep thinking eventually it's going to seem like the right thing. Pretty sure that's my buyer's remorse in denial.

"Definitely the black," she said. As if there was any question. "Unless I can convince you to wear my red one."

"Umm . . . no. Love that dress, but I'm not feeling sexy enough these days to pull it off."

Logek frowned at me, but didn't push.

She insisted on doing my makeup and she certainly has a flair for the dramatic. It was more makeup than I usually wore, but I had to admit, I did feel pretty glamorous. She put some soft curls in my hair and sprayed me till I felt like my hair was bulletproof.

"Enough. Enough. I don't want Kevlar hair."

"It looks awesome."

I looked in the mirror. It did look kind of awesome. Point for Logek.

I shimmied into my black dress and Logek zipped the back for me. The bodice was cut in a low V that angled wide toward my shoulders, giving it something of the '60s Hollywood look. I don't have huge boobs, but with a little help from Victoria's Secret, I could rock this dress. I slipped on my lacy, four-inch heels and stood in front of the mirror. Alrighty, Kate. You got this. I think you might even hold your own against Logek tonight.

Of course, then Logek stepped out of the bathroom in a long red dress with a slit all the way up the side and her hair doing this cool sideswept thing so that it all rested over one shoulder. Damn. She was breathtaking.

"I hate you."

"Oh, stop it. You look incredible."

"Next to anyone else, I'd agree. Ugh."

She laughed and grabbed her purse and keys and we headed out.

"So," I said, once we were pulling away from her apartment building, "I had sex with Jonathan a couple days ago." Because that's what best friends do—they randomly blurt out shocking facts with no lead-in. It's one of the perks of having a best friend.

"Oh my god, Kate!"

Yep, that was about what I expected.

"I know, I know. I'm weak. And shameless."

"How did you go from heartbroken and angry to having sex with him?"

"He's just so hot. And he knows all my buttons. And he kept telling me how much he loves me."

"Douche. Him, not you."

"I know. I regret it. Sort of."

"Sort of, huh? That good?"

"Awesome. Quite the send-off."

I did a half grunt, half growl and hit my head against the headrest. "I think I'm going to miss the sex almost as much as I'm going to miss the rest of him."

"I'm pretty sure if you were open to it, he'd be more than happy to keep screwing you."

"He is generous that way."

"Selfless, really."

I gave her a little pout.

She sighed. "No one died, Kate. Contracts end every day. He didn't even breach, so you can't even cry about that."

"I know. I'm doing my best to put things in perspective."

"Very mature of you."

"Nice to hear since I just moved in with my parents."

"Desperate times, Kitty Kat." And I smiled. Something about that nickname always made me feel like I was back in high school.

"On a related note," I said, "Adam Lucas is no longer after me now that my contract is over."

"Seriously? Like he just wants you bad one day and the next day he's over it?"

"Apparently. He said he likes me though and wants us to be friends." Then I opened my eyes wide at her to let her know how surprising I found that bit of information.

"Really? Friends? How does a woman—a single woman mind you—go about being friends with someone like him? I mean, my nipples get hard around him and he's never even hit on me."

I laughed. "He made a good point. I'm in love with someone else."

"There is that, I guess."

"I am a little disappointed that I won't even get to have dirty, rebound sex with him, though."

"He's not even down for a meaningless hookup?"

"I think he's had too many women claim it was meaningless and then fall madly in love with him twenty-four hours later, or something."

"Twenty-four hours, huh? He must be pretty fucking amazing in bed."

"I'll never know. Maybe you need to get signed so that he'll go after you and then you can fill me in on all the gory details."

She laughed. "Something tells me I'm not his type."

"You're everyone's *type*, Logek. The only flaw you have is that you're single."

"I don't know. I don't think I've ever been so easily dismissed by a man as I was the night he met you. I was invisible."

"Welcome to my world."

"You know what I mean. So? Are you guys buddies now?"

I filled her in on the recent happenings.

"Hmm. Weird. Still, he's kind of a rock star in this town and you had his attention for more than a week. Take it as a compliment."

I laughed at that. "Let's not forget. He's notorious—not famous."

"Same difference," she said. She pulled to the curb near our destination.

The party was at The Met, a posh restaurant in midtown. The trees out front were all decorated with little twinkle lights and the candles in the lanterns on either side of the big wood-paneled front doors were glowing yellow. The Met was widely considered one of the most romantic restaurants in the city. I guess it made sense for a signing party. Yay for being in love.

Logek and I made our way inside. Our college friend, Kimberley, had signed for the first time. I thought for a while that she never would, that commitment just wasn't for her. But that was only until she met Milton. (Yes, Milton. I shit you not. That's his name.) Milton is nice, kind of quiet, and comes from a long family line with lots and lots of money. Not that I'm accusing Kimberley of being a gold digger—'cause that would make me a bitch. But she might be.

I'm not sure if they plan on having kids. Back in the day, children almost entirely took the dad's name because sexism and all that. Then there was this movement about personal identity and so the kids started taking both parents' last names and hyphenating. It only took about two generations to know that wasn't gonna fly, so by the '80s people just decided which last name they liked better—the mom's or the dad's—and wrote it into the contract. Shaw was my mother's. Bunt was my father's. Thank you, Mom and Dad, for picking Shaw. Rhymes in junior high can be a bitch.

Anyway, Kimberley and Milton were both from families big on representation so this contract was between Kimberley Martin-Shaffer-Ramsey-Courtland and Milton Smith-Sutherland-Thompson-Wagner. I hope they plan on breaking tradition so that they don't saddle a kid with Martin-Shaffer-Ramsey-Courtland-Smith-Sutherland-Thompson-Wagner. And on that note, I need a drink.

We started to make our way to the bar when we heard our names.

"Kate! Logek!"

Looking over, we saw Kimberley, working her way through the crowd to get to us. We didn't get together often so whenever she saw us, she always acted like it had been a decade. Her red hair was twisted into an artful updo and she was wearing a gorgeous blue dress that came to the floor. Thank god it was sleek enough to not look like a prom dress. And she looked really, really happy. Aww.

She hugged us both and squealed her excitement, showing us her token bracelet with a big, diamond-studded quill dangling from it. I mentioned the money thing, right?

"It's so pretty!" Logek said, examining the jewels closely.

"Beautiful," I added. "I'm so happy for you, Kimberley."

"Thanks, Kate." And she was back to grinning wildly. "Okay, I have to keep making the rounds. Milton has a bunch of family in from out of state and I have to make a good impression." She rolled her eyes, but I know secretly she loved it. "I really want to catch up with you guys a little later, though."

"Definitely!" I said. I like Kimberley a lot, but being at a signing party four days after my contract went to shit is a little tough to take.

I grabbed Logek's hand and led the way toward the bar and ordered a gin and tonic for me and a martini for her. The bartender set the drinks down in front of us. We picked them up and clinked the glasses before taking a long drink. Good stuff.

"Do you know anybody here?" I asked.

Logek scanned the room. "Mary and Susan are over there." I followed her finger. Mary was our friend that signed with a man when she was only twenty-two and then surprised us all when she signed with a woman at thirty. I thought she and Pete, her first partner, were such a perfect couple, until she signed with Susan, and that actually seemed more perfect. Gotta hand it to the girl.

We made our way over to them and exchanged hugs. They were both super cute—not beautiful—but cute. And charming. The type of girls you like immediately.

Mary and Susan naturally asked all the friendly questions about jobs and partners so I had to run through the Jonathan story again, and Logek took the opportunity to segue into the Adam tidbit as well.

I was starting to feel my cocktail, a nice warm relaxed feeling spreading through me. See? I'm at a signing party and I'm not even wallowing.

My phone buzzed and I looked at the screen. Text from Jonathan. Perfect timing.

You want to come by tonight? I'll make you dinner . . .

Great. I turned the screen to the girls and all three of them quickly read the text.

Mary frowned. "That doesn't exactly sound like a man ending a contract."

"Yeah, I know. This has been my life the last week."

"Confusing," Susan observed.

"Very. I think he just figured I'd be cool with a time-out and we'd high five or something and then get back together in a couple of years."

"Such horseshit," Logek said. I smiled at her.

"Are you going to go?" Susan asked.

"No. Definitely not. I already slipped back into that once. Not doing it again."

"What she means," Logek said, "is that *he* slipped into *her.*"

"Thank you for translating," I said, with a smirk at Logek.

"You're welcome."

I typed back. *At Kimberley's signing party. I'll probably be here till late.*

:(

Sad face? Are you freaking kidding me? That does not even warrant a response.

The four of us migrated back toward the bar, chitchatting here and there with acquaintances. After one more drink with us at the bar, Mary and Susan said they had to get going.

---

* *Subject to the following terms and conditions*

"But we need to go out soon. Celebrate the death of your contract," Mary said, hugging me tightly.

I laughed. "We'll definitely have to do that."

I got a hug from Susan and they headed out, hand in hand, happily signed, in love. I'm happy for them. Mostly. At least 90 percent happy and only 10 percent jealous. Okay, maybe 80 percent happy.

Logek put a fresh drink in my hand. What does that make? Three? Time to sip this bad boy. I need to avoid any drunk dialing and/or texting tonight.

"You're a bad influence on me. It seems like you're always putting a drink in my hand."

"It's my job as BFF. Birthdays, breakups, and, in your case, DA offices. Those are the occasions when it is my duty to get you drunk."

"So once I'm past these events, no more getting me drunk?"

"Well, it's not a hard-and-fast rule."

A stocky guy with a nice face approached us. Of course. Logek could draw men like moths to a flame and I didn't exactly qualify as the ugly friend requiring a wingman, thank you very much. So, yeah, men had been watching. And me . . . first night out with no token. Naked.

"Logek, right?" he said, extending his hand to her.

She nodded, looking suspicious and shaking his hand.

"We met at the media conference." Logek is in radio sales. It was plausible.

"Hmm. What was your name?"

"Daniel. I'm with Comcast. You told me you had a friend that used to be in television? Remember?"

"Oh! Right. Oh my gosh! How are you, Daniel?"

She had no effing clue who he was.

"Great," he said, sidling in by the bar next to her. Yeah—
like we don't know that you use ordering from the bartender
as an excuse to squeeze in close to us. Maybe Adam was
wrong about me—maybe I do have a cynical streak.

Daniel and Logek started chitchatting and I felt like a
third wheel standing there, pretending to be part of the conversation, so I turned around to scan the room again, looking for someone I knew. Come on, reason-to-walk-away.
You must be here somewhere.

As if on cue, a stockier, less-pretty version of Daniel
approached me. Really? This is what I have to look forward
to being single? I did not give him a friendly face.

"Your name is Kate, right? Aren't you new at Samson and
Tule?" Oops. Pretty sure my reaction makes me the asshole,
not him. I think I remember how to be nice. Vaguely.

Trying to make up for my initial bitch impersonation, I
gave him a friendly smile. "Yes. Started there just this last
week."

He nodded, giving me an uncomfortably slow up-and-
down scan with his eyes. "I heard Adam hired you."

Oh, hell. I take back every second of remorse I had over
being shallow about your appearance. Let's just assume I
have really good radar and could tell you were a dick from
three feet away.

"Not directly," I said. Smile gone.

"I work close with Adam on lots of stuff. I may have to
borrow you sometime."

Not likely, dirtbag.

My phone buzzed. I rudely held it up in front of my face to check it. Adam. Irony.

"What did you say your name was?" I asked. Bitter Kate, three drinks in, was not in the mood for bullshit.

"Tom," he said with a nod. His insinuation that somehow *if* I'd been screwing Adam, that would somehow open the door for him to get in on that action? Gag.

I looked at the text.

How's it going?

I been better. Talking to one of hyour coworkers rite now. Seems to think that you two are tight and that he might "borrow" me from you somtiem. WTF? I looked down at the message I'd sent. Drinking and typing do not mix.

Who is it?

Names Tom.

No response.

And then Tom's phone rang. Holy shit. No. Couldn't be.

"Hey," Tom said, answering his phone and turning away slightly. His eyes shot back to me and he walked away. Just like that. No awkward good-bye. Just turned and walked off through the crowd until I couldn't see the asshole anymore. Wow. I was angry . . . but also a little flattered that Adam handled my problem so quickly. If it was really him.

My phone buzzed. Adam again.

Sorry about that.

You called him??

Of course.

For me? Or because he was implicating you? *Why?*

He had no business talking to you like that.

Oh.

So where did this unpleasant encounter take place?

You realize now he's realy going to think we're sleeping together. I mean now he can tell you textd me right when he was talking to me. And you stood up for me. Rumors will fly.

I don't care. People always talk. No stopping it. Where are you, Kate?

Singing party.

signing I corrected. My typing gets pretty bad after three cocktails. Four? Whatever.

Fun.

No. Not *fucking* fun. *Logek is getting hit on and so far the only person talked to me was douche bag Tom. I don't' kno many people. And I think I've had a lot of gin.*

How do you not have men all over you? Are you wearing a token?

No. *fuck tht. Why would I be wearing one?* (I also get really mouthy, apparently.)

Need a ride home?

Yes.

Where are you?

I told you . . . a signing party.

**Where* Kate.*

Oh. Right. *The Met.*

I'll be there in 10.

Oh, my. He's coming to get me?

I turned back to Logek. She seemed genuinely entertained by Daniel, which doesn't happen all the time. I downed the rest of my drink. 'Cause I obviously needed more alcohol. I set the glass on the bar and leaned close to Logek's ear.

"I'm gonna take off."

She whirled around toward me. "What? What do you mean? I drove you."

"I got a ride."

She raised her eyebrows and actually folded her arms over her chest. Oh. I was getting Mama Bear Logek. That was usually my role.

"Adam is gonna pick me up."

She did the exaggerated gesture of dropping her mouth open and looking at me with wide eyes.

"It's a long story. I'll tell you about it tomorrow. Just take my word for it that I've had a lot to drink and I really want to get out of here."

She was disappointed. "Okay. You sure you're okay?"

"Totally." That sounded sloppy.

She was frowning at me. "He's not going to take advantage of you?"

I snickered. "He doesn't even want me. No problem there. I am a fucking man-repellent."

"Kate."

"Shh," I said, doing a sloppy wave in front of my lips with my forefinger, librarian style. "Sorry. I'm fine. I just need away from the crowd. Okay? I'll call you tomorrow." I believe this is what they meant when they coined the term "hot mess."

"You sure? I'm fine leaving now and driving you home. Or you can stay at my house."

"He's already on his way. Trust me. It'll be fine."

"Okay."
"I love you."
"Love you, too."
And I headed for the door.

CHAPTER 6

The cold air hit and helped to clear my head somewhat. I looked up and down the street. Useless. I have no idea what kind of car he drives. It was a Friday night in midtown, so the sidewalks were busy and a steady stream of cars passed by.

Eventually, a black Audi with tinted windows rolled to a stop in front of me. Either I was about to have a *Pretty Woman* moment where I was going to be mistaken for a hooker, or it was Adam.

I waited for the window to roll down, but instead Adam got out of the driver's side and walked around to open my door. Holy hell, he looked good. He was in jeans and a T-shirt. That's all. Doesn't take much on him.

He looked down at me for a minute, assessing.

"What?"

"Nothing. Just trying to figure out how drunk you are."

"Not very. Somewhat. Probably."

He smiled, all beautiful white teeth, and that frickin' dimple again. "You okay?"

He's worried I'm going to get sick in his car. "Don't worry—your upholstery is safe."

"It's leather, and that wasn't what I was worried about."

Oh. And I busted out a wide grin, for no apparent reason other than he was pretty and came here just to give me a ride home. And he was worried about me, not his car.

He laughed and held my hand as I sat down in the passenger seat. He closed the door and climbed back in his side.

"So," he said.

"So," I replied. Still had that big, dumb grin on my face.

"Where do you want to go, Kate?"

Your bed. "I don't know."

"My place?"

"Okay."

"Or I can drive you to your parents'? Whatever you'd prefer."

"Your place." Hey—he offered.

We pulled away from the curb and glided down the dark streets. I realized I had no idea where he lived.

I looked over at him, but he had his eyes on the road. One hand was resting on the gearshift. Ooh. Six speed. Man who likes to drive. He glanced over at me and I looked away quickly. As though somehow he wouldn't have caught me watching him.

"So what exactly did you say to Tom?"

His lips twitched a little. Still angry, I think. "I told him that if he ever disrespected a friend of mine like that again, I'd have him fired."

"Yikes. He pissed me off, but I didn't mean to get him in quite that much trouble."

"He got himself in trouble. Not to mention, he seemed to imply that I share women." And he looked at me. "I never share women."

"Except with their partner."

He laughed. "Yeah. But then they are doing the sharing at that point, aren't they?"

"Aren't you worried about their partners finding out?"

"Not really. I'm not the one that signed a contract. If they want to be mad, maybe they should focus on the person that made the promises to them in the first place."

"Ouch. You've never had guys come after you when they found out you were shagging their partner?"

"Shagging?" That earned a smile from him. "Kate, I'm six foot four, two hundred twenty-five pounds, and I know how to handle myself. No. Not many men have ever come after me."

"Come on. Your size can't scare off everyone."

He smirked at me.

"Pervert," I said. "So, tell me. How do most of your affairs end?" I was relaxed and a little numb so the questions were pouring out. No holding back.

"Well, for one thing, I don't generally have long-running affairs. Those can get tricky even with signed women. But usually I'll cut it off when she starts to seem more interested in me than her partner."

"Have you ever been in love?" Wow. Totally unfiltered. He gave me a long look and then looked back out the front window, and I didn't think he would answer.

"No. I don't think so. I've cared about women, been very fond of them, but nothing that ever changed my mind about the whole paradigm."

"Sad."

"Think so?"

"Yep."

"And people called you an ice goddess."

I laughed and closed my eyes, settling my head back against the rest. "Apparently I don't keep my soft side as well hidden as I thought."

I heard him laugh again and then I must have dozed off. I woke up when he opened my door. He pulled me out by the hand and I realized we were in an empty underground parking garage. We walked toward the elevators and I heard his car chirp as he hit the alarm button. He kept hold of my hand as we got into the elevator like he was worried I'd fall flat on my face without the assistance. I wasn't going to correct him.

He grasped my hand again when we got out on the eleventh floor. As we walked down the quiet hallway, I looked toward the huge picture window at the end of the hall that looked over the lights of downtown. Quite a view, and this was just the hallway. We stopped in front of a door bearing the number 1111. That seemed appropriate somehow.

He unlocked the door and turned on the lights. I followed him as he walked through the living room, flipping on more lights.

* Subject to the following terms and conditions

"Holy cow," I said, standing in front of the huge window that covered most of the living room wall. You could see the river bridge, perfectly illuminated against the black night sky, and you could even see the lights of the ferryboats passing slowly under the bridge. "That's what I call a view."

"Yeah. It's very pretty. It's why I fell in love with the place."

I turned around and he was looking at me. Uh-oh. Butterflies. Settle down, Kate. I don't think any man has ever been clearer about not being interested.

"That's quite a dress."

Oh, my. "Thank you."

"Really. You look beautiful."

"Thank you."

"So why don't you sound like you believe it?"

I shrugged. "Been kicked while I'm down, I guess."

"How about some shorts and a T-shirt?"

"Yes, please."

He emerged from his room and handed me some folded-up clothes and pointed to the bathroom.

I closed the door behind me and got a look at myself in the mirror. Wow. I really had a lot of makeup on. Why does it look like more than when I left Logek's tonight? Overall, though, I was holding up nicely. I slipped out of my dress and tossed on the shirt he gave me. I put on the drawstring shorts and cinched them as tight as they'd go—enough that they'd stay up.

I laughed at my reflection. Kate Shaw—seductress. Adam's T-shirt was faded gray with the Italian flag on it and the

shorts were black and baggy and hit just above the knee.
Yeah. I was a bombshell.

I walked back into the living room and carefully draped
my dress over the recliner nearest the door. He turned from
looking out the window and faced me, grinning.

"I know, I know. I'm hot in everything I wear."

"Exactly what I was thinking," he said with a chuckle.
"Want anything to drink?"

"Water?"

"I think I've got that."

He'd changed, too. He was in long basketball shorts and
a tank top. His arms were big and defined and his shoulders looked even broader out of a shirt. He must look amazing shirtless. Down, girl. Friends with Adam. In love with
Jonathan. You wouldn't think these simple concepts would
be easy to forget.

He came back out and handed me a glass of ice water and
he had a beer in his other hand. He sat down on his big
leather sofa and patted the seat next to him. I sat down and
he tossed a coaster on the coffee table in front of me for my
glass.

"Thanks."

He nodded and turned on the TV and flipped through the
channels. This is kind of surreal. I'm in Adam's apartment.
Wearing Adam's clothes. Sitting next to Adam on the couch
like we're just two buddies having some downtime. Which I
guess we were. But I was buzzed and lonely and I couldn't
help thinking about what it would be like for him to kiss me.

He looked over at me then. Uh-oh. Busted.

"Drink your water, Kate."

Yeah. Water is good. He flipped through the channels and finally settled on some stand-up comedian on Comedy Central. The guy was pretty funny and soon I was into the show, laughing, and *not* thinking about attacking Adam. Which probably wouldn't have gone over so well.

He leaned back onto the arm of the couch and held his arms open to me. Seriously? Dude. This "friends" thing has some serious perks. I crawled up next to him and lay down on his chest and he wrapped his arms around me. So weird. He's awfully cuddly for someone thinking purely platonically. But once there, there was nothing more. No hand brushing dangerously close to any forbidden zones, no awkward shifting to make it feel inappropriate. He just seemed content.

"You said you have no female friends, right?"

"Nope."

"I'm guessing you don't do this with your guy friends."

He laughed and it reverberated through me. "We're trying to cut back."

"And I'm also going to guess, since you've never had a girlfriend, relationship-wise, you've never done much cuddling?"

"No."

"Hmm."

"Hmm?"

"Careful, buddy. If you fall for me, we have to stop being friends, remember?"

"Right. Thanks for reminding me. Have much of a problem with that?"

"Guys accidentally falling in love with me?"

"Yeah."

"You'd be surprised," I said, smiling against his chest. And it was sort of true. Logek was gorgeous and it has always seemed she could get any guy she wanted. I'm more of an acquired taste—most men either think I'm absolutely beautiful or only mildly attractive, but not much in between. And I certainly never got every guy I wanted—not by a long shot. But there were ones that I just hit a certain way, and then I was like catnip. Especially the ones that started out thinking they were just trying to get in my pants. I told them they'd fall for me and it was like a self-fulfilling prophecy. And it was the ones that said it would never happen that fell the hardest. Once I had a guy, I never lost him. But I guess Jonathan is breaking my twenty-year streak on that one.

"Is that right? And you think I'm at risk of accidentally falling for you?" he asked.

I crossed my hands on his chest and rested my chin on them so that I could see him. He was looking down at me, dark brows lowered. In the low light, his eyes were a deeper green and I was close enough to see little flecks of blue and gold in them. It was weird. It was like I could see right through him. I don't know why, but some people, on rare occasions, I just get. Like Mozart with the piano. And Adam— I just got him.

The real Adam was buried so deep, so untouchable, it would be a miracle to ever break through that wall.

I shook my head a little, without lifting my chin. "No. I don't think you are at risk."

He narrowed his eyes, his curiosity piqued. "And why is that?"

"Because you keep the real you tucked so far away, no one will ever really get close."

He frowned but didn't say anything.

"You're so pretty that everything has always come so easy to you, but it's also made you devalue things. And people have always proven you right. They were so delighted with the package that they never cared what was underneath. So you felt like if you were happy or sad deep down, nobody noticed, nobody cared. So you have a permanent game face. And every time someone reinforced this belief, you slipped further away."

His expression didn't change, but his lips pursed.

"Or I could just be drunk and talking shit."

The corner of his mouth quirked up a bit at that. But I'd hit home. Found a crack in the facade.

"Shut up, Kate," he said gently, and pushed my head back down so that my cheek was against his chest again. He settled his arms around me and we both refocused on the television.

*

I woke with a start, disoriented, blinking at the sun coming through the big window. Adam's window. I rolled over and realized I was on his couch with a chenille blanket tucked around me and a pillow under my head. I sat up slowly, thanks to the dull gin-and-tonic ache in the back of my head. I stood and folded the blanket carefully and set it neatly on top of the pillow.

The sun was cutting through the window, but it must be early still. I got my phone out of my little black purse that paired with the little black dress and checked the time. 6:45 a.m. Figuring Adam was still asleep and thinking I probably already overstayed my welcome, I googled cab companies. I was just about to dial when the front door opened and Adam came in.

He was winded and sweaty. Eff me. He was in cycling clothes, including those spandex shorts that leave little to the imagination. Oh, yeah. We cannot be friends anymore. Don't stare. Don't stare. Shit. His hair was damp and messy. His light eyes contrasted with his bronzed skin. His face was flushed and his skin was shimmery. He didn't even look real. Too perfect—too much like the cover of a romance novel. Funny, since he was the icon for anti-romance of any kind.

"You're up," he said, grabbing a towel from the counter and wiping it across his face and hair. "I'll jump in the shower. Give me fifteen minutes."

"K." That was all I could manage. My girlie parts were awake and tingling and he was going to go get in the shower. Naked. Alone. I sighed inwardly. What a waste.

I went into his room and closed the door to change back into my dress. He had a big four-poster bed in dark wood with rich sable-colored sheets. His room smelled delicious, but not like cologne, more like shampoo or really awesome deodorant. I slipped off his clothes, folded them neatly, and put them on the bed. I was sliding my dress over my hips, my back to the door, when he walked into the room.

"Oh, sorry. Didn't know you were in here."

I looked over my shoulder and saw him looking. Ha! I wasn't the only one ogling their "buddy" this morning. Victory.

I put my arms into the sleeves and quickly pulled the dress up over my breasts so that I was (mostly) decent.

"It's okay. Buddy," I said.

He gave me a disapproving look, and I laughed and walked up to him and turned around, pulling my hair to one side. "Will you zip me?"

I felt the pressure of his hand on my lower back, holding the dress in place while his other hand slid the zipper up my back, his fingers brushing my skin lightly between my shoulder blades, and ending at the base of my neck. And I think I almost had an orgasm.

He leaned close to my ear. "There you go. Buddy."

Dick. Turnabout may be fair play, but it sucks.

*

After hitting a Starbucks drive-through, Adam drove me out to my parents' house. I told him Logek would come get me, but he insisted it was no problem.

"Nice area," he said, cruising slowly through my parents' neighborhood.

"It is. I grew up out here."

"Ah. A poor, disadvantaged youth."

I cocked an eyebrow at him. "Something tells me you didn't rough it too much growing up, either."

"Fair enough."

I pointed out the house and we rolled to a stop in front of it and, because my life is *absolutely* perfect these days, parked behind Jonathan's blue Range Rover.

"Shit," I muttered.

Adam was quiet and still for a moment, and then he must have just decided "screw it" because he casually got out of the car, walked around to my side, and opened my door for me.

I took his hand as he helped me out onto the sidewalk and just looked at me, smiling slightly, amused by the whole situation. Ass.

I looked in Jonathan's SUV, but he wasn't in it. Then the front door opened and, just like that, we had a frickin' party. Mom and Dad walked out of the house behind Jonathan. He must have stopped by looking for me, and they were just walking him out, because all three of them were comically surprised to see Adam and me standing on the sidewalk.

"Kate," Mom said, taking a long look at Adam before focusing on me.

Screw it. This is happening.

I gripped Adam's forearm and led him up the walkway.

"Adam, these are my parents, Deanna and Jeff. Mom, Dad, this is my friend Adam Lucas."

They all smiled and shook hands.

"Very nice to meet you both," Adam said, with a voice and smile that could sell ice to Eskimos. And then, turning to Jonathan, Adam said, "And nice to see you again, Jonathan."

"You, too," Jonathan said, shaking Adam's proffered hand. Jonathan was not exuding the same goodwill vibe Adam was, however. It didn't help that I was in a cocktail dress. At nine in the morning. Just getting home.

Hmm. How to untangle this mess. Someone's got to go.

Adam, bless him, turned to me and put his hands lightly on my shoulders. "I've got to run. I'm meeting a friend for racquetball. I'll talk to you later." And he gave me a kiss on the cheek. He waved to the rest of the group and got into his car and drove away.

Mom and Dad looked at each other, uncomfortably. "We'll, uh, go inside," Dad said.

Once the door closed behind them, Jonathan and I faced off on the front walkway. I knew what it looked like and I knew what he had to be thinking. What I didn't know was how Jonathan was going to choose to handle this situation.

"How was Kimberley's signing party?" he asked.

Really? Would it kill someone just once to do something predictable?

"It was nice. She seems really happy."

"Was Adam at the party?"

"No." Sure, I could elaborate. If I wanted to.

He pulled his full lips together. He must want to say many, many things. I know I would. He propped his hands on his hips and looked down at the ground. When he looked up at me again, his brown eyes were all melty and wounded.

"Nothing happened, Jonathan." What the hell, Kate! (I yell at myself a lot these days.) He did not deserve that disclaimer. He didn't deserve anything. I owed him nothing. He chose this. One little, wounded, puppy-dog look and I go brain dead.

"Really?" he asked, perking up.

"Really," I said, with an exasperated sigh. It was none of his business anymore if something happened or not. Yeah, technically the contract wasn't over for a week, but no court will enforce the covenants of a contract that isn't being renewed in that last week. That's why they usually call the last few days of the contract "the termination period." It's not black-letter law—just widely accepted practice that the courts don't typically enforce any big judgments over actions that take place in that window. So this wasn't about the contract—it was about us.

"You can't keep doing this, Jonathan," I said. "It isn't fair."

He nodded. He covered his face with his hands and rubbed them roughly across his face and then over his hair, clasping his hands behind his neck, looking weary. That position made the muscles in his chest and arms show clearly through the shirt, and made me forget a couple of the reasons I was supposed to be angry with him.

"I'm sorry, Kate."

"I'll agree with you there."

"I just somehow told myself that you and I could be independent for a while, take a break from the contract, but still be *together* somehow."

"You thought that I'd be fine with you ending things?"

"I just didn't really think about *ending things*."

"You realize that you make no sense at all, right?"

"Yes."

"I didn't need a break from you, Jonathan. I'm entitled to be hurt that you needed a break from me."

"But I don't want a break from you."

"But you do! You want to live alone, not answer to anyone, sleep with who you want. You want that. That is a *break*. And you don't get *that* and *me*. I don't work that way."

"I know that, Kate. I just . . ."

"You want it all."

"I guess so." And he took a quick step in to me and looked into my face. "I obviously just didn't give enough thought to how impossible it was going to be to let go of you. Even temporarily." He put a hand to the back of my head so that I wouldn't pull away and leaned in to kiss me. I turned my face so that my cheek was to him. He sighed and rested his forehead against my temple a moment and then kissed my cheek. His lips were velvety soft, and I'll be damned if that wasn't the most sensual kiss on the cheek I've ever had.

I needed to be sure not to lose myself again, so I put a hand against his chest and pushed him back. "My dad and I will be over later to get the rest of my stuff."

He frowned. "Okay. Do you want me to help?"

"It might be easier if you weren't there."

Ugh. There was the puppy-dog thing again, but it passed quickly and he looked oddly invigorated. "Okay, I'll be leaving about two p.m. Will that work?"

I nodded.

He smiled and cupped my cheek with his hand before turning away and climbing into his car. I stood looking at the street where his car had been after he drove away.

I walked inside and went straight to my room to change. Then I headed back out to the kitchen to debrief the folks.

"Okay," I said, dropping onto one of the barstools near the counter they were leaning against. Mom looked at me with big, blue eyes over the rim of her coffee cup as she sipped. Mom and I look a lot alike—straight dark hair, light blue eyes—but she is only about five foot five and not as lean as I am. I get my height and build from my dad. He had sandy blond hair, but it's mostly gray now to match his eyes. He's tall and lanky, though. Even at sixty, he's still the type that can eat and eat and eat and not put on weight. I don't quite have it that good, but I'm certainly skinnier than I deserve to be given my eating (and drinking) habits.

Dad looked amused by the situation, wearing a smile that reminded me of Adam's—not because the two looked anything alike, but because they both could find humor in my discomfort.

"In a hundred words or less . . . that was Adam Lucas—yes, the guy that got me the job. Yes, he's beautiful. No, there is nothing going on with us—we are just friends. I was at a signing party with Logek last night, not in the best mood, and Adam asked if I wanted him to come get me. I said yes. We watched TV. I slept on his couch. He bought me Starbucks this morning," I said, gesturing to the cup in my hand as physical evidence that my story was true. "And he drove me home. Which was when you walked out of the house with Jonathan. There. Now you are all caught up."

They both smiled at me and quietly sipped their coffee.

*

That evening I finished putting my clothes away in the closet and the dressers. One of the guest rooms would be the temporary repository of my furniture and other housewares. Jonathan and I didn't sign till I was twenty-seven. We both had our own households set up, so when we moved in together after signing, we already knew what belonged to who. All the items in the house were surprisingly identifiable as being mine or his. There were a couple of things I wasn't sure about, but I wasn't in the mood to bust out the contract to figure out the particulars. We'll figure it out later.

When I finished, I lay back on the bed and dialed Logek. I sent her a quick text this morning to let her know I hadn't been attacked or abducted and she'd insisted on a follow-up call later.

"Hey there," she said.

"Hey."

"So?"

"Well, as I said in my text, I'm home safe and sound."

"Uh-huh, but I'm interested in the hours that led up to you being home safe and sound."

"It's nice to know that my mess of a life has created such an interesting topic of conversation. Between you and my parents, I'm starting to feel like a Kardashian."

"As if a Kardashian ever could have lasted under contract for the full seven years."

"True."

"And your butt is too small to be a Kardashian."

"I love you."

"I know. Now spill it."

*

Once Logek was satisfied that she'd pried out all the relevant details, we said good-bye and I decided to send Adam a quick thank-you text.

Thanks for picking me up last night, letting me stay, and driving me home. I appreciate it a lot.

After a few minutes, he replied.

You're very welcome. How'd it go after I left?

He actually took it pretty well that you and I are sleeping together once he realized how in love we are.

Very understanding guy.

Well, even though he didn't deserve an explanation, I told him right away that nothing happened.

After all the work I did to make the scenario look as damning as possible?

I know. I know. Opportunity to torture him squandered.

And once he knew there was nothing going on?

He was relieved. And he tried to kiss me. Which he really needs to stop doing.

Maybe you should stop letting him?

That's one way to go. And I only let him kiss me on the cheek. I think I deserve a medal or something.

You are a pillar of strength. So he wants to be free, but he'd prefer you aren't.

That's the gist.

Dick.

And I surprised myself by immediately wanting to type fifteen different rebuttals to that accusation and convince Adam what a good guy Jonathan really is. Thankfully, I stopped myself because, a) Jonathan doesn't deserve my protection, and b) it shouldn't matter to me what Adam thinks of Jonathan. I think.

Adam must have read into my lack of reply because he followed it up with another text.

Sorry, Kate. Not my place.

It's okay. You're not exactly seeing him in his finest hour. I'm sure.

Adam's last response took a couple of minutes to arrive so, based on my stellar investigation skills, he either didn't know what to say or he started to type some long reply and then changed his mind. Hmm. Or, I suppose it's possible that he has something to do other than sit around texting me and that's why there was a delay. Nah.

CHAPTER 7

The entire two-week stint at Samson & Tule flew by so fast that it felt a little strange that it was over already.

I tidied up my workstation and deleted any personal passwords I had on the computer before shutting it off and heading for the elevator.

Marnie wished me luck on my way out and Marley came out from behind her desk to give me a hug.

Once outside, I made my way to the parking garage. I was just thinking that I kind of wished I'd seen Adam before I left, when I looked up to see him leaning against my car. He was in black slacks, an ash-gray dress shirt, and a moss-green tie to match his eyes. His hands were in his pockets and his black suit jacket was draped through the crook of his elbow. Delicious.

"Hello, Kate."

"Adam," I said, giving him a regal nod of my head—because I knew he'd think it was funny.

"All done with us here, I guess."

"Looks that way."

"Just use us and walk away."

"Like a cheap whore."

He grinned. "So. Tomorrow's the day?"

"Officially."

"Going out drinking?"

"Highly likely."

"Where? I may need to meet up with you and contribute to your hangover."

I laughed. "Dive Bar."

"*A* dive bar? Or *the* Dive Bar?"

"*The* Dive Bar. I'm determined to finally see the damn mermaid in the tank. They claim she's in there on a regular schedule, but I have yet to see her." The Dive Bar has an aquarium above the bar that runs nearly its entire length. There is a tip jar for the mermaid, but no mermaid. So far, she's just hearsay.

"I've only been there once and she was in there."

"See? Tease. Now you've jinxed me and she won't be in there again."

"What time?"

"Probably nineish."

"Okay. I'll text you." And he hugged me. Like a really good, tight hug where he lifted me off the ground for a moment. "It's been a pleasure having you around the office, Kate Shaw," he said, as he turned and walked away.

*

The next night I was sitting on the (closed) toilet in Logek's bathroom as she did her Kate-just-got-dumped-so-we-need-to-make-her-feel-twice-as-sexy-and-desirable-tonight makeup job.

"Did you bring it?" she asked. She quickly followed up with "Don't move."

"So answer or don't move?"

"Don't move." She blotted my lips with a tissue, made a quick swipe at the corners of my mouth with her fingers, and stood back to look at her finished artwork. "Okay. Answer."

"Yes, I brought it. Not sure I'm up for any black magic tonight, though."

"Well, it does involve matches, but no incantations, so we should be okay."

"Why do people feel the need to symbolically burn their contract?"

"Closure."

"Hmm."

"I assume this is not the original?" she asked, taking the folded papers from me.

"Of course not."

She smiled and led me by the hand into her living room. She knelt in front of the fireplace and pulled me down next to her. She lit the gas flame and held the contract out to me.

I raised my eyebrows at her, not really sure what sort of ceremony she had in mind.

Subject to the following terms and conditions

"Dearly beloved," she began. Oh dear god. "We are here to bid a sad farewell to Kate's youth."

"Excuse me?"

"Sorry. Got this mixed up with your birthday speech." She ignored my glare and cleared her throat dramatically. "We are here to lay to rest Kate's expired contract. We will remember the joy it brought her and think of it fondly." She pulled the first couple of pages off the pack and tossed them into the flames. They quickly turned black and crumpled to ash. "But we are also here to let go of the past . . ." (More pages into the fire.) "So that Kate—and her girlie parts—can move on to a better, if not bigger, future."

"Wow. So touching," I said, tossing a few more pages into the fireplace.

"I know. I should be a minister."

"You're definitely hired for my eulogy."

"Moving on," she said, grabbing the remaining papers of the contract and tossing them irreverently into the flames. "You were a good contract," she said, apparently addressing the ashes, "but you're gone now and life is for the living. Peace out."

I wiped faux tears from my eyes. "You were too young to die," I said, following in Logek's melodramatic footsteps. "But your dad was a dick who killed you before your time."

Logek and I smiled at each other. "Amen," she said.

"Amen. Let's drink."

"Yep. Anyone else you wanted to invite tonight?"

"I told Adam where we'd be."

"You did?"

"He asked. He might come buy me a drink."

"How thoughtful."

"Isn't he, though?"

She picked up her cell and I listened to her order a cab. The plan was for there to be no sober driver tonight. Some of our best nights have started with a cab call.

"Alright," she said, heading back toward her bedroom. "Get your skinny ass in here so that I can finish your hair."

I followed obediently. She did another flip or two. My hair was basically straight and while it wouldn't really hold a curl, it would hold a flip, so Logek put a few flips in some of my layers to give my hair some body. I looked in the mirror. Very dramatic. I think she may have outdone the makeup job she did for the signing party last weekend. I needed the boost.

"Looks good," I said.

"Looks amazing, I think is what you meant to say."

"Yeah, that. I hope this shit is waterproof."

"No." She pointed a finger in my face. "We did the closure thing. That means no tears tonight. Unless of course you were implying that you would be sweating it off later with some hot stranger."

"You know me so well."

"Come on. First night as a free woman. That's fun. Focus on that."

"Yeah. That should be an awesome conversation: 'Hi, I'm Kate, a recently unemployed thirty-four-year-old, living with my parents.'"

"So don't mention you live with your parents. Tell them . . . you have *older roommates*," she said.

I laughed. "Or, I could tell them my parents live *with me*."

"Perfect. You're such a good daughter taking care of your

elderly parents until you can find other arrangements for them."

"I really am." Logek and I were getting the giggles. "Funny how you can use the exact same words, but change the order, and get an entirely different meaning," I said.

"Delivery is everything."

The cab driver called her phone to tell us he was downstairs. So. Logek's rules for the night. Crying not okay. Random sex with stranger okay. Easy enough to remember. I think I'd be okay with avoiding both of those.

Logek and I (elegantly, I assure you) chugged our glasses of wine and headed out.

We climbed in the back of the yellow cab and Logek, as usual, engaged the driver in friendly chitchat. I think it made her feel like she could skimp on the tip without feeling guilty. I'll admit—the two of us have screwed over some cab drivers in our day (unintentionally, usually through cash mismanagement) and they do seem to take it rather cheerfully.

We hopped out of the cab when he stopped in front of Dive Bar and walked past the line of fifty or so people and waited for the bouncer at the rope. Don't judge me. Fact is, bouncers will let cute girls in without waiting in line as long as we don't have guys with us. Many cocktails and a misplaced sense of entitlement helped me figure this out during a girls' trip to Vegas some years ago. They let cute girls into the club for free because then guys are willing to pay $25 a head to get in so that they can buy said cute girls $12 martinis in the hopes that they will get lucky.

The bouncer walked over to us and smiled. He held up his

fingers, communicating that he wanted to see our IDs. Adorable.

"Cover tonight is ten dollars for ladies."

I smiled and held up five fingers. That's right. This girl can negotiate.

He frowned at me, but opened the rope and waived us through. Yeah, I know—who cares? It's $5. But it's not the five bucks, it's the sport, and now I'm starting out the night a winner.

Logek and I were both in our typical bar wear—jeans (because it's not like we're trying too hard), cute tops with cleavage (because men are basically simple creatures), and heels (because I apparently feel the need to be at least six feet tall when we go out). Good times. It was a formula that was tested and approved. Guys turned and watched us walk past, headed for the bar. We, of course, pretended not to notice. It has been a while since I actually wanted men to pay attention to me, which is usually the best way to ensure that it wouldn't happen. Damn.

Logek ordered us drinks, and I downed the first one pretty fast and ordered a second. Now I don't have to be drunk to have a good time—just thought I'd throw that out there.

The alcohol started to do its trick, making me feel warm and relaxed. And in my own mind, I was getting funnier and more charming. This did not always mirror reality, but for tonight, let's say it does.

I stole a peek at my phone to make sure I didn't have any new texts. Not totally certain who I was expecting a text from.

Logek turned up the smile. Incoming. I turned around to

see two really good-looking guys headed our way. Hmm. The night is off to a decent start. Then they grasped hands and the lead guy leaned to the far side of Logek to order drinks from the bartender. Swing and a miss.

I felt a tap on my shoulder and turned around to see Adam smiling down at me. And I lit up like a freaking Christmas tree. Pathetic. He wrapped me in a big hug and then actually leaned in and gave Logek a one-armed hug. "How are you, Logek?"

"Good," she said, looking a little stunned at his friendliness. Pleased, but stunned.

"Are you drunk yet?" he asked, focusing on me again.

"Nope," I said, putting a little too much oomph on the "p" sound. He grinned. "I'll help. Logek, whatcha drinking?"

"Martini."

"And from the smell of you, you're drinking gin again."

I just smiled, feeling borderline giddy. He was so great. Talk about a pick-me-up. Out to drown my sorrows and this totally beautiful, sweet *friend* shows up to hang out. *And* try to be friends with my friend. How awesome is that? Everything was feeling pretty awesome.

Adam turned toward us again and he had four shots in his hands.

Logek took the one he offered her. She held the little glass up toward her face. "This doesn't look like a martini."

"That's because it's Patrón."

"That explains it," she said.

He put one in my hand, and just as I was about to ask why there were four, another guy walked up to our group. Interesting. He was almost as tall as Adam, but sort of a light doppelgänger version. Sandy blond hair, blue eyes, and fair-skinned. He had a strong jaw and a small cleft in his chin. Apparently good-looking guys run in packs. I wonder if that means he's a contract killer, too?

"Dave, this is Kate and Logek."

Dave and I shook hands. "Congrats and/or condolences." I laughed at that.

"Thank you. I think."

He turned to Logek and took her outstretched hand. "Logek?"

"Yes, pronounced 'logic' but not spelled the same."

"Gotcha. Clever."

"Thanks."

"So, Dave," I said. Shit. "You are a friend of Adam's?"

"Sometimes." Cute.

"Does that mean you're a contract killer, too?" I swear to god. I'm like a five-year-old when I drink. Filterless.

Adam and Dave started laughing.

"Yes, Kate. Dave is another soulless bastard, like me," Adam said, smirking.

I smiled, turning back to Dave. "Well, lucky for you I kind of have a soft spot for soulless bastards."

"Then my night is looking up." Wow. Great smile. And he's flirting. Which seems like breaking some rules, right? I mean, he knows I'm expiring tonight. Ignore it.

"So what are you two gentlemen up to tonight?" Logek asked.

"Isn't this enough?" Dave asked.

Logek smiled, all seductive and gorgeous. She can't help it. Playing with men is hardwired into her DNA. And contract killer or not, they were not immune.

"Well it should be, but you two have peculiar interests."

Adam's mouth dropped at that, as did Dave's. Adam recovered first. "Thank you for making it sound so perverse."

"I do what I can," Logek said.

Adam finally put the fourth shot in Dave's hand and then held his out in the middle of us. "To Kate."

We clinked glasses and downed the tequila. Yuck. Don't care if it is fancy tequila. Tequila is still tequila. Adam chuckled at my expression and turned back to the bar, grabbing the cocktails we originally requested, and handed them to Logek and me. Nothing like chasing a tequila shot with a gin and tonic. This night has the potential to go seriously awry.

"Tell us about yourself, Dave," Logek said.

Dave gave her a long look (most men do) and did a little one-sided smile. "Well, I'm a Sagittarius, I like surfing, snow-skiing, and movies starring Bruce Willis."

"Thank you for that very dating-profilish answer," she said.

He laughed all good-naturedly and friendly. Yeah. He's probably (almost) as good as Adam at getting women into bed.

"Actually, I'm a sportscaster for channel forty."

"I watch seven." Logek was sparring. Good-looking men were so used to women fawning, and I think they were rarely prepared for a girl like Logek.

"I can change that."

Ooh. Point, Dave.

And Logek erupted into laughter, surprised at such a forward challenge. She, too, was used to being the intimidating one. They were like two big-game hunters, squaring off for a pissing contest. My money, as usual, was on Logek. I'm sure to her, being single and all, taking down a contract killer would be like downing a rhino or something. I looked over at Adam, taking in his cool, distant look as he observed their banter. Taking down Adam would be like downing a friggin' unicorn.

"What about you, Kate?" Dave asked.

"What about me?"

"Seven or forty?"

"Oh. Neither. I've been in law school and haven't watched local news in years."

"Well played," Adam said, nudging me with his elbow.

"Adam didn't mention you were a lawyer." Which made me raise my eyebrows because, really, what would Adam mention about me?

"And what did he mention about me?" See? Like a damn five-year-old. Every little thought just spills out.

"That you were a friend of his going out to celebrate the demise of your contract." He stopped, and I thought he was finished, but then he added, "And he said you were beautiful."

"Oh." Weren't prepared for that, were you, smarty-pants? I looked at the floor, back up at Dave, anywhere but at Adam. And I'm pretty sure I was getting all flushed, too. Awesome.

Dave looked at me appraisingly. Not sure what he thought he was seeing, but I don't think it was what he expected.

"Women that look like you are usually better at taking a compliment," he said.

I didn't say anything, just looked him in the eye. He looked away first, refocusing on Logek.

"You're beautiful, too," he said, grinning at her.

She smiled. "Thank you."

He immediately turned back to me and said, "See?"

Why was I the epicenter of this little group? I was getting uncomfortable with all the commentary. And Adam was quiet, but also entirely focused on me. I'm used to being the sidekick around Logek. This was new to me and, oddly, I was finding it pretty unpleasant.

"I'm not drunk enough for this much scrutiny," I said with a laugh.

"Sorry," Dave said, all boyish charm. "Can I get you a drink?"

"Still working on this one," I said, holding up my glass.

"Logek?"

"Not quite."

"Alright." He leaned in close next to me to order from the bartender. Like really close, actually putting a hand to the small of my back, like he was trying not to squish me. Man, he smelled good. And it felt really conspicuous, like he was somehow making a pass at me in front of Adam and Logek. I inched forward a bit to give him a little more room and looked up at Adam, who was smiling at me faintly.

Adam grabbed my hand and pulled me to his side, away from Dave. Realizing I'd moved, Dave turned around innocently and said, "Sorry—didn't mean to crowd you."

"Not a problem."

Dave was now leaning against the bar in my former spot, standing next to Logek. He handed a glass to Adam.

"Macallan," he said. Scotch. Love the smell—the taste makes me want to vomit.

Dave turned to Logek. "What do you do? Aside from watch channel seven."

"I'm in radio sales for the Sandstone Group."

"Oh. I know a guy over there. Ricky Martin?"

"Pretty sure he goes by Rich."

"I know, but I call him Ricky to piss him off."

"You guys must be close."

Dave laughed. "We go back to high school. I think there's a rule that if you know someone for fifteen years or more, embarrassing nicknames are fair game."

"Kate and I have been friends since high school."

"Lucky you," he said to her, before looking at me again. Dude. Seriously? I'm single! The absurdity of that statement in my head—that it was the *complete* opposite of what a woman would normally use to protest being hit on—made me start giggling. Now they all looked at me, but for good reason. And once the giggles started, they took on a life of their own, all from an inside thought they knew nothing about.

"What?" Dave asked.

I waved my hands in front of me. "Nothing. Just," and I pointed to my head like that would somehow explain it. When I realized how stupid *that* was, I started laughing all over again. "Sorry," I said, taking deep breaths. "Dead puppies, dead puppies, dead puppies."

"What?" Adam asked, regarding me curiously.

"Dead puppies. You know," I said, turning to him. "When you are trying to stop laughing, you think of something sad?"

He chuckled low and shook his head. "Never heard that one."

"There you go—I'm educational." Oh, yeah. Tequila and gin is always a good idea. And let us not forget the wine at Logek's.

I started wiping the tears out of my eyes and then remembered I had about a pound of makeup on and fixing this would require a mirror. "I'm going to go to the bathroom and fix this," I said, with an exaggerated flourish of my hand past my face.

"Thank god," Dave said. "Do something because you are a train wreck."

I wrinkled my nose at him, because I was too mature to stick out my tongue, and turned and headed to the back of the bar where the restrooms were. I looked up at the fish tank that ran horizontally along the ceiling nearly the whole length of the bar and I'll be damned. There she was. The mermaid. She was a redhead with long, flowy hair, wearing a shell bra and a long shimmering green tail. She moved gracefully through the water, did a somersault like the Olympic swimmers do at the end of the pool, and headed back the other direction.

"Adam!" I called out. The music was loud and he was a distance away, but he still turned when I yelled. When he looked at me, I pointed frantically at the mermaid swimming past in the tank. He looked at her and then back at me, laughing, no doubt, at my childishness. I was grinning ear

to ear, did a little giddy dance thing (cute, not at all humili-
ating, I'm sure) and turned down the dark hall that led to
the bathroom.

I got inside and waited for a spot by the mirror. When one
opened up, I grabbed a paper towel and dabbed my eyes dry.
So ironic. I remember asking Logek if the makeup was waterproof. Never in a million years would have guessed that I
would need waterproof makeup tonight because I'd laugh
till I cried. Score. The makeup *was* waterproof. I blotted the
corners of my eyes, tossed the towel, and headed back out.

As I headed down the hallway, I saw Adam waiting for
me. When he saw me coming, he stretched a twenty-dollar
bill between his hands and held it up to show me before
stuffing it into the mermaid's tip jar that was at the end of
the bar, and then he kept walking toward me. I stopped and
waited for him to get to me, leaning against the wall in the
hallway. He was graceful when he moved, confident. He was
still wearing a broad smile, making his face more genuinely
warm than I'd ever seen it. The dimple was helping.

"Twenty bucks, huh?"

He reached me and tucked his hands in the pockets of his
jeans. "Are you kidding? That little dance you did was worth
every penny."

I laughed. "Yeah—took me years to learn that one. If
you're nice, I'll teach it to you."

He tipped his head to the side as he looked down at me.
He looked relaxed. Happy. Not that he normally looked
unhappy, he just usually seemed so guarded. I'm going to go
ahead and take credit for this.

Without thinking it through, even a little bit, I reached

out and put my hands on the sides of his face, stood up on my tippy-toes, and kissed him. His lips were soft, but firm. So different from Jonathan's. Adam's body stiffened. I definitely caught him off guard. Please kiss me back. Please, oh please, oh please.

He turned us so that my back was up against the wall and gripped my jaw with one big hand. I went for it before he could change his mind. I slipped my tongue between his lips, kissed each lip individually, running my tongue along the edge of it. And I won. He kissed me back. The kiss felt a little out of hand after that. His whole body pressed against me. When he slipped his tongue into my mouth, I sucked on it, making him lean into me harder. His hand slid down my jaw so that it was wrapped gently across my throat, keeping me pinned against the wall. I pulled one of his full lips between mine and bit it lightly. He gripped my throat a little tighter and kissed me hard on the lips. And then he stopped.

He abruptly took a step back and put his hands into his pockets as though he needed to keep control of them. He looked at me intensely, frowning, frustrated. He looked down at the ground and shook his head. Then he sighed. Just what every girl dreams of hearing after a kiss like that. I, on the other hand, was exhilarated, weak-kneed, and tingling in all the right spots. All I wanted to do was grab him and keep kissing him, which I guess may have been why he'd stepped away from me in the first place. Damn. My heart was still pounding. If a kiss does this, sex with him might give me a stroke. So. For the best, Kate. Best to stop it here.

"Kate . . ."

My turn to sigh. I was about to get the talk. Not sure which talk exactly, but I was pretty sure my guess would be close.

"Shit, Kate."

Interesting beginning. "Well, hell, Adam."

He was looking at me again. He was completely at odds with himself—I could see the war waging in his eyes. I bet I could tip the scales. I took a step toward him.

He reached a long arm out and planted his hand firmly against my chest—the top of my chest, near the base of my neck. Unfortunately, nothing inappropriate. I really, really wanted inappropriate right now. He pushed me back against the wall, but kept his hand on me—which—I gotta say, was kinda working for me. I dropped my chin and rubbed it against the back of his hand.

"Stop."

I did.

"Kate. This really can't happen. I am *not* a relationship guy and you are *majorly* a relationship girl. There's no way that works out. But you know that I'm attracted to you. And I like you." His arm relaxed and he stepped in closer to me. "I care about you. I do. But that doesn't change the way that I feel about relationships. Fuck, Kate," he said, dropping his hand from my chest and running it roughly through his hair. "This wasn't supposed to go there. We were going to be friends. Now what?"

"Friends with benefits?"

He looked at me like I was an idiot. I was. There was no way I'd be able to keep it friendly if we were sleeping together. He was right. Everything he said was right. I could never be with him, and our friendship will never work if I want to be.

I was staring at the ground. I'd made a mess. He put a couple of fingers under my chin and lifted my face so that he could see my eyes. The butterflies I was getting from looking into his green eyes were a bad sign. Time for a salvage operation.

"We are friends," I said.

"I want to be. You're adorable and really odd. And you seem to . . . *see me* . . . which is kind of a new thing for me. I don't want to lose you, but if you've decided you want more from me, then we part ways now."

Ouch. Harsh. He's right, though. And being fair—in a dickish sort of way.

"I don't want more," I said (a little sulkily, I'll admit). "But it does kind of suck to have a hot *friend* that you can't even have meaningless, rebound sex with."

He laughed and hugged me. "I don't think 'meaningless' is a word that ever really applies to you, Kate."

I smiled against his shoulder.

CHAPTER 8

We walked back over to Logek and Dave and they seemed to be having a heated discussion about something. Uh-oh.

"Should we have left them unchaperoned?" I asked Adam.

He frowned and shrugged.

"But Bond was always supposed to be more tongue-in-cheek. Daniel Craig just isn't Bond," Dave said, shaking his head in exasperation.

"Look, I'm not saying Sean Connery wasn't great—he was. I'm just saying that to say that Daniel Craig barely qualifies as Bond? Ridiculous."

They saw us approaching and Dave walked up to me quickly, putting a hand around my forearm. "Kate. I know you'll have the right answer to this," he said. "Sean Connery or Daniel Craig?"

"You are shitting me right now. The two of you are about to come to blows over who you think is the best Bond?"

He smiled at me, emanating that boyish charm. Hey—if it works, go with it, I guess. "Never blows. Well . . ."

I held up a hand, laughing. "Okay, stop there. Sean Connery owned it and is the classic. Daniel Craig is more of a Bond for the twenty-first century. And he's obscenely hot. You're both right."

"I hope you don't plan to be a litigator," Dave said, winking at me.

"Oh, don't you worry your pretty little head about it," I said to him. "In my other life, I'm a total bitch."

He smiled and seemed like he was going to say something, but opted against it. He turned to the bar and picked up a drink and handed it to me.

"Sorry. It's a little melted down. Didn't expect you to be gone so long."

"Line at the bathroom?" Logek asked, but she also did this eyebrow quirk that meant she was suspicious. And rightly so.

"We were discussing the feasibility of being 'friends with benefits.'" Thank you, Adam Lucas. So glad we could just blurt that out.

Logek turned to me with a look of such intense interest, I laughed.

"We," I said, gesturing between Adam and me, "decided it was not in his best interests because he would get too emotionally attached and that would just make things awkward."

Adam nodded. "True. She stuck her tongue in my mouth one time and I'm already half in love with her. We just don't want me to wind up getting hurt."

"He's very fragile," I said sympathetically, matching his somber tone. "And not everyone is cut out for meaningless sex." I patted his shoulder.

He nodded.

"Well, Kate," Dave said, "if you're looking to fill that position . . ." Even when he was dishing out sexual innuendo, his sort of all-American-boy face made it seem harmless. Even charming.

"Dave. Sweetie. I'm not your type."

"How do you know?"

" 'Cause I'm single. Duh. You," I said, putting my index finger against his chest, "are a contract killer. I have no contract to kill. I apparently was capable of doing that all on my own." Alrighty. Quick 180 into a little pity party for me. He grabbed onto my finger tightly and stared at me.

Logek grabbed my hand away from him and started walking us away from them. So that's what was happening here. The abrupt change in direction made me stumble a little. I *hate* when that happens. I'm not drunk enough to be stumbling, but no one would believe that I just tripped.

"I need Kate to come to the bathroom with me," Logek said to Dave and Adam. She was still smiling, not coming across bitchy or anything. And naturally I had a dumb grin since absolutely everything was amusing me.

We walked back toward the hallway and stopped.

"What's going on, Kitty Kat?"

I shrugged. "Be more specific?"

"Adam? Dave? What's going on?"

I sighed dramatically. "I did sort of kiss Adam. And he scolded me and said I was going to blow our friendship." Then I laughed. "Blow." Logek chuckled at that, too. "I said fine. Friends. All good." She just kept looking at me like I was holding back part of the story. "It was one of the most amazing kisses I've ever had. I think I saw God."

"For some reason, I don't doubt that. So what about Dave?"

"What about Dave?"

"Are you interested in him?"

"Logek. He's a contract killer. He's not interested in me."

"I wouldn't be so sure. What is it with you? You're like fucking contract killer catnip or something."

I giggled. It couldn't be helped. "Maybe Dave is interested in *you*."

"Pretty sure no on that one."

"How is that possible?"

"Contrary to what you believe, not every man on the planet is after me."

"Ninety percent?"

"Kate!" she said, snapping her fingers in front of my face. Wow. Forceful. "What do you want tonight?"

"I don't know what you mean?"

"I mean, if you aren't interested in hooking up with Dave, then I'll run interference. But if you are . . . and you feel like a dirty one-nighter, I think he's an awfully good candidate."

I frowned.

"Oh god. You want Adam, don't you?"

I nodded. "I wanted a dirty little one-nighter with him, but he doesn't think I'm a meaningless sex kind of girl."

"You aren't a meaningless sex kind of girl."

"Then what makes you think I'd be okay with that with Dave?"

"Because Dave is not the love of your life like Jonathan, and he's not completely irresistible like Adam. He's in-between. And I'd bet he'd rock your world."

"Hmm. Okay. Back to reality—I'm single. He's not going to go for a single girl. Isn't that their golden rule?"

"I don't know. I'm getting the vibe that you have a way of fucking up that golden rule."

"Hmm. Interesting."

"So. Tell me. Let him pick you up? Or nonchalantly cock-block him?" Logek asked.

"I can't make this kind of decision!"

"Okay. I'll improvise."

"Do you think Adam would be okay with it?"

"No. I'm pretty sure it will bug the shit out of him," Logek said with a smirk.

"Why?"

"Because he's got a total thing for you."

"Hello. Tongue down his throat and he still shot me down."

"Irrelevant."

My phone buzzed. Text from Jonathan.

Regretting this so much.

Wow. Nice timing, asshole. *You'll get over it.*

Unlikely, but thanks for the vote of confidence.

You're welcome.

Where are you?

At a bar contemplating meaningless sex with a stranger.

Ouch. Which bar?

Why?

Just wondering. Not because I'm thinking of going there and trying to be the stranger that picks you up.

Hmm. Jonathan sex. That does sound like a good ending to the night. Logek had her hands on her hips, waiting for me to explain.

"Jonathan wants to come here and try to pick me up. Not pick me up like a ride pick me up—like a take me home and screw me pick me up."

"Yeah—I got your meaning. And?"

"I don't know."

"Katie! He's messing you up!" When Logek gets annoyed, she talks with her hands, and they were waving around a lot right now.

"True story."

"He thinks he can have it both ways. He doesn't want the commitment, but he still wants you."

"Absolutely right. But . . ."

"But?"

"But if I'm thinking about having meaningless sex tonight—couldn't it be with him?"

Logek grunted and pulled out her phone and started typing. Curious. Then she turned her screen to me: **mean·ing·less [mee-ning-lis]** *adjective* **without meaning, significance, purpose, or value; purposeless; insignificant.**

Unbelievable. Bitch pulled up the definition.

"Now, doll, which part of that do you think would apply if you went home with Jonathan tonight?"

I scowled at her. She deserved it. Using all that common sense and bullshit.

"I rest my case," she said, folding her arms across her chest.

"Fine, fine, fine, fine, fine." Because one "fine" would not have sufficed.

I texted Jonathan back. *Not going to happen.*

I figured. I'm such a dick. I saw all of this going such a different way.

What way?

I don't know . . . you and me taking a break for a year or so . . . then signing another contract and having kids. I somehow didn't envision my life without you.

You're right. You're a dick.

I know. I really am sorry, baby.

Don't.

Ok, fine. Dinner next week? Celebrate your new job?

I'll consider it.

:) I'll take it.

Good night.

Good night, Kate. Don't fuck anyone tonight.

None of your business.

Ok, but if you do—DO NOT think about me. Don't think about what I WOULD BE DOING TO YOU.

I hate you.

I love you.

I looked up and pouted at Logek. I handed her my phone

so that she could scroll through the texts. So much easier than trying to communicate.

We headed back to our spot at the bar. I didn't want to say "back to the guys" because that would imply that we were somehow "with" them tonight—which of course we were not. They did, however, happen to still be there. I was certainly deflated a bit since when we walked away. Adam lifted his brows at me in question. I ignored it. Wow. When I came down, I came down hard. Weird that I was having so much fun just fifteen minutes ago and now I want to go to bed and ignore everything. Well done, Jonathan. You aren't even here and you managed to ruin my night.

"What's up, Kate?" Dave asked. He didn't know me well enough to pull off Adam's unspoken communication.

"Nothing."

"Her ex just cockblocked her via text."

"Ouch," Dave said, making a hissing sound through his teeth.

Adam put his hand on my back, which, for whatever reason, made me angry.

"Whose cock was he blocking exactly?" Adam asked, frowning.

"Don't worry. It wasn't yours," I said coolly. Okay. Game over for Kate. Things were going south fast, along with my mood. Adam looked at me with a solemn expression with one eyebrow raised, but didn't seem overly offended by my snide remark. I kind of wanted him to be. When guys are always supposed to want sex, getting turned down was quite a blow to the ego. I was able to brush it off when I was in such a good mood. Without the cheery disposition, his rebuff was leaving a bad taste in my mouth. Why does every-thing in my head sound like an innuendo for a blow job?

Logek had started chatting with someone, and when I looked over I realized it was the guy from last weekend.

Logek turned to me. "Kate, remember Daniel? We met him last weekend?"

"Of course," I said, smiling and shaking his hand. "Good to see you again."

Logek seemed genuinely happy to see him again. Enough so that I had to wonder if maybe she didn't text him and let him know we'd be here so that she could see him again. It's possible Logek has a crush. Daniel was nice-looking. He didn't look like the two contract killers we'd been hanging with, but that didn't mean he was unattractive, just that he didn't immediately make you think of porn and chocolate.

Logek seemed immediately engrossed in Daniel so I turned back to Dave and Adam. Yep. This night is over. I don't feel like I can handle either of them right now.

"I think I'm going to catch a cab," I said, pointing a thumb toward the door.

"That's silly, Kate," Adam said. "I'll drive you home."

"No." I held up a hand. "It's fine, Adam. It's way out of your way."

"Where do you live?" Dave asked. I was originally just going to crash at Logek's, but if there was a chance she'd have company, I'd just as soon go home. I told Dave where I lived.

"I actually live really close to there. I'll drive you home," Dave said.

I looked at him. Then I looked over at Adam. Screw this.

It shouldn't be this hard. I worry too much about how everyone else feels about everything.

"I'd hate to make you leave before you're ready to," I said to Dave.

"Nah, I'm good now. Better now than if I have a couple more drinks and shouldn't be driving."

"Sold."

I turned to Adam. "Thanks for coming out." Damn. He looked hurt somehow. Since he didn't reply, I turned away slowly—trying to give him time to stop me—hug me—say good night. Something. Nothing. Perfect.

I interrupted Logek and Daniel.

"Dave is going to drive me home—he actually lives out that way."

"You sure?" she asked. But it was halfhearted. She knew I was done and she really wanted to hang with Daniel. Plus, she may have been holding out hope that I was going to end up having some sweet monkey love with Dave after we left.

"I'm sure." I kissed her on the cheek. "Have fun," I whispered. "And call me tomorrow."

I turned to look at Dave who seemed to be talking to Adam.

"I'll wait for you outside, okay?"

"Yeah. Right behind you."

Adam did not look very happy. Too effing bad. I'd reached my bullshit limit tonight for men who didn't want me, but didn't seem to want me with anyone else, either.

I walked outside the club. The bouncer gave me a nod as I wandered down the sidewalk a bit, away from the entrance. I walked only about five steps when someone grabbed my arm. I guess those couple of self-defense classes my mom dragged me to taught me something because I reacted with a quick defensive turn, inverting the hand that was holding me, and quickly twisted the arm. Dave's arm. Should have thought of that—he'd said he'd only be a minute.

"Sorry," I said, quickly releasing his wrist from the uncomfortable hold.

"I am so turned on right now," he said.

I laughed, which helped to lighten my mood considerably.

We walked quietly to Dave's car, which turned out to be a pickup truck. Not what I expected. A nice truck, but still. He opened the passenger door first and closed it after I climbed in. He got in and we started to drive out of town. He was quiet all the way until we were on the dark freeway taking us to the suburbs of the city.

"You sure you're okay?" he asked.

Loud, exaggerated sigh. "Yeah. I'm fine. Just. I don't know. I was having a good time and then after the texts . . . I just lost it. And fast."

"I get that. So. The ex. What does he do?"

"Aside from dump me and then torment me?"

"Yeah. Aside from that."

"He's the CFO of a midsize tech company."

"How long were you together?"

"About a year before we signed."

He whistled. "Eight years. That's no joke."

"You're telling me."

"And you wanted to re-up."

"I made the mistake of thinking it was a foregone conclusion."

"There's no such thing." The sincerity of the statement made me look over at him. He was looking at me.

"So what's your deal?" I asked, trying to get back to casual chitchat.

"My deal?"

"Well, you're a TV sports guy. Single, obviously. I've got the gist of Adam's story. What turned you into a cynic, Dave?"

He laughed. "I'm actually not a cynic."

"Isn't it kind of a prerequisite for a contract killer?"

"Stop with the 'contract killer' thing. It's not my defining characteristic, you know."

"It isn't?" I asked.

"I'm not religious about it. It's just sort of my starting point."

"Starting point. Interesting."

"You, I gather, are not a cynic."

"I wish I was, but no. My stupid idealism always wins out. Makes disappointment inevitable."

"Wow. You really are a wounded puppy, aren't you?"

I laughed then frowned at him. "Wounded puppy? Not sure I'd go that far."

"So what was so great about the ex?"

"Hmm. I've just never been so compatible with a person. I'm a little . . . overpassionate, impulsive, opinionated . . . and he's really easygoing, didn't sweat my moods, appreciated my eccentricities. It was just the perfect mix, I guess. We never argued."

"Impressive."

"And then, of course, he's incredibly hot, smart, and

successful. Amazing in bed. And we laughed all the time. After eight years, I still missed him when he was gone during the day."

"Damn. That is a tough act to follow."

"Yes, it is." My throat felt constricted and I looked out the window.

We got quiet. I was lost in thoughts of Jonathan's broad shoulders and dark eyes. The way he looked at me whenever he saw me naked, you would have thought he was seeing me naked for the first time . . . and that I was a *Playboy* centerfold.

"You know the movie *Airplane*?" I asked. "You know—the really goofy one with Leslie Nielsen?"

"Who doesn't?"

"You know the part where they're landing the plane and all hell is breaking loose and Leslie Nielsen comes in and says, 'I just wanted to tell you both: good luck—we're all counting on you,' and then I think he comes in and says the same thing a couple more times during the landing?"

He chuckled. "Yeah, I know that movie pretty well."

"I was super stressed before some of my law school finals. Naturally. And one of the first ones I took that I was *really* worked up over, I get this text from him, literally like five minutes before the exam starts and it says, 'I just wanted to say good luck—we're all counting on you.' And it cracked me up, as stressed as I was.

"And then the bar exam was pretty much the worst three days of my life. I even stayed in a hotel near the convention center where the exam was held for the last couple of days before the actual bar just so that I could focus and not be distracted. I was going to bed the night before it started and I thought about the handful of those stupid *Airplane* texts he'd sent me during law school. I figured he'd probably feel like this was too big a deal to make light of that way. I was walking a very fine line those last few days," I said, looking over at Dave with wild eyes. "But I got an e-mail from him . . . with the YouTube link to that scene from the movie."

"And it made it okay?"

"It was the California bar exam. Nothing could make it okay." He laughed. "But it made me smile. And at that point in time, even that was a lot. We had a thousand of those kind of little inside jokes."

Dave was nodding, thoughtfully. Maybe he understood. Then again, if he was anything like Adam, he was at least partially socially dysfunctional and wouldn't get the concept.

Dave took the freeway exit that led to my parents' neighborhood. I rattled off quick directions so that he could get to the general vicinity.

A relatively quiet five minutes later, he pulled to a stop in front of my parents' house. The porch light was left on for me.

"Nice," Dave said, nodding toward the house.

"Thanks."

And then some more awkward Dave-staring, so I glared at him.

He laughed. "What?" He smiled broadly after the question, waiting for me to answer. His teeth were pristine—straight, even, crazy white.

"Your teeth are fake, huh?" Alrighty. Not quite sober yet, apparently. Or maybe I'm just rude. Can't always blame the alcohol, Kate. "I just mean they are incredibly perfect . . ."

He dropped his head back and laughed. Then he turned to me. "Yes. They are mostly caps. But I have a good excuse that doesn't have to do with vanity."

"Really? Not something most TV personalities just do?"

"No. I've had them a lot longer than that."

"Let's hear it."

"When I was about twelve years old, I decided that I was going to be an NHL star, so I joined the youth ice hockey team to start off my career."

"Oh. I like where this story is going."

"Hockey puck to the face." He pointed to three or four of his top teeth and a couple of his lower ones. "All these were broken. Capping them was the only option, really."

"Well, you aren't an NHL star, are you?"

"I am not."

"All that dental work for nothing."

"Not entirely. I'm a pretty mean ice-skater."

"Quite a useful talent to have."

"You're kind of a smart-ass."

"That has been mentioned to me once or twice."

"So, come ice-skating with me."

I glared at him again.

"What? What did I say?"

"That sounded like you asking me out."

"Funny. That's sort of the way it was intended."

"You're a contract killer. I'm single."

"I'm willing to overlook your flaws."

Now I dropped my head back and laughed. "You suck at being a contract killer if you are so ready to ask out a single woman."

"For all you know, you're the first time in years I've broken my rule."

"Am I?"

He nodded. Oh. Butterflies. God, I'm easy. Or maybe just in desperate need of anything to stroke my bruised ego.

"How do you know Adam?" I asked.

He frowned a little. "Met him through some friends a few years ago when we all went kayaking on the river."

"Are you guys close?"

"What does this have to do with me asking you out?" And he meant that. He wasn't suggesting that I was just trying to change the subject—he wanted to know how Adam played into the matter of whether or not I would go out with him. Fair enough. Unfortunately, I didn't have an answer to that.

"Nothing. But you two are friends and for some reason he seemed a little put out that you were driving me home."

"Yeah, I noticed. Answer me this—what is the deal with you two?"

"There is no deal." When he looked skeptical, I added, "Really. You know how he is. He *is* religious about the contract killer thing. He's made very clear to me that it fully applies to me, as well. We're just friends."

"He doesn't typically have female friends."

"Which would explain why he sucks at it." Dave laughed. "Did he say anything to you about driving me home?"

"Not really. Just the vibe he was giving off. Want to come to my place for a bit? Have a glass of wine?"

Shit. Yes. No. Yes. We were getting along well enough that the mere suggestion of being alone with him at his house sparked the tingles. When I just kept staring at him with a stupid look on my face, he grabbed my hand and gently pulled me toward him. I went. Okay. Yes. I kissed Adam tonight. And now apparently I'm going to kiss Dave. I'm a lip slut. So sue me.

When I didn't pull away, he leaned down and kissed me. Don't compare. Don't compare. Yeah—this was so different than Adam. Or Jonathan for that matter. Jonathan was all humor and sexy charm. Adam was passionate, forceful, and a little (awesomely) terrifying.

Dave, though. Despite his looks and his contract killer status—he was sweet. His hands, his mouth, were both gentle and patient. He put his lips to mine softly and moved them slowly. He wrapped his arms around me and trailed one of his hands lightly up and down my back. He slid his mouth from my lips to my cheek, trailing soft kisses along my skin. When he reached my neck, I could feel his tongue mixed in with the kisses and he worked his way down my neck to my shoulder.

As unassuming as he was, I was starting to feel lightheaded and my breath quickened. At a pace that was practically slow-motion, he slid my shirt off my shoulder and down my arm. His kisses continued lower, down my chest. At the same achingly slow speed, he slipped his fingers into the cup of my bra and pulled my breast out so that it was exposed to him. He dipped his head and covered my nipple with his mouth. I hissed through my teeth and arched against him and he sucked harder based on my reaction.

Holy shit. How did a kiss turn into my wanting to screw him right here in the cab of his truck? Yeah. Sweet, my ass.

His subtlety is an art form. He expertly aroused my antici-pation and made me impatient for more. More than I'd in-tended to want or allow tonight. And if I don't stop this pretty quick, I'm going to be giving him a whole lot more than credit for his technique. But it will feel *so* good, Kate—don't stop him. (That was the little devil on my shoulder talking. She's kind of a slut.) I waited. Apparently the angel on my other shoulder was on sabbatical. Bitch.

Don't think about what I WOULD BE DOING TO YOU.

Son of a bitch! I hate you, Jonathan. He'd be using more teeth, btw.

I pushed Dave back and quickly put my girl parts back in their clothes. Dammit. "Sorry," I said.

He sighed. "Don't be. I hope I wasn't being too pushy."

"I was game, too. Until my ex mentally cockblocked me—well, you—about ten seconds ago."

"I'm really starting to hate that guy."

"You and me both."

He was watching closely like he was trying to see if I'd change my mind. "So, how about that glass of wine?"

"No. Thanks for the offer." Since we both knew what he was actually offering.

He looked disappointed. Frustrated. Couldn't really blame him. If I had balls, they'd be blue right now, too.

"Thanks for the ride. I appreciate it," I said, opening the door and climbing out of the truck. I headed toward the walk-way and heard his door open and close so I stopped and turned around. He jogged up to me and stood, slightly slouch-ing, with his hands in his back pockets.

"Can I get your number?"

Let's see, you're presently placing third among the men in my life and I think I've played out the *tease* thing to its max tonight, so if I give you my number . . . you'll think you're getting in my pants. See? That was a damn fine explanation. I probably should have said it out loud.

"Why?"

"So I can call you? Or text you?"

"Why?"

"Well, to be frank, on the off chance I might get to kiss you again," he said, leaning in closer to me, hands still safely in his back pockets.

Something in my brain flickered and I realized—I'm being totally played. This boyish come-on, the sweet vibe, the slo-mo moves, the "I hardly ever break my rule" bullshit— all game. I remembered thinking of him and Logek as big-game hunters earlier in the night. And I just almost fell prey to a big-game hunter without even knowing it.

I tipped my head to the side. "You must get laid *a lot*."

"What?"

"Your moves are so smooth. I'm guessing lots of girls never pick up on them."

His mouth hung open a little. I gave him a minute, curious whether he would drop the act or feign innocence. His blue eyes lost some of their puppy-dog quality and he looked more shrewd. Apparently he couldn't decide which way to take this.

I'll make it easier for him. "You may not be a strict contract killer, but you are definitely all player."

"Not always."

"Maybe. But I doubt it."

"Harsh."

"True."

He stepped in closer to me. No good-ol'-boy charm, here. He had undergone a transformation before my eyes. Now I could see some similarity to Adam—the intensity, the manipulation, the cynicism—but without Adam's honesty and depth. No. Dave was so much more calculating. Adam had his reasons for making the choices he did. Dave seemed more like he was in it for sport.

"Go out with me."

"Why would I want to do that?"

"Because you need something to take your mind off the ex. And I'm willing to be that something."

"All you're thinking about right now is strategy. Doesn't that get tiring?"

"I like a challenge."

"I get that. I don't really care to be sport, however."

"But you know I see you as a challenge, so what's the risk?"

Not sure, but I feel like there is one. "You're kind of a cold fish, Dave."

"So thaw me out."

"Trying to appeal to the player in *me*?"

"Maybe."

"What makes you think I have one?"

"All beautiful women do. Come on. I have a feeling we're pretty evenly matched."

"You sound like you're setting up a challenge."

"I am."

"I'm afraid to ask."

"I think that I can get you to sleep with me—even though you know I'm only in it for the sport."

Don't let the shock show on your face, Kate. I cocked an eyebrow at him. Well done. "And what is my challenge in this little scenario?"

"What do you want?" he asked, giving me a wicked grin. I was disgusted, but also sort of excited. And yes, I am ashamed of that fact.

"Right now? I just sort of want to go to bed."

"That can be arranged."

"Okay, stop. What makes you think I care enough to put any time into you?"

"You don't. But you're coming out of an ugly breakup and could use the distraction."

"You're assuming that I'm into games the way you are."

"Games make life fun. That's why they're so popular."

"Yeah—beer pong and bowling. Not screwing with people's heads."

"Games are games. Don't kid yourself."

"The problem with this whole thing is that I liked the fake you. This Dave is kind of a heartless prick that I'm not sure I want to be around."

"Maybe you just don't know the real me."

"I'm not sure there is a *real* you."

"Ouch."

I shrugged.

"So what do you want?" he asked again, leaning in toward me a little.

"To not make drunken wagers with strange men in the middle of the night."

"Come on. We were getting along really good when we were just talking. What's the harm in a little more of that?"

"It's not the talking you want more of."

"Based on what I've seen, I wouldn't mind seeing more, true. But you're so certain you can resist me. Prove it."

He was getting my hackles up, which I'm pretty sure was his goal. Enough so that I was ready to accept the challenge just to prove that he wasn't as irresistible as he thinks he is.

"Fine."

"Fine, you'll go out with me?"

"Against my better judgment, yes. Thanks for the ride home."

"You haven't given me your number, yet." I took his phone from his hand and added my number to his contacts.

He surprised me by wrapping me in a hug and even sneaking a quick peck on my lips.

"Good night, beautiful girl," he said, heading for his truck.

"Good night, Lucifer."

He laughed. "I'm a pussycat. Really," he said, climbing into his truck.

"With rabies," I called to him, before he shut the door.

CHAPTER *9*

I awoke the next morning to my phone vibrating on my nightstand. Let me sleep, people. Truth be told, I would put it on silent, but then what if Logek or Jonathan had an emergency and couldn't reach me?

I looked at the screen. Logek. Then I looked at the time in the corner of the screen. 9:15 a.m. Oh. Not exactly the crack of dawn.

Get lucky?

Nope. You?

Nope, but I did get a pretty awesome kiss good night :)

I got a kiss, too, but I'm not sure if it was awesome or not. Jury is still out.

Meaning?

Meaning Dave is a broken toy just like Adam and I'm

pretty sure I may have accidentally made some sort of deal with the devil last night.

And what was the deal?

He'll try to get me to have meaningless sex with him even though I know it's just a game for him . . .

And you?

Resist.

Doesn't sound like much in it for you . . . unless you decide meaningless sex could be a win for you, too ;)

He comes off nice but he's a major player. Don't think good sex makes it worth being a notch on someone's headboard.

He was pretty hot though . . . maybe just keep him in your back pocket in case you change your mind.

There's a thought.

So you made an actual bet with him?

I don't really know what it is. We kissed—there was some touchy-feely and then he asked me out. Then of course I realized it was because I'm a challenge and he was in the mood for a new conquest.

So why did you go for it?

Cause I'm insane.

Worried about what Adam will think of you playing around with Dave?

We're friends. He shouldn't have a say.

Shouldn't but does.

So what's up with Daniel?

:)

Yeah, I got that part.

He drove me back to my place and we stood outside talk-ing for 2 hours.

Talking?

Mostly ;)

Logek has a crush??

She does :)

Yay! When do you see him again?

Today. Lunch.

Get it, girl.

Gonna run. I'll text later and let you know how it goes.

Definitely. Bye.

Logek ends up with a crush on a sweet guy and I end up with a twisted battle of wills with a narcissist. Possibly time to reevaluate some choices in my life.

I lay in bed on my side and stretched my arm across the bed in front of me. So much empty space. Jonathan was a stomach sleeper so most mornings his face would be turned toward me with his arms wrapped under his pillow. The position always made his shoulders look big and defined. His hair was usually long enough to look messy across his forehead and his eyelashes always looked thick and black against his cheeks. Sigh. Needless to say, we had a lot of morning sex. I'd wake up first and wind up watching him for a few minutes, which would then turn into my brushing my fingers against his full lips or caressing his bare back. And then once he woke up to my attention, it was game on.

Shake it off. These are not useful thoughts.

I got out of bed, blissfully hangover free. I used to try to run three or four days a week, but I sort of fell off the wagon after I moved out of Jonathan's house. Time to get back at it, girl. I threw on my running clothes and headed out. I did my typical four-mile run on the trails near my parents' house and got back to the house extra winded after my two weeks off, but feeling empowered regardless. About damn time.

When I got out of the shower, I checked my phone. No text from Adam. Yes, I'll admit, I had an as-yet unidentifiable emotion brewing after last night. A little hurt by his brush-off, frustrated with his stoicism, and downright annoyed with that weird possessive thing he seemed to pull when I was leaving. But on top of that there was a hope that he'd text me, that he wasn't going to cut me off, that he still liked me, cared about me even, and still wanted to be my friend. Shameless. Or shameful. One of the two.

After I was dressed, I started going through my clothes to figure out what I was going to wear to my new job tomorrow. Gag. Think positively. It could be epic. Maybe you'll love signing law. Yeah. Mental pep talk not effective today.

My phone buzzed.

Dave. Wow, that actually came with an unpleasant wave of disappointment.

Hey, beautiful girl.

You can stop with the flattery. I think we're sorta past that.

Not flattery. It just seems to fit you. How you feeling?

Good. No hangover. Already went for a run.

Shoulda called me. I would have gone with you.

Next time.

What are you doing today?

Mentally preparing for my first day at the new job tomorrow.

Oh, that's right. Congrats on that.

Eh.

You sound thrilled.

Never wanted to do signing law. But Single Kate has no choice.

It'll be good experience.

Everyone says that.

Okay. Then it'll suck and you should just save yourself the headache and jump off the Tower Bridge.

Lol. Okay. Pity party over. Yay! New job tomorrow!

Ha-ha. You're not opposed to contracts . . . why so opposed to signing law?

Because the majority of the work—at least with this firm—is working on breaches, so that means I'll be spending 50 hours a week buried in other people's misery. Not my idea of fun.

I see your point. Wanna hang out today?

Not particularly. Then, because my inner whore was wide awake, I had an unbidden flashback to my boob in his mouth last night and had a hot flash. Yikes. *Kind of in job prep mode so probably not today.*

Okay. Soon though ;)

Ominous.

*

I was dressed in a snazzy black suit and three-inch heels (they might as well get used to the tall girl early on, because

I refuse to wear ugly flats instead of cute heels to make short men feel better). Manetti, Markson, and Mann was in a swanky high-rise downtown, not far from Samson & Tule, actually. Which means the commute sucked. Thirty miles in from the suburbs in rush-hour traffic. Finding an apartment just moved to the top of my list of priorities.

I got out of the elevator on the tenth floor and was in the lobby of the firm. The carpet was plush and charcoal colored. The furniture was inviting, but dignified. The walls were covered with high-contrast black-and-white photographs of the city and were accompanied by similar photos of other major cities worldwide—Paris, London, Tokyo. All very classic and cool. Very un-Tony.

The receptionist was around fifty, I'd guess. Short, graying hair, glasses, friendly smile.

"You must be Kate," she said, standing and extending her hand.

"Yes," I said, shaking her hand.

"Tony said to buzz him when you got here. It'll just be a minute."

I wandered around taking a closer look at the pictures until I heard my name called.

"Kate. So glad you're here, darling."

Tony looked the same as when I saw him last—a year ago at my law school grad party. Tony is my mom's brother. My grandparents decided to go fifty-fifty when naming their children. Mom got Shaw, which was Grandma's last name, and Tony got Manetti after Grandpa. Funny that he got the Italian name since he definitely got the more Italian features, too. He had olive skin like Grandpa and hazel eyes. He was only about my height (when I'm not in three-inch heels) and he's . . . well . . . not fat. Stocky, I guess would be the word. Basically he looks like a goombah. I don't know how else to describe him. His salt-and-pepper hair was combed straight back and he had a pinkie ring. Yes, really. And he fiddled with it when he talked. Personally, I think he comes off creepy, but women *love* Uncle Tony.

I smiled and we hugged. He turned to the receptionist.

"Rita, did I tell you she was gorgeous? Look at this girl."

Rita was nodding politely and I didn't try too hard to hide my discomfort. Please don't do this with everyone. Oh, please.

He looped my hand through the crook of his elbow and led me into the back office. There was a sea of cubicles filling the center of the office space, and offices lined the entire perimeter.

"That's my office," he said, making a quick gesture to the left. Damn. That office was almost as big as Logek's whole apartment. He pulled me into the next office. Very nice. Mahogany desk and matching armoire, leather chairs facing the desk, and a great view of the river.

"And this is yours."

Holy crap. "Really? This is amazing, Tony!" This job just got significantly better.

"Thought you'd like it. Okay. Let me introduce you around."

I set my satchel by the door and followed Tony, admittedly with a little more spring in my step.

Tony, being Tony, didn't bother to introduce me to any of the secretaries, only the other attorneys. He started with the other two named partners. Joe Markson looked like he was about a hundred years old. I felt kind of bad when he stood up from his desk to shake my hand. Once he was up, though, he seemed a little more spry. A little.

Jared Mann was the polar opposite. He looked about thirty. Can you become a named partner in a firm this size by thirty? Maybe if you graduate from law school before you're thirty-four, Kate. Jared was nice-looking, about my height *with* the heels, and did the two-handed handshake where he takes my hand and cups it in both of his. Charming. He must be awesome with clients.

"Well, Kate. Tony said you were lovely, and I will say, he did not exaggerate." Danger, Will Robinson. That felt odd coming from one of my new, young, handsome bosses. Don't make a big deal out of it. Let it go.

"That's very kind of you."

"Yeah. Jared's our lady-killer. Any pain-in-the-ass women clients—we just send them to Jared and he charms their panties off." Then Tony laughed and I swear to god my eyes glazed over. Shit. I've been here fifteen minutes. And this is to be my life.

"Tony, you're going to give Kate the wrong impression of me."

"Whatever, just keep your hands off *her* panties and things'll be fine." Then he laughed in a loud, crass way and I wanted to run for the door. Jared laughed a little, but it seemed more to placate Tony. He looked at me and mouthed "sorry." Earning points with me already, Jared.

So Tony, Joe, and Jared had the big corner offices. After that he took me past the other offices, fifteen or so, doing more cursory introductions. I was never going to remember all these names. Brandon, Andrew, Martin, Mike, Tom, Cliff, Steve, Paul . . . holy shit. They were all men. He didn't introduce me to a single female attorney. When I got the rest of the names I wouldn't remember, we went back into my office.

"Tony. Am I the only woman?"

"There's lots of women."

"Attorneys?"

"Oh. No. Just you, darling. What can I say? Most ladies just don't have the stomach for signing law."

I was losing my stomach, myself. Well, I was Tony's niece. At least I didn't have to worry about the paralegals and secretaries thinking I got the job by sleeping with the boss. Okay. Focus on the office. Focus on the salary. This is temporary.

"Okay," he said. "I've got to get back to work. I'm going to turn you over to Mags. She's going to be your paralegal. Then I'm going to have you sit in on a lot of client meetings so you can get the feel of it. I think you know this, but we don't *write* a lot of contracts here—we fight over them." I nodded. Their reputation precedes them. "Frank, I introduced you to him, handles all the contract writing we do. He likes it because he doesn't like conflict—which is probably code for gay, but he gets it done so I don't have to so I don't complain." Wow. How is it he hasn't been sued like fifty times?

I guessed it showed on my face because he added, "Darling, you better get that stick out of your ass if you're going to make it here." And he walked out of the office. Oh my god. As impossible as it seems, this could actually turn out *worse* than I'd imagined.

A thirtysomething woman walked into my office. Her hair was big and her clothes were small. She had brown hair and either spent too much time in the sun or had found some fairly decent spray tan (since I couldn't tell the difference). She was really curvy and liked to show it off, apparently.

"I'm Mags," she said, smiling. No handshake.

"Kate. Very nice to meet you."

"Tony has talked about you a lot. We've been hoping you'd take the job." She held a hand (with freakishly long, pink fingernails) up to the side of her mouth. " 'Cause it's a sausage fest around here and even though they think they do, they don't know shit about women."

I laughed. Holy shit. Is everyone in the office this un-PC? Awesome.

I opened my eyes wide. "I noticed that *all* the attorneys are men."

"Not anymore," she said in a singsongy voice. She was entertaining—I'll give her that.

"Okay, well, take a look around your office and let me know what you need. There are some things in the desk, but it looks like someone took your stapler so I'll track one down for you. Otherwise, let me know if you have any special requests for pens, paper, planners, whatever."

"Thank you."

"That's my job," she said. "So questions about anything, just let me know. I put instructions on getting you logged in and whatnot on your desk. Once you're in, they were supposed to e-mail you your passwords for Lexis, Westlaw, and the other programs we use."

"Okay. Got it."

"You're going to be great. I can tell."

Mags was getting more awesome by the minute. "Thanks for the vote of confidence."

She left and I sat down at my desk. I opened up my satchel and pulled out my favorite coffee mug (the Starbucks one with the moose on it) and two framed photos—one of Logek and me and, since I won't be putting out a picture with my loving partner, the other photo is of me with my parents after being sworn in to the bar. Okay. Refocus.

This office really did kick ass. I walked over to the door so I could get a wide-angle shot of the office so you could see the view and snapped a picture of it with my phone and texted it to Logek and my parents. I went through the desk and the armoire taking stock of the supplies left behind by the office's former inhabitant. I was just about to run out of things to do when one of the attorneys came in.

"Kate, I've got a client meeting I'd like you to sit in on."

"Great. Tell me your name again?"

"Brad." Brad didn't seem overly friendly. Cordial, maybe—buddy-buddy, no. He was probably about my age, six foot and lanky, average-looking, and he was wearing glasses that were a little too big for his face. "Our client is Mario Sanchez. We've already filed a complaint for breach based on his partner John's infidelity. I think John's attorney is trying to set up some sort of anticipatory repudiation defense based on statements Mario made about ending things. Mario is a little on the dramatic side."

"So what is the topic of the meeting?" I asked, grabbing a pad of paper and a pen from my desk.

"John and his attorney are coming to meet with us. They

want to take a stab at dissolving the contract without further litigation."

"Any chance of that?"

He smiled. I was being naïve. "You'll understand when
you meet Mario. Not to mention John's lawyer, Beth Erickson.
She smiles and nods and then rips your balls off when you
aren't looking."

"Thanks for the warning," I said, and Brad laughed.

"Who knows? Maybe she won't be such a raging bitch to
another woman." So I'm basically batting three for three
with the inappropriate coworker conversations. But I'm
trying to fit in here. Close your mouth, Kate. "Oh. Sorry,"
he added.

I shrugged. No biggie, Brad. I'm realizing that being
mouthy and inappropriate is apparently a requisite to work
here. Of course, I'm usually only mouthy and inappropriate
when I drink, so it's possible that will by *my* requisite to
work here.

"Ready?"

I nodded and followed him out the door. Eager to learn
the ropes and grow as an attorney. So that I can get the hell
out of here.

I followed Brad back out through the lobby and over to the
other end of our floor where the conference rooms were. He
went into one ahead of me and the petite Hispanic man stood
and hugged him. From the look on Brad's face, he wasn't much
of a hugger, but Mario apparently didn't catch on.

"Mario, this is Kate Shaw. She's a brand-new associate
with the firm and I've asked her to join us because she'll
probably be helping me out on your case."

Mario faced me. He was about five foot three and maybe 120 pounds. He had big brown eyes, heavy on the eyeliner. He was in capri pants and a tank top. And he looked like he'd been crying recently.

"Nice to meet you, Ms. Shaw," he said in a light accent, while extending a perfectly manicured hand.

"Please, call me Kate." He warmed up to me at that. Winning.

"So," Brad said, as we all sat down at the end of the long conference table. "How have you been, Mario?"

"How have I been?" Big sigh. "How do you think I have been? I still have to go to the salon and see that bitch all the time." His voice fluttered and he waved his hands. Right. Dramatic.

Brad turned to me. "Unfortunately, Mario and John own a hair salon together so they still have to see each other frequently even with all of this going on."

Mario put his hand over mine. "That bitch was fucking two of my clients. Do you believe that?"

I shook my head sympathetically. See? Bright side. Jonathan didn't cheat on me.

"I caught this slut rubbing his cock by the hair dryers. *A woman!* Do you believe this shit?"

When he gets on a roll, his accent gets thicker and every "s" sounds like "sss." And he does this thing where he puts his fingertips to his forehead like he's feeling faint. He's Scarlett O'Hara.

"And the other one . . . well, I probably would have fucked him, too. He was beautiful. Mario can't compete with that." And he talks about himself in the third person. I mean, yes, I do that, but not out loud . . . and usually because I'm talking to myself. Yeah. Much better.

I patted his hand. I have no response. I got nothing.

"Were you able to find any e-mails?" Brad asked.

"No. The harlot changed his passwords once he knew I knew."

"Letters? Any proof?" Brad asked.

"Proof?" Mario shrieked. "I saw that slut Heidi's hand on him right in the salon!"

"Right," Brad said in a super calm tone. "But it was in public, over the clothes. Not exactly proof he was screwing her."

"A partner always knows, Brad. I could see it on his lying face when I asked him."

Brad worked his jaw back and forth a bit. I think he'd been fighting against this particular client for a while now.

"Phone records?" I asked. Stupid probably, since obviously Brad would've covered all these bases already.

Mario shook his head. "I think they were hooking up through the work line so I can't tell when he actually spoke to her."

"Hmm. Are they Facebook friends?"

"Yes."

"Did he change his Facebook password, too?"

Mario tilted his head at me, but didn't reply. "I'll have to check," he said.

Brad nodded at me. Kudos to Kate.

Just then, the door to the conference room opened and Rita held the door open for a man and woman. Beth and John, I presume. Beth the Bitch was lovely and definitely came across all sugar and spice. John was . . . one of the most hetero-looking hairdressers I've ever seen. He was about six feet, brawny, had a neatly trimmed beard, and he was in jeans and a plaid shirt. And he looked really pissed. I'm starting to get the feeling this job won't ever be boring.

Brad introduced me to them. Beth smiled and shook my hand. John gave me a cool nod. Gotta say—he didn't look like a harlot.

We sat at the table. Mario sat next to Brad on one side and Beth and John sat on the other so I sat at the end. I felt a little like a referee.

"John and I wanted to meet with you at least once to see if we could reach any resolution before things get more out of hand," Beth said. Well, that didn't sound particularly bitchy, Brad.

"And what were you thinking by way of resolution?" Brad asked.

"John would be willing to agree to an early termination on the terms that would have been in place had the contract gone to term."

"Of course he would!" Mario shouted, slapping his palms to the table. "He doesn't want to face the penalty for being a whore."

"I never fucked Heidi!" John bellowed.

Okay. So apparently these meetings escalate quickly. Beth and Brad looked calm so I guess it's commonplace. Keep cool. Wait for the experts to reel it in. Brad reached over with his hand like he was going to put it on Mario's arm, but Mario got up from his chair and started pacing back and forth in front of the door.

"I was so stupid," Mario said. "All the times you told me nothing was going on, I believed you!"

"Nothing was going on, you crazy bitch!"

Yikes. Beth put a firm hand on John's shoulder, clearly intending to keep him from leaping up from his chair like Mario had done. Thank you. Because having them both on their feet and ranting would probably be a bad scenario.

"I'm a bitch? You fucked a *woman*!"

"Beth, you know full well that your client breached and that my client is entitled to damages," Brad said, holding out a hand to Mario with the intent of calming him.

"No, Brad. I don't know that *full well*."

"You told me you wanted out of the contract," John shouted.

"I was mad at you!"

"Yeah, I was pissed, too, but I didn't tell you that the contract was over."

"You knew I didn't mean it."

"How? How am I supposed to know which of your threats are real and which ones are you just being a drama queen?"

Uh-oh. Mario looked like he'd been slapped. "So that made it okay for you to go fuck around? That's what you're saying?"

"Nothing happened with Heidi! Please! That wrinkled hag. You really think if I wanted some, I couldn't get something a little fresher than that?"

Oh, geez. I really want to leave the room. Are the attorneys allowed to leave?

"What about Fared? Are you going to tell me you didn't

fuck him, either?" Mario was half yelling, half crying now. And much like a car accident, I wanted to look away, but was somewhat mesmerized by the carnage.

"No, him I did. It was incredible."

And then everything went to hell in a handbasket. Mario came running toward John, who was on the other side of me. Oh shit. I tried to scramble out of my chair so that I could get out of the way. I was halfway out of my chair and leaning back to try to stand clear of Mario. Unfortunately, Mario went for the roundhouse technique, and even leaning back like I was, I couldn't get out of his rage-fueled swing. Damn.

It looked like it was going to be openhanded, but apparently good ol' Mario changed his mind mid-swing because I distinctly felt a knuckle connect with my cheekbone. Between my awkward lean and the punch to the face, I tumbled backward in the chair and landed on my back on the ground. I put my hand to my face, because that's what you do when you get punched. I guess. Not like I've had experience with this.

Brad bent over me, looking like he was doing his damnedest to not laugh. I'd like to think it was only funny once he knew I wasn't really hurt. Then again, I just got hit in the face by a tiny man half my size, so it was probably more of a bitch slap than a punch.

Beth knelt down next to me and looked in my face. She pulled my hand away from my cheek so that she could see where I got hit. "You definitely need ice." Then she stood up, infuriated, and pointed in Brad's face. "We'll see you two in court." I was aware of her and John leaving the room although

* Subject to the following terms and conditions

I didn't sit up to actually watch them. Mario was sitting at the conference table crying.

Brad held a hand out to me and helped me to my feet. Now he was grinning, looking the friendliest I've seen him so far. Okay. Getting punched by a client makes friends. Check. Rita rushed into the conference room.

"Oh my god! Beth said you got hit! Are you okay?"

I still had my hand to my cheek. Bitch slap or not, it really effing hurt. My whole eye socket was throbbing. I nodded to Rita and smiled, sort of, even though I really wanted to cry.

"You poor thing! Let's get you to your office and I'll get you some ice."

We walked back through the lobby to the offices. And that sea of cubicles now looked like that whack-a-mole game with little female heads poking up out of more than half of them. All the faces I could see were wide-eyed and shocked. You and me both, ladies.

Rita guided me into my chair and closed the blinds a little so the sun wasn't in my eyes. "I'll be right back, honey." And she hustled out, I'm guessing, in search of ice.

My face was throbbing, but really, how bad could it be? Rita returned with a towel wrapped up into a neat little square.

"Okay, honey, lean back and let's put this on your eye." Aww. Rita was being so sweet, it almost felt like my mom was here.

I put my feet up on the desk so that I could lean back a little more and rest the towel-wrapped ice on my face. I closed my eyes, trying to relax. And not cry. 'Cause that would be super lame.

"What the fuck happened?" Tony yelled, storming into my office.

"She got caught in the cross fire," I heard Brad say. I wasn't aware he'd come in.

Someone pulled the ice pack off my face and I opened my eyes to see a very angry Tony looking down at me. "I didn't tell you to start her off with fighters, Brad, goddammit."

"First time, Tony," Brad said nonchalantly. "They've never come to blows in the past."

"Your mom is going to chew my ass for this, darling." He settled the ice back on my cheek. "Next time, duck."

"Gee, Tony, wish I'd thought of that," I said.

"It happened really fast. No time to react," Brad said, chiming in with support that was much appreciated.

"I wasn't exactly in fight-or-flight mode since I was *at the office*, Tony."

"Well, why don't you take off for the day and go get some rest," Tony said, on his way out the door.

"Thanks. I just need to sit a few more minutes before driving." Truth be told, I wasn't feeling so hot now that the adrenaline was ebbing and I was starting to feel some of that post-injury queasiness. Best day ever!

"I'll get you a Coke," I heard Mags say from the doorway. "You probably could use a little sugar now that you're coming down from the rush."

"Please. You and Rita are amazing." And then I felt Rita brush my hair back from my forehead. So Mom.

"I'll be back in a few minutes," Rita said. And finally my office was quiet.

I set the ice down on the desk and pulled a mirror out of

my satchel. Motherfucker! That little bitch! The whole corner of my cheekbone was turning purple and the skin under my eye was looking a little dark, likely foreshadowing a full-blown black eye. I must be psychic. Didn't I say this could actually turn out *worse* than I'd anticipated?

Okay. Logek always says "You can either laugh or you can cry." Don't cry. And on that little piece of wisdom, I got the giggles and started laughing. At the absurdity of this day . . . and this week . . . and this month. Laugh it out, girl.

CHAPTER 10

When Rita came back into my office, I was nearly in a fit. Tears were streaming down my cheeks. I was laughing so hard that my shoulders were shaking but no sound was coming out. Rita looked worried. Reasonably so.

"You okay, honey?"

I sucked in some air and held it. "Yes," I said, a few more giggles leaking out. "I just looked at my face. How many people can say that they got decked by a ninety-pound man on their first day at the office?" And then I was reduced to laughing again, tears running down my face.

Rita chuckled. "I'm guessing not many."

I shook my head at her. "This is one for the books, Rita!"

She came back by my side and put the ice pack back to my face. Mags showed up with a Coke with a straw in it. Who is thoughtful enough to put a straw in a soda can to make it easier for someone to drink? These two ladies may just make this place bearable.

Mags held the can out to me and I sucked on the straw— not like I was going to let that little gem go to waste. Her and Rita exchanged glances, probably wondering if I was really laughing or simply on the verge of hysterics.

"Thank you," I said, after a long drink. "Don't worry, ladies. I'm not losing it. Just getting a little perspective. And I've decided this is pretty funny shit."

They both smiled down at me. Mags hopped up onto my desk and tugged down her micromini so that it wasn't (totally) indecent and crossed her long legs and looked content.

"I better get back to the front desk," Rita said, as though just remembering that she was the sole welcoming committee for the lobby.

"Thank you, Rita. Really. So much," I said.

She smiled at me and scurried out of the room.

"So," Mags said, swinging her legs back and forth over the edge of my desk. "I need the play-by-play. How exactly does an attorney get punched on her first day, by her first client?"

I looked at her with my good eye, glaring just enough to make her laugh. Her brown hair was wavy and slightly ratted to make it bigger. She was wearing light blue eye shadow and pink lip gloss. And somehow it fit her. She was actually pulling it off.

I handed her my phone. "Take a picture for me, 'cause no one is going to believe this without photographic evidence."

She grinned and held my phone out in front of me. "Smile.

Okay, one more. There you go," she said, handing my phone back to me.

I picked the more dramatic of the two pix and texted it to Logek saying, *Having a super first day! Only got punched once! :)*

I should send it to Adam, too. No. It would seem like a desperate cry for attention. And I am definitely *not* a desperate-cry-for-attentioner. Definitely.

I finished the soda and felt more like myself. "Okay, Mags. I'm going to take Tony up on the offer to leave early and go home."

"I hear ya. You are coming back, right?"

I smiled. "See you tomorrow."

I headed down in the elevator, after getting a quick hug from Rita, and made my way to the parking garage. Oddly, not the worst day I've ever had. Guess that says something about the days I've had.

I sat down in my car and checked my phone. Logek had replied.

Holy shit. Holy shit. I can't think of anything else to say. Call me.

About the reaction I expected.

And another text. From Adam. I'm going to overlook the fact that I'm probably way more excited about that than I should be.

How's the first day going?

Screw it. I texted him the picture. With no explanation. Then I waited.

WTF Kate?

Rough day at the office.

Someone hit you??? What the hell happened?

Not on purpose. Wow. He sounds kinda pissed. How cute. *Wrong place at the wrong time.*

Are you ok?

Yeah. Taking the rest of the day off so I'm just leaving.

Good. Get some rest.

Hmm. Not gonna lie. I was hoping for something a little warmer. Oh, well. As much as I give myself credit for knowing that guy, he's still a mystery in many ways.

I drove home aware that a significant ache was developing behind my right eye. Ice. Tylenol. Bed. Stat.

I parked in the driveway and went into the house. Mom was in the kitchen. Better get this over with.

"So, I had an interesting first day."

"Dear god, Kate!" She was frozen with a glass of juice midway to her mouth. She reached out and put a hand on the counter to steady herself.

"It's okay. It looks worse than it is." Not entirely true. "I was in a client meeting and unfortunately happened to be standing between a very pissed-off partner and his cheating soon-to-be-ex-partner."

Now she smiled. "Are you sure you're okay?"

"Yeah. I mean—I'm obviously going to have a spiffy black eye, but no major injury."

"I'm going to kill Tony."

I smiled. "He said you'd say that."

"He was correct. Have you taken anything?"

"Not yet. I need Tylenol. And an ice pack. And cookies."

She smiled and put her hand lightly to my cheek, reminding me of the way Rita had treated me. "I can make all of those wishes come true. Why don't you go get into your comfy clothes and I'll bring them up."

"Thanks, Mom."

I headed upstairs and changed out of my suit and into my yoga pants and a T-shirt. I crawled onto my bed and turned on my television. I flipped through the channels. Sweet. Shark Week on Discovery Channel. Best week of the year. I settled back against the pillows and started watching *Anatomy of a Shark Bite*. I've seen it before, but it never gets old for some reason.

I heard my mom coming up the stairs and looked over when she reached my door.

Adam. What the hell was he doing here? I sat up, no doubt looking completely shocked. He was holding all of the items my mom was supposed to bring me. He set the bottle of Tylenol, a glass of milk, and the box of cookies on my nightstand and pulled out the ice pack that he'd tucked under his arm so that he could carry everything and handed it to me.

"What are you doing here?" I asked.

He looked down at me with just a hint of a smile and shook his head. "I thought you might need an ice pack."

"You forget. I live with my doting parents who," I shook the ice pack, "insist on taking care of me."

"Well, friends want to take care of you, too. Your mom seemed willing to share in the task. Scoot over."

I did. He was wearing jeans and a T-shirt. He kicked off his shoes before sitting on the bed next to me. "Put that on your face. It needs it."

"Thanks," I said, with a little sarcasm. I put the pack to

my cheek gingerly. It was getting pretty sore, but I didn't want to seem like a wuss.

"It's Monday. Shouldn't you be working?"

"I was actually at a client's furniture store where they were shooting a commercial. I hadn't planned on going into the office today, anyway."

He took a couple Tylenol from the bottle and handed me the glass of milk. Then he picked up the box of cookies.

"Girl Scout cookies?" he asked, with an amused expression.

"Thin Mints are my favorite," I said unapologetically. After handing me one, he took one for himself.

"Why are they cold?"

"Because Mom stockpiles them in the freezer. She's hoarding them for the apocalypse. She thinks they'll be the new currency."

He laughed. "It's important to plan ahead." He looked at me a moment before continuing. "Well, here's to your new job," he said, frowning.

I laughed. After taking a drink of milk, I held the glass out to him. He shook his head.

"So, you got hit by a man or a woman?"

"A tiny little man."

"It's the knuckles. You'd have been better off getting hit by a fat guy. Bony little knuckles make for bigger shiners."

"This guy was definitely bony."

"And he wasn't aiming for you, right?" He still had this protective vibe that . . . was kind of awesome. Screw women's lib. Yes, I can take care of myself, but that doesn't mean I don't get butterflies when a man tries to do it for me. Jonathan mostly let me handle things, but on a rare occasion he'd try to take care of me, though, and I did like it.

I shook my head, which caused a throbbing in my eye. I closed my eyes and did a quick intake of air. I looked back over at him and he was frowning again and had a deep crease between his eyebrows. My blinds were closed so the light in the room was dim and his green eyes looked darker.

I smiled. "You're sweet. No—I, unfortunately, was standing between two very pissed-off people. But I'm fine. It looks worse than it is."

His face softened. He ate the cookie he'd been holding in his hand and then held an arm out to me. I nestled into the crook of his arm, holding the ice against my face and eating another cookie. I'm not gonna lie. I can do some serious damage to a box of Girl Scout cookies. But, since I had an audience, I'd try to keep it to five. Maybe six. No more than seven.

I went back to watching Shark Week. This feels too good. But while lying here like this with Adam was awesome, lying with Jonathan like this . . . would be home.

My phone buzzed from where it was sitting on the nightstand. Adam picked it up to hand it to me and looked at the screen. And instantly didn't look happy anymore.

Uh-oh. I looked at the screen. Dave. What Adam could see was: *Hey, beautiful girl. I need to see you again so I can finish what I.* And the rest of the text was cut off. Super. I tossed the phone on the bed next to me. Adam shifted a little. I sat up and looked at him. I sighed and did the palms up "what is your problem?" gesture. He shook his head and acted like he was going to just go back to watching TV. I don't think so.

"Talk to me."

"No, Kate. Drop it. And put the ice back on your eye."

"Hell with the ice. You need to straighten some shit out, Adam, because you're throwing some majorly mixed signals here."

He looked at me, but didn't say anything.

"We are friends," I said. "Just friends. You've made that abundantly clear. So why do you keep acting jealous?"

"I'm not jealous."

"You're full of shit."

He paused. "I'm *trying* to not be jealous."

"You're failing. Explain yourself."

"What is there to explain?"

"Adam!" I said emphatically. "You only want to be my friend so why does it bother you that Dave is texting me?"

He shook his head. He didn't know. Or he knew but he wasn't willing to admit it.

I put my hand on his slightly stubbly chin and turned his face to me. His mouth was set in a hard line, molding his full lips into a perfect shape. His lids were lowered and he was determined to be stoic.

"You didn't want Dave to drive me home the other night," I said softly.

"No."

"Why?"

"I don't like the thought of him manipulating you."

Oh. See, that's totally reasonable and doesn't have anything to do with him being jealous in a romantic way. Maybe I'm reading too much into it.

"He tried. He failed," I said, gripping his chin a little tighter, trying to lighten his mood. Wasn't all that successful, however.

"What did he try?"

"To play me."

"How?"

"Doing the whole sweet, all-American-boy thing."

"And it didn't work?"

Hmm. "Not for long."

"How long?"

Holy shit. He seems to want a play-by-play of everything that happened after I left his sight. "At first he came off really sweet. But then I realized he's a total player."

"So you didn't sleep with him?"

"Jesus, Adam! No. I didn't."

He relaxed a little. "Sorry."

"We kissed, though." Yeah, I was lobbing a grenade. So what?

His jaw tightened.

"Why does that look like it really bothers you?"

He reached out and put a big hand on the side of my face and rubbed his thumb over my lips. Is he going to kiss me? It's amazing that I can read someone so well and still find him entirely unpredictable.

He pulled his hand back, picked up my glass of milk, and took a drink. "You're right, Kate." He still uses my name more than anyone I've ever known. "I'm overstepping my bounds."

Ugh. I kinda want to smack him right now. "He's definitely not a contract killer like you." He was watching me, looking casual, but I knew it was phony. "He just wants a challenge whether the woman is single or not."

Adam raised an eyebrow. "And you intend to put up with someone like that?"

"Since I know what he's up to, he seems harmless enough."

"You realize he just wants to get you in bed."

I nodded.

Adam sat up a little and turned toward me more fully. "Then why go out with him at all?"

"I don't really know. I mean, I thought he was like you and would have zero interest in me because I was single." Feel free to disagree with me. Truly.

"But he is interested in you."

"Wanting to sleep with me and being interested in me are not the same thing."

"Hmm." He seemed disappointed in me, either as part of his jealous twitch when it comes to me or, worse, that he likes me less thinking I'm the kind of girl that would allow herself to be sport in such a shallow game. But Adam meant something to me. Something undefined, but something important, and the thought that I might have damaged that with what I'd just told him was freaking me out.

"Adam, I'm not falling for anything. He was just persistent about us going out and I figured . . . what the hell."

"Hmm."

"If you don't want me to talk to him, I won't."

That got his attention. "Why?"

"Because I care about you and I don't care about him."

He smiled, perfect white teeth, dimple and all. I was conscious of my heart beating hard and a warmth spreading across my chest. He's like a virus attacking my whole system at once. "Good answer," he said.

"That being said, you're awfully possessive for a friend." He nodded. "I'll work on that."

"So? Is that a 'don't ever speak to him again' or a 'we're just friends and you're free to do whatever you want'?"

He leaned in closer to me. Whoa, buddy. Stop with the tingles. "We're friends and you're free to do what you want, but please, be careful around that guy."

"Because he's unscrupulous like you?"

"Because he's unscrupulous, *unlike* me. I never deceive women, Kate. You may not like my objectives, but I never lie about them. Ever."

Oh. I nodded.

He ran a hand through his dark hair.

"Okay, get the ice back on your eye and lie down or your mom is going to fire me."

I lay back against his chest and put the ice to my eye again. This is definitely the most confusing friendship I've ever had.

My phone buzzed again and Adam pretended not to notice. I looked at the screen. It was my mother letting me know that Jonathan dropped off flowers and saw my car and knows I'm home. Perfect. Seriously. My life was so ordinary just one month ago! Now it's a frickin' circus. How can anyone's timing be this consistently bad?

Stall?

For how long? Are you getting dressed?

---

* *Subject to the following terms and conditions*

Mom!!!!

Just kidding. Tell me what you want me to do ... I can tell him you're sleeping.

I looked at Adam. "Apparently Jonathan is here."

"Unfortunate timing."

"Yeah."

"I can go."

Not like he was going to spend the whole day here, anyway, but I certainly wasn't going to kick him out. "You don't have to, but he saw my car so I guess I have to go talk to him."

"I should probably go anyway," he said, looking at his watch. He sat up and slipped his shoes on and stood. I climbed off the bed and stood in front of him. When I'm barefoot he seems really tall.

"Why are you pouting?" he asked. Good question.

Instead of answering, I wrapped my arms around his waist and put my cheek (my good cheek) to his chest. He hugged me to him and put a hand on my hair. I've got a crush. I was finally admitting that to myself—guess I'm a little late to the party.

He stepped back from me, turned me around, and guided me out the bedroom door with a hand to my back.

I walked down the stairs slowly. So, for the second time, I'm about to have an awkward encounter between these two men. I reached the bottom of the stairs and looked into the kitchen and saw my ex-main squeeze leaning against the kitchen counter with a dozen white roses (my favorite) in his hand. His hair was getting a little long, so it looked all sexy and messy. He looked over when he saw me coming in and his mouth dropped open.

Yeah, I guess seeing Adam again, when we were likely coming down from my bedroom, would catch him off guard.

"Jesus, Kate! What happened to your eye?"

Oh, right. That.

"Oh," I said, putting a fingertip to my eye. "Wrong place at the wrong time at the office today."

He stood close to me and put his hands to my face, turning it so that he could see the bruise more closely. My body let out an inner sigh. He smelled good. He looked back in my eyes, all concern and sympathy.

"Does it hurt?"

"A little. It'll be fine," I said, stepping away, out of his hands.

"These are for you. They were to congratulate you on your first day, but I guess now they're a 'get well soon.'"

I smiled and smelled them ('cause that's what you do when someone gives you roses).

"Thank you. They're beautiful."

He finally looked past me and his eyes settled on Adam. This should be fun.

"You remember Adam?"

"Of course," Jonathan said, reaching out with a hand. They shook.

Adam put a hand on my shoulder. "I should run." He pointed a finger in my face. "Ice."

"Yes, sir."

Adam leaned into the kitchen farther so that he could see my mom. "Deanna, very nice to see you again."

"You, too, Adam," she said.

And he left. Doesn't take a genius to know why this little scenario is giving me déjà vu.

"So," Jonathan said. He'd folded his arms across his chest, but quickly released them down to his sides, probably worried about what I'd make of his body language. "Are you *seeing* him?"

"I'll let you two talk," Mom said with an uncomfortable smile before she disappeared into some unknown corner of the house.

I went into the kitchen and sat down on a barstool at the kitchen counter. Jonathan sat down next to me.

"No, we're friends."

He nodded. I don't think he wanted to press his luck. "So," he said, making a slight gesture to my eye. "You broke the first rule of Fight Club, huh?"

And I smiled, in spite of myself.

He started to lean in toward me like he was going to try to kiss me so I leaned back. He stopped where he was and instead, he tucked my hair behind my ear and kissed my cheek lightly.

"Dinner tonight?" he asked.

"Not tonight. Look at me. I'm gonna lay low for a few days."

"I see nothing wrong."

"Jonathan."

"Would you take me back if we signed another contract?"

This is what stunned silence feels like. I just stared at him. I couldn't think of anything to say.

"Kate?"

"I have no response to that."

"Should I take that as a good sign or a bad sign?"

"You should take it as no sign."

"Oh."

Shit. I guess he's serious about regretting this whole thing. But he felt strongly enough about it to start us down this whole path . . . it's not as though he changed his mind before our contract actually ended. And there it was. Completely unbidden and complicating: I thought about Adam. If I signed with Jonathan again, there would be no way I could be friends with Adam. I have feelings for him. Not to mention, I would fit his target again and having feelings for Adam *and* having him try to sleep with me? Pretty sure that would end badly. Well, it would probably end freaking amazing . . . and then I'd hate myself forever.

So here's what I know for sure: 1) if I sign with Jonathan again, I have to completely cut Adam out of my life, and 2) number one is a much bigger factor in this than I ever thought it would be.

"Jonathan, I was happy and content and you pulled the rug out from under me. It's not that I doubt you're sincere now, but how am I supposed to trust that in another year you won't be itching for freedom again?" I sighed. "Look, it's just that you've already put us through this . . . and it seems like we need to ride it out."

"Sorry, I have no idea what that means."

Yeah. Me, either. "I didn't want to be single, but now I am. And so are you. I think it makes sense for us to take some time to be on our own since we're already here."

"Oh. Are you seeing anyone?"

"No, but I will if I feel like it. And you wanted your

freedom enough to put this in motion. You need to be sure wanting me back isn't just some knee-jerk reaction. Here we are, Jonathan. Contract is over. I've moved out. The damage is done. We may as well take this time to be really sure what we want. If it's meant to be, we'll know."

"You're not sure it's what you want anymore," he said softly.

"Hey, I wouldn't have given it a second thought if we had just re-upped like I thought we would."

"I know. Believe me—I know."

I put my hand over his where it was resting on the counter. He bent over and kissed the back of my hand.

"I'm tired," I said. "I'm going to try to take a nap."

"Okay. Dinner this week?"

"Fine, but let me give this," I waved a hand in front of my eye, "a couple of days to see if it looks any better."

"I still say you look perfect."

I smiled. "You would."

He leaned in and hugged me and then headed out.

After he left, I made my way back upstairs to my room. I ate a couple more cookies and looked at the glass of milk Adam and I had been sharing. Not like I was worried about catching his cooties at this point. I crawled onto my bed and fiddled with the ice pack. I laid back just enough so that the pack would stay on my eye, but not too far that I couldn't drink from the glass. Multitasking skills. It took me about sixty seconds to know I wasn't going to be able to sleep. I looked at the clock. Almost five. Logek might be out of the office.

She picked up on the first ring.

"Hey, Rocky."

"Hey. You out of work yet?"

"Yep, on my way home."

I picked up a mirror from my nightstand. Shit. Why is it that a glancing blow to the cheekbone results in a black eye? Where does all that bruising come from?

"So, how does one go about covering up a black eye?"

"Well, what I normally do is . . . how the hell would I know? Not exactly a common occurrence. We'll look it up online. I'm sure there are certain colors to use that neutralize the color. And what color is it at this point?"

"Eggplant."

"Awesome."

"Logek, when did my life get so crazy?"

"When you decided to go to law school."

Hmm. Hadn't considered that. I had it pegged for two weeks ago when Jonathan dumped me. Okay, or maybe the week before when I didn't land the job I'd considered a sure thing. "So Adam showed up here."

"And?"

"He'd texted so I sent him the pic of the eye and he showed up here to take care of me."

"Aww. That's actually really sweet. That guy is just full of surprises."

"I know. So he was up here in my room, cuddling with me while I iced my face."

"There was cuddling?"

"Oh, yes. He cuddles with his female friends. Which is a very lonely club, I might add."

"Of which you are the sole member."

"Exactly. So, I'm reasonably sure I've got a pretty decent crush going."

She sighed. "Yeah."

"And then Jonathan shows up. Which, by the way, puts him two for two on showing up here when I'm with Adam."

"Fun."

"And Jonathan sort of asked if I would take him back if we signed another contract."

"What the fuck?" It was sort of a shriek. Her reaction is clearly similar to mine. And I smiled because I could picture her in her car, her Bluetooth coming through the car speakers and her gripping the steering wheel with both hands and yelling. Anyone driving past her would think she had Tourette's.

"Right? What the hell is that?"

"Oh my god. What did you say?"

"Nothing. But I did realize that I couldn't stay friends with Adam if I did get back together with him."

"Definitely not. Not now."

"Exactly."

"But that can't be part of your decision."

"I know." Lies. Why can't it be?

"I mean, Kate, if you had a crush on a normal guy, I'd say don't rush into another contract with Jonathan until you're sure there's nothing real with the other guy. But he's not normal. Not even close."

"I know." Sort of.

"I do think he likes you, too, but I don't know that it's enough to actually overcome any of his . . . idiosyncrasies."

"Idiosyncrasies?"

"Well, you know him better than I do, but isn't he sort of fundamentally and psychologically opposed to actual relationships?"

"Yes," I said, heavy on the sulk.

"See? If Jonathan hadn't put you into this situation, you never would have actually gotten to *know* Adam Lucas. You just would have been his conquest and, you being you, would have been completely unswayed by him. But now . . ."

"Now I'm swayed."

"Oh, Kitty Kat," she said sympathetically. "And he's not making it any easier on you by being all sweet and thoughtful, either."

"Right? Bastard."

"Maybe you need a little space from those two. Go out with Dave. You don't give two shits for that guy."

I laughed. Then I growled in frustration. "Enough. How was your day?"

"Good, but I may kill our new general sales manager."

"Asshole?"

"Bitch."

"Ah."

"Oh. I did get a bit of good news, though. Looks like Derek came into some money."

Derek was the only partner that had breached on her. She was awarded damages in the suit, but he was "judgment proof" (i.e., broke) so all Logek could do was file an abstract of judgment in his county of residence in case he was ever worth anything. This was good news indeed. "How much?"

"Enough to pay me off."

"That's awesome. Then you can pay off Evan."

"Exactly." She sighed. "Then I'm only paying Marcus. Don't ever let me sign another contract, okay?"

"You always say that, but you don't exactly listen to reason when you're swept up."

She grunted in reply.

"Speaking of contracts, how's it going with Daniel?"

"Great. He's a doll. He's never been under contract."

"So does that mean he's averse to them or that he takes them seriously and doesn't rush into anything?"

"The latter."

"Does he know you're a serial signer?"

"Thanks for that."

"You're welcome."

"Yeah. I told him. He seemed a little freaked, but he keeps calling so I guess he's not too put off by it."

"Is he worried that you're going to want to sign right away?"

"Just the opposite, I think. He's worried that I've had so many failures that I won't be up for it again even if it's finally with the right person."

"Hmm. You're too much of a romantic to ever be that jaded."

"Yeah—you and me both, doll."

True.

CHAPTER 11

By morning, the black eye was impressive, but at least it didn't hurt. Apparently yellow concealer is the supposed answer to my shiner, but so far, not too impressed. I patted on a third layer on top of the purple, but the purple was a very determined color. Damn. I patted my normal skin-colored foundation on top of the concealer, then some powder. It toned it down, but definitely didn't conceal it. I put extra eye makeup on—like it was somehow going to compensate for the black eye. My light blue eyes looked even lighter in contrast to the bruise since they were so much closer to the color of the white of my eyes than the purple skin under the eye. I look like an effing zombie. Gonna be an awesome day.

Thanks to a stall on the freeway, my forty-minute commute took fifty and I got to work right at eight o'clock. I got off the elevator and Rita ran up to me as soon as she saw me coming.

She put her hands on my shoulders and looked into my face. "Nice cover-up job."

"Thanks. For all the good it did."

"Oh, you look fine. He sure got you, though."

"Yep. One little knuckle can do all this."

She smiled sympathetically. "You might be able to get a spot as an extra on *The Walking Dead*, though."

My dream.

I went to my office and set my bag down. I smiled when I saw a set of boxing gloves on my desk. A Post-it note stuck on them said, "Welcome aboard, Bruiser. —B." Brad, I'm guessing. I chuckled. I tied the laces on the back of the gloves together and hung the gloves on my coatrack. Definitely gave my office some flare.

"Okay. Let's see it," Mags said, strolling in. She was in a leopard-print skirt today and a pink top. It was tied together with leopard-print five-inch heels with a pink platform on them. She apparently didn't mess around when it came to accessorizing.

I smiled at her as she came closer to study me.

"Damn."

"Thanks."

"You kind of look like a zombie."

"So I've been told."

"A really, really pretty zombie. Like a supermodel zombie. Who was killed by a blow to the face."

I laughed. "Stop with the compliments."

She winked and headed back out my door.

I logged into my computer and checked my e-mail. Wow. Second day and the requests from other attorneys were rolling in. Draft two letters to opposing counsel, write a mediation brief, and research the requirements for claiming a breach of a procreation clause. Procreation clause? I never took a signing class in law school, because, you know, I was *never* going to do signing law.

I started looking through the electronic files for the cases I was being asked to work on. About twenty minutes later, Jared Mann walked into my office.

"Hi, Kate. I heard what happened yesterday. How are you feeling?"

He was wearing a charcoal suit with a barely noticeable pinstripe and a solid royal-blue silk tie. He had a really square jaw that kept him from looking too pretty, 'cause otherwise, damn, he was a pretty man.

"Oh, it's fine. Looks worse than it is."

He tipped his head to the side and . . . stared. It was getting a little uncomfortable when he made a little "hmph" sound and sat down in one of the leather chairs facing my desk.

"Well, glad to see you weren't scared off."

I smiled in reply.

"So, did you see my e-mail?"

I looked at my computer. Oh. The "procreation clause" research request was from him.

"Yes, I'm not sure what it means, but I'll figure it out."

He laughed. "Well, you can't require sex in a contract."

"Right. Prostitution. Bad."

"Right. But that didn't stop people from trying to put booty clauses in their contracts."

"Booty clauses?"

"I actually think Tony is the one that coined the term thirty years ago, but now I hear it all over town."

"Nice."

"A booty clause would require certain performance in the bedroom—either frequency or fun and games. Whatever. So basically some guy would put in the contract that his partner was in breach if she didn't give it up at least four times a week. Or if she didn't let him tie her up. Or if she didn't spank him."

My mouth was hanging open a little.

"Oh, trust me. We see everything here."

Close your mouth. You look like a rookie. Which I am.

"And all of those were, of course, unenforceable," he continued. "But, procreation clauses are a different story."

I picked up a pen and waited. Might need to take notes on this lesson.

"A person has a right to know before signing that their partner will have children. So attorneys started crafting carefully worded procreation clauses that basically say that the couple will work toward having a child—or children, and they agree to participate in these efforts at least twice a week until conception, or four times a week, or daily."

"Ooh. I can see where that can get sticky."

"Pun intended?"

I laughed. And possibly blushed.

He smiled. "Exactly. So now people have a work-around

to require sex. No fetishes or anything, but regularity. There's a lot of case law out there from people breaching these because it happens all the time. Our client is a woman and she's got one of these procreation clauses in her contract and it requires that she *try to get pregnant*," and he did the "air quotes" thing with his fingers, "at least three times a week. So she's about six months into her contract and her dick-head partner keeps pulling out."

I raised my eyebrows. Holy crap this job gets personal.

"Yeah, he doesn't come inside her. I realize—too much information, but welcome to signing law. She's been having sex three times a week pursuant to the contract and he pulls out every time, so she finally stopped having sex with him and now he's suing her for breach."

"Asshole."

"Yeah. So I need you to find a case along those lines. I can't imagine something like this hasn't happened in the past. If we'd written the contract, this wouldn't have happened. Our procreation clauses have all kinds of safeguards to be sure both partners are equally obligated to try to conceive. We go so far as to put in exactly how much infertility testing they have to participate in and if they will be required to go as far as artificial insemination or in vitro. Her contract just said 'three times a week till she's knocked up' and not much more."

"Yikes. So she never realized this guy was a dick before she signed with him?"

He shrugged. "She probably should have. Not like people change that much."

I did a quick, hopefully inconspicuous, scan of his clothing.

Tie tack, cuff links, watch. No—no token, at least not that he's wearing. Oh, hell. Just ask.

"Are you signed?"

He smiled. "No. You won't find a lot of attorneys that do signing law who actually sign. At least ones that specialize in breach the way we do."

"Too cynical?"

"Occupational hazard." Then he stared again without saying anything. Okay. This is going to be tough to take if he does this regularly. Not sure if I should feel flattered or self-conscious. I'm gonna go with the latter. Since it's my nature.

After a minute he seemed to remember himself and he stood up, smiling. "So, in a couple of days?"

"A couple of days?"

"You can have that research to me?"

Duh. "Oh, absolutely."

"Great. Thanks, Kate." And he left. Hmm. Kind of a strange guy. Not bad strange, but . . . unusual.

I spent the next couple of hours running Westlaw searches for my booty clause research. It's a little shocking how much case law there is on lawsuits over people's sex lives. Makes you realize how sneaky people get to try to incorporate sex into their contract. Nothing so far on pulling out, though. I did find a case where they wrote "no children" into the contract and the woman poked holes in the condom with a safety pin. That's dedication. And one where the man put in that, as a means of water conservation, they had to shower together. I'm thinking that woman did not read that contract too closely before signing. But don't worry—the court found the water conservation clause unenforceable.

My phone buzzed. Adam.

How's the eye?

Ugly.

I'm sure. How did it go after I left yesterday?

Weird.

Want to talk about it?

Yeah, Adam, let me tell you all about my crush on you so that you can run screaming from my life. *He's a very confusing man.* Technically, you both are.

Oh? What did he say?

Okay, this is the first time Adam has wanted to know how things were going with Jonathan. Tell him? Don't tell him? Tell him because secretly I want to see how he'll react? God, I'm such a girl sometimes. *He asked if I'd take him back if we signed another contract.*

One minute. Two minutes. Apparently Mr. Lucas didn't know how to respond to that.

Finally he replied with, *And?*

And I don't know.

Hmm.

How very insightful. Men. They just never shut up.

How about lunch, beautiful?

What the hell? *Since when do you call me 'beautiful'?*

Not sure what you mean, Kate.

Shit. I looked down at my messages again. Oh. Lunch invite was from Dave. And I accidentally replied to Adam. I laughed—because that's kind of an awesome snafu.

Oops. Misread a text.

From who?

Dave.

Oh. He calls you 'beautiful'?

Yep. More a nickname than commentary.

Maybe both.

Ooh. Butterflies. He just *sorta* called me beautiful. I sighed. This was the most useless crush I've ever had. And I can't think of a response. Maybe it doesn't require one.

Dave. Logek said to use him to distract me. Starting to sound like pretty good advice.

Sure. Want to meet somewhere?

I'm actually by your office. How about if I come to you?

Sure. 12:30?

Perfect. See you soon.

So there. I have a very unexciting lunch date with Dave to avoid thinking about the man I like or the man I love. I have to say, there is something comforting about being with a guy that isn't tangling up my head.

And since I had invoked him by thinking about him like an evil spirit, Mags walked into my office carrying a vase with a dozen or so white roses. Jonathan. Two dozen roses in two days. Can you say "overkill?" She was grinning with one eyebrow raised. She set them on the corner of my desk and then, instead of sitting in one of my chairs, sat on the desk next to the flowers and waited for me to read the card.

Turns out I'm totally over you. Just thought I'd let you know.

And I chuckled. He's such a nerd. My kind of nerd. I sighed and handed the card to Mags. She smiled and looked at me, waiting for me to elaborate. I gave her the quick rundown—turns out you *can* distill eight years down to two minutes fairly easily.

"Ouch," she said. "So? Are you gonna sign again?"

"I don't know. Things are . . . complicated now."

"How so?"

There was a soft knock on my door and I looked over to see Dave leaning against the doorframe. He was in black slacks and a light blue, button-down shirt. He had his hands deep in the pockets of his slacks and his legs were crossed casually at the ankle.

Mags looked at Dave and then back at me with wide eyes. "Jonathan?" she asked in a hushed voice. I shook my head. "Complication," she said, naturally assuming Dave was the man at issue. "That is one hell of a complication," she said softly, after taking another long look at Dave.

I stood up and walked over to him. When I was close enough, he stepped in to hug me, but stopped and put his hands on my shoulders. He looked down at me, frowning. Oh, right. The eye. It's funny how easily I forget until someone looks at me.

"What in the world happened to you?"

"There were a couple of guys holding up the liquor store. I wrestled the gun away from one of them, but when I was beating up the other guy, he got in a lucky shot."

He didn't laugh, but I could tell he was amused. He looked over my shoulder to where Mags was still sitting on my desk.

"She accidentally got caught in between two angry partners," Mags said.

"I see," he said, looking at me once more. It was kind of sweet—he looked genuinely concerned. He rubbed a thumb lightly across my cheek. "Does it hurt?"

"Not anymore. It just looks awful."

"Yeah. It kinda does. Can I get a rain check for lunch? Not sure I want to be seen in public with you like this."

"Ha-ha. And no. I'm hungry."

He grinned at me with his too-perfect smile. So cute. Mags hopped off my desk and walked over to us.

"Dave, this is Mags. Mags, Dave."

They shook hands and Dave gave her the full-on charm thing. "Mags is short for?"

"Magdalena." I'd been curious, but hadn't gotten around to asking.

"Beautiful," he said, making her actually glow a little.

Mags passed him on her way out of my office and turned back to look at me from behind his back and mouthed "oh my god," and fanned herself with her hands. Yeah. He was easy on the eyes.

I grabbed my purse and we headed out. I did a quick introduction to Rita as we crossed the lobby.

Once we were alone in the elevator, he quickly pressed me up against the wall and kissed me. It wasn't the soft and gentle thing he did in his truck that night. This one had a lot more fire. Oh, my. He wrapped a hand around my waist and gripped my side tightly as he slipped his tongue into my mouth. After a thorough invasion of my mouth, he trailed some soft kisses on my neck before letting go of me and stepping back just in time for the elevator doors to open. Losing this competition wouldn't be so bad, right?

My skin was tingling and I think my nipple was fondly remembering his mouth. I smoothed my hair and straightened my suit jacket.

He chuckled when he took in my flushed, startled expression. "We could just get a hotel room instead of lunch."

Okay. "No, lunch sounds better."

"Only because you haven't sampled my menu."

My smile drooped and he laughed. "Fine. Food. Nice to know where your priorities are."

"Yes. Always feed me before hitting on me," I said.

"I don't need to sleep with you—I just like being around you," he said, leaning in and giving me a sincere expression.

"Bullshit. Nice try, though."

"Well, I *do* like you. More than most girls."

"That I do believe. If only because you don't have to work so hard to keep up the facade."

We walked out of the building and he took my hand. Holding my hand in public was weirding me out a little. PDA usually implied something, but it seemed that he was doing it casually, and pulling my hand away would only make it a bigger deal than it was meant to be.

We walked down Capitol three blocks to the Zinfandel Grille. He held the door for me and I walked in ahead of him. The hostess knew him. She was pretty cute and very young. Made me wonder if Dave was a cradle robber on top of being a letch. Or she may just be a little dazzled by his local star quality.

She sat us at a table and I could tell she was checking me out. Whether it was because I was competition or because she was curious what kind of women he went for, I couldn't tell. But I definitely interested her. Oh shit. Or it could be the eye. She set menus on the table and left us.

"No," he said.

"No, what?"

"I've never slept with her."

"I didn't ask."

"You didn't have to."

We looked at each other quietly for a minute, aware that we were so onto each other. This was the shortest game of bullshit in history.

The waitress came by and took drink orders and, since we already knew what we wanted, our lunch order as well.

Once she was gone, we went back to quietly regarding each other. This was such a weird situation. It was like playing poker with all your cards showing. Poker faces were pointless.

"So how do we do this?" I asked.

"What?"

"Pretend we're two people on a date and not just a guy scheming to get a girl into bed."

He didn't answer right away. "I can want to get you into bed *and* want to date you. In fact, I'm pretty sure the two usually go hand in hand."

"Maybe, when a guy is genuinely interested in a woman, but wanting to sleep with a woman does just fine all on its own. Considering what I already know about you, it still feels like the most likely scenario."

"You know I like you."

"Because I didn't fall into your bed."

"Actually, no, that would really win me over." He was giving me his best naughty grin. "You should give that some serious consideration."

"Are there that many women that sleep with you just 'cause you're pretty?"

He frowned. "I'd like to think there's a little more to it."

I raised my eyebrows.

"Yes. Women, in general, are not as evolved as you'd like to believe."

"Tragic."

"Says you. I sort of like women the way they are." He was serious. So much for men being the ones that think with their Johnsons. So what would that be called in a woman?

"But, you know, sometimes relationships are supposed to make you happy and not just be for the challenge."

He looked at me for a minute with dead, unemotional eyes. "So show me."

I laughed a little . . . without real amusement. "But you're sort of Helen Keller and I'm no Miracle Worker."

"You might be. Give yourself a little credit."

I didn't know how to react when he acted like he wanted to date me for real. I guess that's the trouble with him—I'll never really know for sure if he's sincere.

"What did you do before law school?" Alrighty. Changing subjects.

"I was at channel seven for about ten years."

"Seriously?" He lit up at this bit of info. "Why didn't you tell me? I told you I was at forty and you never told me you'd worked in TV."

"It didn't come up."

"What did you do?"

"I was in sales—research director."

He nodded. If you were in TV, you knew exactly what a research director did. Market research, TV ratings, competitive tracking. Pretty mundane, really. But being in the TV business was fun for a while.

Before he replied, a middle-aged woman stopped at the table. She looked at me apologetically before focusing on Dave. "I'm so sorry to bother you, but are you Dave Hunter from channel forty?"

"Guilty," he said, smiling. All fake charm and sincerity. Good lord. This guy was so screwed up—he must be at least 75 percent bullshit and only 25 percent real.

"My partner and my son are huge fans. Would it be possible to get your autograph?"

"Of course," he said. He took the pen she offered and snatched the cocktail napkin from under his glass. He scribbled on it and handed it to her.

"Thanks so much." Then she looked at me and thanked me, for allowing the interruption, I guess.

When she was gone, he looked at me and shrugged. Oddly, the TV Dave charm that lit him up when he was signing the autograph ebbed once she was gone, and he seemed more real.

"What?" he asked, at my assessing expression.

"Nothing."

"You say about ten percent of everything you think."

I shrugged. "It's probably closer to twenty-five percent." Ninety-five percent if I've had cocktails.

"Well, I can see all those thoughts rolling around in your

head and I can't help wonder what is going on in there," he said, pointing a finger toward my forehead.

"I say the important stuff, I think."

"So why do you keep so much inside?"

"Because if everyone said everything they think, half the time they would just be hurting people's feelings."

"Does that apply to me?"

"Assuming you have feelings to hurt?"

"For the sake of argument."

"Yes, that applies to you." Stop this now. No good can come from this path of conversation.

"And what do you think about me?" He leaned in toward me from across the table.

"I think that I'm between a rock and a hard place. And you are neither. So here I am."

"You're here because I'm easy?"

I nodded.

He shrugged and fiddled with his water glass. "Everyone has to start somewhere."

"See, I'm never going to trust myself to know when you're being real and when you're maneuvering."

"I'm being real."

"Sure. Of course I can trust *you* to tell me whether or not I can trust *you*."

He just looked at me intently, but didn't reply.

"Tell me something real," I said, trying to lighten things up with a smile. "Something no one else knows."

"I hate college football."

I laughed.

"It's not funny—that's serious stuff. Do you have any idea how much college football I have to cover? And pretend I care?"

"I see your point. I'll keep your secret."

"And I like you."

"You said that earlier."

"But now I want you to actually hear it."

Inward sigh. Maybe I should flip a coin every time he says something to decide whether it's bullshit or not. Because watching his face isn't doing me any good.

"Shit," he said. I raised my eyebrows, asking the question. "You're gonna break my heart."

"That seems highly unlikely."

"It's been a long time since I actually *liked* a girl," he said. "Not just wanted her, but liked her."

Oh. I have no response to that. If it's true, it's very flattering. If it's a ploy to butter me up . . . I won't fall for it. Probably.

"What do you think, Kate?"

"I have *no* idea what I'm doing these days. None at all. That's the only thing I know for sure."

He gripped my wrist and pulled me toward him. He leaned across the table. While his lips were just a hair's breadth away from mine, he whispered, "Sometimes things work out best when you don't overthink them."

He sat back and released my hand just in time for the waitress to bring our food. I wasn't as hungry as I was when we left my office. Too much . . . confusion . . . kills the appetite.

We started eating. "So you're a planner, huh?"

"A planner?" I asked.

"You keep things very orderly in your life and according to plan."

I laughed. "I'm about a thousand miles from the plan I had just two months ago. So maybe I *was,* but I think I'm giving up on trying to control things. It doesn't work."

He smiled. "Embrace the chaos."

"I liked things better when they were under my control," I said, gesturing at him with my fork. I took another bite. "But, then again, I guess that control was an illusion, so maybe I'm better off."

"I predict things are going to work out just fine for you."

"You're a fortune-teller?"

He smiled and swiped his mouth with his napkin. "Maybe."

"Got any winning lottery numbers for me?"

He closed his eyes and touched the tines of his fork to the space between his eyebrows. "Hmm. Check back later."

I giggled. "Perfect. I'm dating a Magic Eight Ball."

He grinned. "It is decidedly so."

I laughed some more and we went back to more eating and less talking.

"So, you agree to date me, then?" he asked.

"I really don't see the point in it."

"You don't have to see a point in it. You just decide that you like hanging out with me and say 'what the hell?' "

"Why, Dave? You don't date. You hunt. I get that you like a challenge, but why are you willing to invest this much time into getting into my pants?"

"We're never going to get past that, are we? You know what? I'm sorry, Kate, I think you're beautiful and everything, but I'm taking sex off the table. I know you had your heart set on it, but it is just getting in the way."

"Is that right?"

"Yep. Now that it's no longer an option, maybe we can just spend some time together without all the hang-ups."

"Maybe," I said. Uh-oh. I like talking to him. What was it Logek said? I didn't give two shits about him? It's possible that ratio is changing. How is it that now I have multiple men in my life? This is new territory for me. Really rocky, slippery territory. With land mines.

We finished eating and the waitress cleared the plates and left the check, which Dave grabbed before I had a chance. Come on, Dave. I need you to show a little more of that asshole I know you're capable of.

He took my hand as we headed out of the restaurant. Holding hands in public makes you look like a couple. Period. And I got the impression Adam agreed with me when I looked up and saw him come in through the door. His eyes immediately flickered down to our joined hands.

"Hey, man," Dave said, greeting him.

Adam did not look all that friendly. He gave Dave a nod in reply and focused on me. I'm not sure what sort of friendship he and Dave had, but of the two of us, it was me he expected more from. And somehow I'd let him down.

He put his hand under my chin and tipped my face up, examining my eye. "It looks a lot better than it did yesterday. Less swelling, anyway."

Was he just being nice or subtly letting Dave know that he was with me yesterday? "Yeah, now it's just the color I have to deal with."

Now I got the full smile. And the butterflies that accompanied it. Land mines.

"It certainly is interesting. The blue of your eyes against the purple bruise."

"I know. Zombie."

He laughed. "Someone beat me to that?"

"A few people. But thank you for reinforcing the fact that I look like a freak."

"Yes, but you make a very pretty zombie, so there's that."

I laughed at that. It was sweet. And complimentary. And not helping my crush any.

He looked over my shoulder and waved to someone. I did a quick glance. Quick. Don't make it look like you care who he's having lunch with. Even if she's beautiful. Which she was. Poker face, Kate. Misplaced jealousy is his thing, not yours. He looked at me and lowered his eyebrows a touch.

"I have a client lunch," he explained. And now the butterflies were knots. What the hell is going on with us?

And just when I actually felt a little light-headed because my heart was beating too fast, Dave gave my hand a firm squeeze and brought me back. He looked down at me in a way that made me realize he picked up on a lot more of what was transpiring than I thought he would. Dave to the rescue. I smiled at him. And meant it.

"Well, I've got to get back to the office," I said to Adam.

He nodded. "I'll talk to you later." Then he looked at Dave and said, "See ya, Dave."

And Dave and I hustled out of that painfully awkward situation.

He held my hand all the way back to my office in silence. He stopped us before we went into the lobby.

He took both my hands in his and bent down and kissed me. Nothing too forward, thankfully, since we were on a public street. "I'm okay with being the easy option. For now," he said.

I had no response, but I smiled at him, which he seemed to take as answer enough.

He winked at me. "I'll talk to you later, beautiful."

CHAPTER 12

I was crossing the lobby when Rita rushed me from behind her desk.

"That was Dave Hunter!"

"I know!" I said, teasing her by using the same emphasis.

"From channel forty."

I laughed. "Apparently so."

"Is he your recently ex-partner?"

"Nope. Just a friend. I met him a few days ago."

"Oh, I just love him. And I don't even like sports." Dang, she was so excited.

"Well, now that I know you're such a fan, we'll be sure to stop and chat the next time he's in."

"You're the best," she said, heading back to her desk.

I got to my office and looked at the vase of roses. I sat

down and picked up Jonathan's card and read it again. He was really good at getting a smile out of me. I tossed the card into my desk drawer and dove back into my highlighting of the cases I'd pulled for the procreation clause case.

"Kate!"

It was Tony, apparently beckoning me from his office. Hope he doesn't make a habit of that. I hurried over there and leaned in his doorway, waiting for him to look up from the paperwork on his desk.

"Hey, darling," he said, smiling. "How's the shiner?"

"Colorful."

"I see that. How's it going so far?"

"Aside from the assault, you mean?"

"Aside from that."

"Good. Interesting. So much to learn."

"Great. I want you to go to a child support hearing for me on Monday. Think your eye will be normal by then?"

"I don't really know. I certainly hope so. Or at least coverable by then."

"The hearing is in front of Judge Stanford and he's kind of an old pervert so I think we've got a better shot if you go."

"Um. Thanks?"

"It's called 'maximizing our assets,' darling."

Super. I was the only female "asset" so does that mean I'm going to get fed to the lions on a regular basis?

"Before Monday have Mags pull the Britton file for you so you can familiarize yourself with it. Let me know if you have questions."

"Aside from the obvious 'I've never even seen a child support hearing let alone done one' question?"

He looked at me with a blank stare for a minute. "Ask around. Someone probably has one this week and you can tag along."

"Alrighty." I left his office and looked around. The only attorneys I'd actually talked to so far were Jared and Brad. I started walking the perimeter peeking in offices. Brad would be my first choice. We had a strange camaraderie based on me getting punched by his client that could lead to us actually being friends. That's a delightful bit of dysfunction right there. I passed the offices slowly, aware that I did not remember a single name.

"Kate?"

I turned around and Jared was standing in his doorway.

"Were you looking for me?"

"Actually, Brad. Well, anyone, but Brad is the only attorney I've really met so far."

"And me."

"And you."

"What do you need?"

"I need to find someone who has a child support hearing this week so that I can sit in. Tony wants me to cover one next week."

"I've got one tomorrow. Afternoon calendar so we have to be there at one."

"Great. Thank you." Yes, thank you, Awkward Staring Man. Without another word he turned around and went back into his office. He may be pretty, but he is definitely a strange bird.

I went back to my office and the rest of the afternoon blew by. I shut down my computer and debated on whether or not to leave the flowers at work. Nope. Too much commentary and I don't feel like trying to explain to everyone that walks into my office how my partner that dumped me is now oddly trying to woo me. I waved to Rita and stepped into the elevator that Mags was holding for me. The doors closed and it was just the two of us in there.

"Okay. I was slammed this afternoon, but I've been dying to know. Is that the guy keeping you from re-upping with the ex?"

"Nope. Believe it or not, it's another guy."

"You are my hero. God. What is that even like to have that many men after you?"

I laughed. "Trust me. This is virgin territory for me. I've never been a guy magnet before. And now . . . apparently I am, but they are all kind of damaged. So, not an actual guy magnet—more like a broken toy magnet. Yay me."

She laughed. "Well, if that guy is currently in third place, I can't wait to see the other two."

"There are no places. There's no nothing. Just a big ol' mess."

"Shit, girl. Let yourself have some fun with it."

She did have a point. I've never had more attention than I could handle. And given the fact that my self-esteem has been dragged through the mud for the last few weeks, maybe I should stop lamenting over it and enjoy it a little.

"I think I worry too much about hurting people," I said.

"Most women worry about being the ones that get hurt."

I shrugged and the elevator doors opened.

"Want to hit happy hour?" Mags asked.

No reason to hurry home. "Sure," I said, smiling. "Where?"

"The Irish pub, Mallory's, on Tenth Street has a good happy hour."

"Okay. I'll meet you there," I said, lifting up the vase to imply that I needed to put those in my car. "What's the cross street?"

"K Street. It's only about three blocks from here. Parking kind of sucks so you probably want to leave your car here and walk."

"Alright. I'll dump these in the car and meet you there."

I got to my car and sat down while I situated the vase on the floor of the passenger seat so that it wouldn't tip over. I grabbed my wallet out of my bag and tucked the bag in my backseat. I looked at my phone. Two texts. Do I even want to know? Of course I do, dammit.

From Jonathan. *Now that I'm completely over you, we should probably have dinner so that I can tell you all about it.* Nerd.

And one from Adam. *Busy tonight?* Hmm. Brief. Cryptic.

Heading to happy hour with one of the paralegals from the office.

Where?

Mallory's on 10th. What are you up to tonight?

Thinking about doing happy hour with a friend.

A friend. Me? Or is "friend" code for a woman he's sleeping with?

Lucky friend.

Glad you think so. See you in a bit.

Me! Deep breath. Guess I better warn Mags.

I looked in the mirror on my visor and touched up my makeup to tone down the eye some more. It helped, but it was certainly still there. I locked up the car and headed to the bar at a brisk pace.

I walked in the door of Mallory's and looked for Mags. The pub has a long, rustic wood bar that stretches the length of the place. The rest of the place looked like your run-of-the-mill restaurant: hardwood floors, booths, tables, all with that pub feel. And, of course, an Irish flag hanging above the bar.

The bar was already packed, but I quickly spotted Mags at one of the booths nearest to it. She waved to me. I sat down across from her and leaned toward her.

"You're not going to believe this."

"Try me," she said. Her dark hair was freshly puffed up and her pink lipstick had been reapplied. Like I said, somehow the girl pulled it off. Ordinary just wouldn't do.

"My complication? Wants to meet up with us." I gave her my best wide-eyed, deer in the headlights look, which she quickly mirrored.

"But not lunch guy, right?"

"Nope. Lunch guy I can handle. This is my crush. Who will only be my friend. For real. As in, if he thinks I want more, he won't be my friend anymore. He's made that clear."

"After the guy today, I can't imagine what kind of guy would have you so . . ." and she stopped midsentence. It was Adam. It had to be.

I followed her gaze behind me. Yep. There he was, all six foot four inches of deliciousness.

She looked at me. "No."

"Yep."

"Fuck me."

"Yep."

Adam strolled up to us and dropped a kiss on the top of my head, sort of brotherly, sort of confusing. I scooted over so he could sit down next to me.

I gestured to Mags who had managed to close her mouth and regain some composure. "Adam, this is my friend, Mags." Yes. I used the word "friend." And it felt good. I had a new friend. "Mags, my friend, Adam." Yes, *unfortunately* I also used the word "friend" here. Big inward sigh.

He shook her hand.

"I'm gonna get a Scotch. You ladies want something?" He pointed at me. "Gin and tonic, two limes?" I nodded. He looked at Mags.

"Scotch, neat," she said.

"Mmm. What a woman," he said, all friendly and adorable, and headed off to the bar.

The expression on Mags's face made me laugh. She was in shock. Literally.

"Is he real?" she asked.

"Afraid so."

"Just friends?"

"Afraid so," I said, frowning. I gave her the short version of how we met, Adam's *contract killer* status, and how I was tragically friend-zoned since I was now a single girl.

When I finished, she mirrored my pout for a second.

Adam came back and set our drinks in front of us and then scooted back into the booth next to me. Right next to me.

"So, Mags, do people get into fistfights at the firm often? Or does Kate just bring it out in people?"

"We've had some client-on-client violence before, but never client on attorney. Kate is a trailblazer."

Adam smiled. "How long have you been there?"

"Five years."

"That's a while," he said. "What do you think of Jared Mann?"

"He's brilliant, beautiful, and a little cruel." Wow. Guess I should have asked her for the inside track on the people in the office.

I looked at Adam and he looked at me. And I almost forgot what I was going to ask him. His eyes looked so intensely green beneath his long dark lashes. And I knew how his lips felt. Enough! Mental slap upside the head.

"You know Jared?" I asked.

"I went to college with him."

"Interesting."

"And what do you think of him?" Mags asked.

"Smart, ambitious . . . kind of odd," Adam said.

"I get the odd part," I said.

He raised an eyebrow at me in question.

"His mannerisms are just kind of strange. And he stares," I said, before taking a sip from my glass.

"You probably encounter a lot of men with that problem," Adam said.

I laughed. "It's not in a flirty way," I said. "More like he's thinking about eating my liver with some fava beans and a nice Chianti."

Adam just smiled.

"Are you guys still friends?" Mags asked.

"We talk once in a while. Not too often." He moved his focus from Mags to me. "So, Kate, how's it going with Dave?"

Really, Adam? We're doing this now? "Good. We're friends. That's all."

"You definitely looked friendly."

This is getting old. Mostly because it doesn't mean anything is changing between us—more just that he doesn't like sharing his toys.

"Yeah, I got the feeling he was half gone over Kate," Mags said. Alrighty. Mags was in the game, too. She was apparently going to poke the bear and see if she could get a reaction.

"You met him?" Adam asked, looking at Mags again.

"He came to the office to meet Kate for lunch. He looked like he was going to kill someone when he saw her face." Not really true, but okay.

"You hadn't told him?" he asked me.

"It didn't come up." I looked back at Mags. "Dave is a friend of Adam's."

"More of an acquaintance," he said. Interesting. He checked his watch and finished the rest of the Scotch in his glass. "I need to get going. Kate, can I talk to you for a second? Outside?"

I lowered my eyebrows a little then nodded. "I'll be right back, okay?"

"Sure, take your time," Mags said.

"It was great meeting you," Adam said to her, reaching out to shake her hand again.

"You, too. Thanks for the Scotch. I'm sure I'll see you again."

I followed Adam's broad back out the door. Right as I was walking through the door I looked back at Mags's puzzled expression. I shrugged. You and me both, sister.

He walked past the front of the building and rounded the corner into the narrow alley that ran between the two buildings. My heart sped up a little. This was strange. Very.

"Adam . . ."

He turned around and pulled me into the alley by my hand. Once we were (somewhat) out of sight, he grabbed my shoulders and pushed me up against the outside wall of the bar. He wrapped one hand across my jaw the way he did that night at Dive Bar. He pushed his other hand through the side of my hair, gripping it tightly. Both of his hands angled my face upward and his mouth came down on mine hard. His lips were firm and fierce. His tongue entered my mouth with the same ferocity and rubbed across my tongue, my lips, my teeth. I could taste the sweet remnant of Scotch on his lips. He pulled my lower lip between his and I felt him graze it lightly with his teeth. As he did, he pressed against me with the full length of his body and one of his knees pushed between mine invasively. An ache started growing in my stomach and radiating outward.

His grip on my jaw and my hair was so tight that it was erotic. I felt light-headed as he continued his assault on my mouth. I was lost, but aware enough that I was afraid he would stop, and that once he did he would immediately come to his senses and walk away.

I grabbed the tight muscles on his sides through his shirt

and held him against me. I could hear him breathing heavy, as he pulled back from my mouth a little. He continued rubbing his soft lips across mine, back and forth. His hand on my jaw slid down my neck and went to the back of my hair where he buried his fingers in it. He tugged on it, firm, but gentle, forcing my head back a little more so that my face was turned up to him more fully. He looked into my eyes and then down at my mouth.

My heart was pounding. I knew it was inevitable that he would let me go, but I wanted this to continue so badly. Just when I thought he would let me go and step away, he lowered his mouth to mine again and ran his tongue across my lips and then rubbed his lips against mine again, part kiss, part caress. His hands loosened their grip in my hair. It wasn't the abrupt, regretful release I'd expected. Instead he slowly moved away from me, holding my face in his hands for a minute before letting me go.

He looked at me with a deep, fathomless expression.

I was leaning against the wall with my chest heaving. The kiss was so intense and so confusing, I felt my eyes well up a little. Breathe, girl. Blink. No tears.

When he just stood there, quietly watching me, I finally shook my head. "Adam, you can't do this. You made yourself quite clear, but now you're muddying the water with your actions." His square jaw clenched as he looked at me, but he remained silent. He was confused, too. I could see it. I didn't fit within his carefully created guidelines.

"I know," I said. He narrowed his eyes at me a little. "This was not the plan." He just looked at me. Seriously? He has nothing to say? I can't do this. He's so close, but so far away.

Like petting a lion through the bars at the zoo, but when he retreats to the corner, you can't reach him unless he decides to come back within reach. Then, of course, there's the possibility he could rip your throat out at any moment.

"Maybe we both ruined our chance at being friends," I said quietly. He looked down at the ground. Perfect. "Good night, Adam." I turned and walked back toward the front of the building. The romantic in me wanted desperately for him to stop me, but the realist knew he wouldn't. I walked back into the bar and never heard a word from him.

I gave Mags the uber-short version of what happened and called it a night. She didn't fight me on it. She could tell that my mood was wrecked.

*

I lay in bed, staring at the ceiling, trying to sleep. I'd replayed the kiss in my head about a hundred times. But now I'm resolved. No more Adam. My silly little crush is impacting everything in my life. And it just can't. I need to give Jonathan some serious thought, not get hung up on ridiculous thoughts about some man I hardly know.

*

I wore my favorite charcoal-gray suit to the office the next day so that I'd be appropriately dressed for court. I got to the office early and got straight to work. I had a lot more tasks coming in than I was getting out—that's for sure.

The beauty of law is that plagiarism is totally allowed.

Our type, anyway. Sure, I'd never written a demand letter before, but I could go surf through the network drive and find some demand letters for cases with similar grounds. Change a few names, dates, details, and voilà. Yes, this exposes the glaring lack of originality in the legal profession. Oh, well. My massive student loans are here to remind me to suck it up because I'm not changing careers anytime soon.

The morning flew by. I'd brought a sandwich to eat at my desk since I figured Jared and I would be leaving before one o'clock to head over to the courthouse. Sure enough, I'd just finished when he showed up in my office. He looked like a TV lawyer—handsome, thousand-dollar suit, expensive brief-case in hand.

"Ready?"

"Ready," I said. I thought about what Mags said about him being cruel. Pretty sure I do not want to see that side of him.

I followed him out and to the parking garage. We got into his black Jaguar (naturally) and he took off toward the courthouse.

"Our client is Robert Patton," he began, giving me a long look when we sat at a red light. "He and his ex, Sara, have one child, three years old. The contract had your basic child support formula based on the parents' income. Sara had a well-paying job when they were together and so at the end of contract he was only required to pay eighteen hundred dollars a month. Since then, she quit her job and made a motion to recalculate the child support, which, with her unemployed, would now be thirty-one hundred dollars a month."

"Yikes," I said.

"Yeah. She didn't seem to have any explanation for leaving her job. We think she was fucking her boss and when his partner found out, she got the ax."

Yes. Fucking the boss is very bad. And it's no picnic when one of your bosses has a bad habit of staring, either. Eyes on the road, buddy.

"Anyway, the goal is to make her look like a lazy gold digger. If she plays the whole 'I wanted to have more time to spend with my daughter' thing, we're screwed."

"Is she a lazy gold digger?" I asked.

"Not our job to care, Kate."

Alrighty. This should be fun.

He parked in the parking garage across from the courthouse. I had to walk pretty fast to keep up with his pace as we walked into the building. We zipped through the "attorney" line—which is awesome, by the way. With the major security at the courts, the line gets pretty backed up. We have a special line where they take us ahead of everyone else. Totally worth my six-figure student loan debt.

We stopped in front of Department 4 and Jared approached a man who I presumed to be Robert Patton. He was nice-looking, salt-and-pepper hair, late fifties, maybe. A little on the old side to have a three-year-old.

"Robert," Jared was saying, holding a hand out toward me. "This is Kate Shaw. She's a new associate at the firm. I brought her along today to observe the hearing."

He smiled and extended his hand. "Nice to see you've added a pretty face to the firm." Awesome. Pretty sure he just took twenty-five IQ points from me.

"Mr. Patton," I said, giving a firm handshake.

"Robert," he said.

I nodded.

"So, here to watch Jared nail this bitch to the wall?"

I laughed. Noncommittal. He won't know if it meant "Yeah! Nail her to the wall!" or "Surely you must be joking because you sound like a total dickhead." Read it as you will.

"There she is," Robert said, taking a quick glance to his right. It worked out because I could see her coming without being obvious and turning around. Sara was about twenty-two years old. Tops. What exactly was this job she had where she was making a lot of money? Might it have involved a pole? Because her size-two frame, I'm guessing, did not come standard with the double Ds. To say nothing of her waist-length, dyed-within-an-inch-of-its-life blonde hair and ridiculously dark tan.

The bailiff unlocked the doors and we filed in. Jared checked the calendar and signed in.

"We're third on the calendar," he told Robert and me.

This was good. I could watch a couple of other hearings as well. Maybe everyone wasn't out to nail the bitch to the wall so I could see different methods aside from the "fry the bitch" tactic.

The judge appeared and the bailiff did the whole "all rise" bit and we stood until Judge Warner said we could sit. The judge was about ten years past retirement. He actually reminded me a little of Mark Twain—white hair, bushy white mustache and eyebrows, glasses, grumpy expression.

He called the first item on the calendar and one of the attorneys asked the judge for a continuance. The other attorney agreed. Judge said fine. And we all moved on. Not much to observe with that one. He called the second item on the calendar, which was also pretty uneventful and only took a few minutes.

Jared and Robert stood since they were next on the calendar. The courtroom was quiet while the parties in the former case exited and the parties for our case approached the table.

And in that quiet, a cell phone went off. Oh my god. This is why I left my purse in the car, so I didn't even have to worry about whether or not my phone was completely on silent. The tune was the *Law & Order* theme song. Which is my ringtone. I looked down at my suit jacket and patted the front pocket. Fuck. Oh fuck, fuck, fuck. I'd slipped it into my pocket when I was getting stuff out of my car. I pulled it out and quickly hit every damn button that might silence the goddamn thing, short of smashing it under the heel of my shoe. Which was next. This is not happening. I need to quit my job. And move to Alaska. This is the story law professors tell to scare the shit out of their students. Can having your phone go off in court get you disbarred? My face felt like it was on fire. I was afraid to look up since I'd have bet a kidney that everyone in the courtroom was looking at me.

"Whose phone is ringing?" Judge Warner said (sternly). Shit.

I stood. Fall on the sword like a grown-up. I hate my life. "I'm so sorry, your honor. I thought I'd left it in the car. I didn't realize I had it on me."

"Who are you, young lady?"

"Kate Shaw, your honor. I'm a new associate with Mr. Mann's firm." Sorry, Jared. Now you're guilty by association.

"I don't tolerate cell phones in my courtroom, Ms. Shaw."

"Yes, your honor. I can't tell you how sorry I am." Truly. I can't even express it.

He frowned at me and looked over the rim of his glasses. Did I mention that I hate my life? He fiddled in his robe for a moment and pulled out his cell phone and held it up for me to see. "This is my phone."

I nodded. If you say so. What the hell is happening?

"And this is my ringtone." He pressed a button and sure as shit the theme song for *Law & Order* played. When it stopped, he pointed a finger at me. "I like your taste, Ms. Shaw, but put it on silent."

I smiled. Couldn't be helped. This judge was pretty awesome. "Absolutely, your honor. I apologize again," I said, taking my seat once more.

He smiled at me. Actually smiled at me. I turned my phone *off*. Then I pulled the battery out. Not gonna risk this get-out-of-jail-free card. Breathe. My heart was still racing. Keeping my bar card for another day, I guess.

"Good afternoon, counsel. Please state your appearances for the record."

"Good afternoon, your honor. Jennifer Moore on behalf of Sara O'Neill."

"Good afternoon, your honor. Jared Mann on behalf of Robert Patton."

"Thank you. Your motion, Ms. Moore."

"Thank you, your honor. When the original child support

order was created, Ms. O'Neill had a job where she was earning approximately sixty thousand dollars a year. She has primary physical custody of the couple's three-year-old child. Based on her income and Mr. Patton's income at the time, child support was set to be paid by Mr. Patton at only one thousand eight hundred dollars per month. Recently, Ms. O'Neill has become unemployed and the current support is insufficient. Based on current incomes, child support should now be set at three thousand one hundred dollars a month."

I looked at Sara O'Neill sitting at the table next to her attorney. She was wearing a little white top stretched tightly across her huge boobs. Her tan was too brown and her hair was too blonde. Seriously. Can you really make $60,000 a year as a stripper? I could pay off student loans pretty fast with some extra income . . .

"Mr. Mann?"

"Thank you, your honor. Ms. O'Neill only lost her job through reckless behavior and she has no valid reason for not finding another job."

The judge looked back at Sara's attorney. "Your honor, through no fault of her own, Ms. O'Neill encountered inter-personal difficulties at her job and was unfairly terminated. She is currently consulting with an employment attorney over her wrongful termination."

"Ms. Moore, may I address your client?" the judge asked. Ms. Moore nodded. The judge looked at Sara. "What was your previous employment, Ms. O'Neill?"

"I was in the entertainment industry, your honor." Nailed it.

Judge Warner looked nonplussed. "In what capacity?"

"I was an exotic dancer."

"Making sixty thousand dollars a year?"

"Yes, your honor."

"Are you planning a career change? Or are you looking for a job in the same field?"

"I haven't started looking."

"Why is that?"

Uh-oh. Don't say it. Don't say it. "I really want to be able to spend more time with my daughter." There it is. Jared called it. Who can fault a mom for that?

Judge Warner looked back at Jared. "Mr. Mann?"

"Your honor, Ms. O'Neill was fired four weeks ago. In those four weeks, her daughter has been with her *father* about eighty percent of the time."

Ooh. It was on. Judge Warner did not look amused. "Is this true, Ms. O'Neill?"

"Um, I don't know that it's been that much."

Time for her attorney to jump in and try to save her. "Your honor, the parties have not been keeping an actual custody schedule so we can't say for certain how much time the child has spent with each parent."

"Mr. Mann, may I address your client?"

"Of course, your honor."

"Mr. Patton, how many days would you say your daughter has been at your house in the last week?"

"She's spent the night at my house five of the last seven days."

The judge looked back at Sara and her attorney. "Do you have anything further, Ms. Moore?"

"Just, as I was saying, they haven't been keeping an actual calendar so we can't say for sure if Mr. Patton's estimation is correct. And Ms. O'Neill does wish to have more time to spend with her daughter and the hours she was working got in the way of that." Nice try, sweetie, but I'm pretty sure that ship has sailed.

"Okay. It is the ruling of this court that child support will increase from one thousand eight hundred dollars per month to two thousand dollars per month for a period of three months. At the next court appearance I would like to see an actual schedule of the child's custody over that period, as well as what efforts Ms. O'Neill has made to find employment. Ms. O'Neill, if at the end of those three months Mr. Patton shows evidence that he has become the primary caregiver for the child, support may need to be recalculated on that basis." He smacked his gavel. I love that part. "Court is adjourned."

I followed Jared out of the courtroom with Robert trailing behind me. We stepped to the far side of the door and kept quiet while the other parties exited. When Sara and her attorney walked past us (none too happy) Robert turned to Jared and shook his hand.

"Nicely done, Jared."

"No problem, Robert. We'll be in touch closer to the three-month mark and you can let me know exactly how things are playing out custody-wise."

"Will do." He turned to me with a very charming smile. "Kate, it was lovely meeting you. Hopefully, I will see you again."

"Nice to meet you as well."

Jared and I parted ways from Robert and exited the courthouse and made our way to his car.

Once we were on our way back to the office, he seemed more relaxed . . . more real. "Nicely done."

"Yeah. As far as monumental screwups go—I guess that was okay," I said. I needed to be sure he knew I was remorseful over the whole phone thing, even if it didn't entirely blow up in my face.

He nodded, still smiling. "True. But you seem to have made a friend of Judge Warner. And Judge Warner doesn't make friends." He looked over at me as we stopped at a red light. Partly to impart the significance of what he was saying, and, likely, partly just because he had a bad habit of staring.

I smiled. "Well, if I manage to get punched in the face on my first day and disrupt a courtroom on the third, I bet you can hardly wait to see how the rest of the week goes."

He laughed. Warm. Genuine. Not cruel. Not yet. There is something about him that makes me not want to get on his bad side, though. Something dangerous just under the surface, well-contained, but there, nonetheless.

"I can't wait to see how the rest of your year goes, Kate."

CHAPTER 13

The rest of the workweek was blessedly uneventful. I managed to finish off my first week at Manetti, Markson, and Mann without being fired or disbarred. Things were looking up.

I'd brought comfy clothes to change into so that I could head straight to Logek's after work. It was time for wine and whining. Well, a little whining. I'll try to keep it short. I pulled up in front of Logek's cute, little 1920s rental house in midtown. It was one house that had been sort of converted into a duplex, hence the one-bedroom situation. Still, cute house, cute neighborhood. Perfect for a single girl. Which reminds me that *this* single girl needs to start looking for her own place as well.

I knocked once and opened the door. Once inside, I set

down my bag and a bottle of wine on the counter. Logek popped her head out from her bedroom and smiled with her cell phone to her ear. I opened my bag and pulled out a T-shirt and yoga pants. I slipped off my jacket, followed by my slacks, eager to get out of my suit. I bent over, picked up my slacks, and began folding them carefully, when Daniel emerged from Logek's bedroom. Naturally.

I yelped like a scared dog. Overreaction? Probably, but I was not expecting to be standing half-naked in front of a stranger this evening. Given my track record of late, I suppose I should start making allowances for occurrences like this since shit just *keeps* happening.

"Oh, god. Sorry, Kate," Daniel said, doing the quickest 180 in history and disappearing back in Logek's bedroom.

I slipped on my pants and changed my shirt really quick and then headed into the bedroom to make a proper, albeit awkward, greeting.

Daniel was sitting on Logek's bed and Logek was still on the phone with someone. He looked up at me apologetically.

"Good to see you again," I said, smiling.

"At the risk of sounding perverted, good to see you, too."

I laughed.

"Sorry about that," he said again.

"Yeah—shame on you for not expecting a woman to strip naked in Logek's living room."

"Well, yeah."

Logek finally hung up and came over and hugged me.

"Daniel caught my striptease in the living room. Sorry."

She laughed and looked at Daniel. "Took me years to get Kate to stop stripping in public. I guess old habits die hard."

Daniel chuckled and walked over to Logek. "Okay, I'll leave you girls to your witchcraft." He gave her a sweet kiss on the lips and smiled at me before heading out the front door.

"You didn't tell me he was here when I called to tell you I was on my way," I said.

"He wasn't. He surprised me and just popped in for a minute."

"How much popping in did he do?"

"Less than I would have liked," she said, laughing.

"So I guess that's still going well?"

"It is," she said, as we walked back to the living room. She grabbed glasses and I brought the bottle of wine over to the couch. She started opening the bottle. "No fireworks or anything, but I just really like being with him."

"No fireworks?"

She shrugged. "He's one of the nicer guys I've dated. Kinda tame. But we have a lot in common and I just find myself calling him to hang out." She poured wine into our glasses. "A lot."

I raised my eyebrows. "How much time are you spending with him?"

"Let's see. Monday night I asked him if he wanted to come over to watch that stupid reality show where the guy dates a dozen girls till he picks one to sign with because Daniel admitted to me that he was secretly addicted to that show. So he came over and watched it with me." She took a sip from her glass. "Tuesday we went to Home Depot because he said he could help me swap out the faucet in the bathroom. Wednesday he came over to actually install the faucet we'd bought so I made dinner to thank him. Then last night we went to a cocktail party thrown by a mutual client."

My mouth was hanging open. "No wonder he popped in tonight. The poor guy is going to go through withdrawals not hanging out with you tonight."

"Probably."

"All that and no fireworks?"

"Not really. Just fun. And comfortable. And easy."

"Hmm. That's saying something."

"Don't I know it. So, catch me up. You sent me that quick text about Adam kissing you, but I need the rest of the story."

I gave her a little more of the nitty-gritty of the kiss that nearly made me weep. "And I haven't heard from him since."

She looked at me and frowned. She knew it mattered to me . . . that I was more bummed about it than I was letting on. She got it.

"Nothing, huh?"

I shook my head. "And I really don't expect I will. So I guess that situation sort of resolved itself."

She sighed. "Are you going to text him?"

"No. I need to take this opportunity to get away from that predicament. It was never going to be anything for me but trouble. You know that."

"I know. It does suck that there isn't a way you could at least be friends with him. But, I know, too messy."

"Way too messy."

"So what else is going on?"

"I'm having dinner with Jonathan tomorrow."

"Hmm. Leave your pens at home."

"Sound advice. No—I'm clear on that. I'm not ready to get right back into it with Jonathan after everything that's happened. Our relationship was great, but it's not as though another contract is just going to make the last few weeks disappear."

"Good girl."

"I had lunch with Dave this week."

"How's that sadistic little wager going?"

"He claims he just wants to hang out and isn't trying to sleep with me anymore."

Logek pushed her thick blonde hair back from her face and rested her chin in her hand. "And is he full of shit?"

"I don't know. He seems sincere but I think there is a decent chance he's just the best liar I've ever met."

"You are usually pretty good at detecting bullshit."

I shrugged. "Maybe."

"So do you like him?"

"A little. He's a little like Daniel is to you, I guess. Easy to be around."

"Except I could sleep with Daniel without losing a bet."

I laughed. "There is that. And are you going to?"

She shrugged. "I *like* him, but I definitely don't get the urge to get naked with him. We'll see. Do you have the urge to get naked around Dave?"

I laughed. "We did have one hell of a kiss but I don't really know him. I just think I have zero expectations when I'm with him and he may have devious motives, but he basically acts like a cool guy around me."

"Hmm. That sounds a little contradictory, but okay."

"Thank you."

"Your eye looks way better."

"Yeah—it's to the point where I can pretty much cover it up with makeup, which is awesome. Now I just need to avoid getting hit again."

"Baby steps."

*

I woke up the next morning and did my obligatory four-mile run. I'd hate to get carried away with the whole fitness thing. When I got back I did a quick cup of coffee with the folks before hitting the shower.

Afterward, I got comfy on my bed and started reviewing the Britton file for my hearing on Monday. Rochelle Britton had an ugly breach that the firm handled for her. Her partner breached by sleeping with the neighbor, the babysitter, and their daughter's kindergarten teacher. Busy boy. Their contract lasted for five years (since it took Rochelle five years to catch on to her partner's extracurricular activities) and they settled just shy of trial about a year ago. Tony's notes in the file all refer to her ex-partner as "dickhead." While I agree, I'm a little shocked that he made all of those notations in the file. Oh, well. "Attorney Work Product" keeps it all from being discoverable if anything ever went to trial, so I guess no harm no foul?

Apparently Rochelle held down the fort while Dickhead went to dental school and then he breached before he'd graduated. She still got a sizable settlement (payable over ten years), but the child support order was based on current incomes so it was pretty small. Well, now Dr. Dickhead is making a ton of money and it's time to recalculate child support. Alrighty. This should be a slam dunk.

My phone buzzed. Dave. *Hey, beautiful.* I smiled.

Hey there.

Whatcha doin?

Work. I have my first hearing on Monday.

Fun. Want a distraction?

I looked at the clock. It was already three o'clock and I was going to dinner with Jonathan at 5:30 p.m. *Can't. I have plans a little later.*

:(

No pouting.

What are you doing tonight?

Awkward. Okay. *Dinner with the ex.*

Business or pleasure?

Damn fine question, Dave. *Remains to be seen.*

Oh. So not just finalizing details of the contract?

Not really. He's trying to get me back.

Oh. Tell him no.

Lol. Okay.

Should I be jealous?

No. Because you barely know me.

I know you.

And because you are just trying to get me in bed, remember? ;)

Right. Somehow that keeps slipping my mind.

Damn. He was fun to flirt with. *What are you doing tonight?*

Apparently trying to get you to ditch your ex and go out with me.

Probably not gonna happen.

Probably?

Oops. *Not gonna happen.*

Fine. When do I get you?

Don't do it. Don't do it. Hell with it. *When I lose the bet?*

Tease.

I noticed that as well. *I don't know—what did you have in mind?*

Tomorrow?

Ok. Lunch? Dinner?

Morning run . . . lunch . . . movie . . . dinner . . .

An 8-hour date? We may kill each other, Dave.

You're worth the risk.

God. So cute. *Ha-ha. Sweet of you to say. Okay, but I'm sleeping in so no run before 9 am.*

Works for me. I'll come to your house at 9.

Okay.

Have a terrible time tonight.

Thanks.

Really. Awful.

Lol. See you tomorrow, Dave.

;)

Well. And just like that, my entire Sunday is booked. Adam who?

*

By 5:30 p.m. I was dolled up and ready for dinner. Jonathan was punctual as always in picking me up. He was wearing jeans with my favorite blue button-down shirt, which I bought for him. The color was amazing against his bronze coloring. His black hair was still kind of overgrown, so it curled a little at the ends around his ears and the back of his neck. He also had a five o'clock shadow so he looked entirely scruffy and amazing. Sigh.

We walked out to the car and he held the door for me while I climbed up into the passenger seat of Jonathan's Range Rover. Dating someone you've had an eight-year relationship with is weird, especially when it's been tainted by the hurt of the last few weeks.

He climbed into the driver's seat and looked over at me, dropping an eyebrow. "What's the matter?"

"Us. On a date. Again."

"That's right, baby doll. I'm gonna date the hell out of you."

I laughed. "That sounds perverted."

"Really?" he asked, mock innocence and all.

He reached over and grasped my hand and he took off toward the restaurant. He linked his fingers through mine and I looked down at our hands where they rested on my leg. It felt like we hadn't broken up—like our contract hadn't lapsed—like I wasn't dating other men. And it was confusing as hell. I love Jonathan. Like—a lot. Maybe I'm an idiot for not taking him back. Maybe. Maybe not. I pulled my hand from his grasp.

"What's on your mind?" he asked.

I looked at his hand still resting on my leg in response.

"You can't expect me to sit in the car with you and not try to hold your hand. You know how much I love your hands. Long fingers, smooth skin, and always on the cool side so they always feel so good against my skin." He reached for my hand again so I grabbed his instead and set it back on his own leg. Sigh. Yes—again. Sometimes I have to repeat myself.

With Jonathan, even just holding hands can seem like something more. He's this very sensory-oriented person so when it comes to me he has a list of a thousand little details that he claims to have fallen in love with. Case in point—he tells me that when the sun is in my eyes, he can actually see a couple of green flecks in my blue eyes, that the skin on the tops of my feet is incredibly soft, that the barely notice-able dimple in my cheek shows more when I'm crying than it does when I'm smiling, and so on and so forth.

It was *so* easy to be like this with him. So much so that I almost regretted pulling my hand away.

"Gotta work for that. I get it," he said.

"I'm not trying to make you work for anything, Jona-than."

"What then, Kate? You don't want to hold my hand? Don't want to be with me? What?"

"I don't know."

"You don't know. Kind of a big thing to not know." He sounded frustrated, but it seemed to pass quickly, and he just sighed.

"You don't get to be short-tempered with me. I didn't get us here." My voice may have been a little raised. A little.

So he raised his voice a little, too. "I don't know what to say. I can't take it back. I wish I could, but I can't. I don't know what else I'm supposed to do!"

"I don't, either!" Shit. Tears. I looked out my window and dabbed subtly at my eyes.

*   * Subject to the following terms and conditions*

Jonathan turned down a side street and pulled to the curb. He abruptly got out of the car and came around to my door. Once he opened it, he yanked me out by my arm and crushed me to his chest. He pulled me back a little and looked into my face. He brushed a couple of tears off my cheeks with his fingertips.

"Fuck, Kate. Tell me. I'll do anything. I fucked this all up. I know that. But there *has* to be a way for me to fix it."

Is there?

"I'm not angry," I said. "This isn't some passive-aggressive attempt to punish you, Jonathan."

"Then what? Do you still love me?"

"Yes."

"Okay." But he said it like a question, like a "What's the problem, then?" question.

I pushed him back slightly with a hand to his chest. "It's just . . ."

"Is it a something or a some*one*?"

I immediately thought of Adam, but no. I shook my head. "Just me. I think I was just so safe with you. I was in this little cocoon and . . . I was naïve. I thought I knew exactly what I had. You were the one thing I was certain of. And I was so *wrong*."

"Kate, no . . ."

"Please let me finish. I'm trying to explain something I haven't even figured out yet, so just let me get it out." He closed his mouth and waited. "I *was* wrong. And I was blind. I honestly don't think I would have been more surprised that night if you told me you killed someone and needed help burying the body."

He smiled. Just for a second. So did I.

"I'm trying to figure out how I let myself be duped into a false belief."

He was quiet a minute, making sure I was done. "You weren't the one duped—I was."

"But that's not true. You had one foot out the door for months and I was *clueless*. How could I be so oblivious?"

"You weren't oblivious. You just knew how much I loved you and that only an idiot doesn't re-up with someone when he's completely in love with her."

"Then we were both blind. And here we are."

"Where is that again?" And he did a quick look around.

I laughed. "Hopefully, not in a shady neighborhood."

"Can't we both just go back into this thing with our eyes open and figure we've learned our lesson?"

"It's not that easy. Not for me anyway. You know, it's funny—I'm so good at reading people. After all our years together, you would've thought I'd be better at reading you."

"Pretty sure you know me better than I know myself."

I shook my head. "I don't think so or I would have seen it coming."

He sighed. "Then what do I do, Katie? How do we get past this?"

"I don't know." The knot in my stomach told me where I was going before the words left my mouth. "I think we need to take a step back. I think you need to have a little of that freedom you wanted. And I need to come to terms with this wake-up call."

"I don't want anyone else. That freedom sounds like such a stupid idea now."

I threw my hands up in the air. "I don't know what else to say. There's this new jaded part of me that, at least for now, seems to be calling the shots." I brushed at new tears and took a deep breath.

Jonathan put his palm to my cheek. "You never would have been jaded if it wasn't for me."

I shrugged. "Everyone should have a *little* cynicism when it comes to love. My complete lack of it was probably a disadvantage." I gave a lame smile that I knew didn't cover up the fact that I was still on the verge of tears. "I think I need to call it a night."

He looked at me a minute, trying to decide if it was worth arguing with me, and then nodded. We got back into the car and drove in silence back to my house. He came around and opened my door and helped me out. We walked up to the front door and stopped.

He wrapped his arms around me and held me against him. For like five minutes. Just when I started to wonder if he was ever going to let go, he pulled back just enough to kiss me. His full lips melted against mine—soft, velvety. And let's not forget, I haven't had sex in weeks and Jonathan always knew what buttons to push. I wanted him, but I already gave in on that front once and still have the regret to prove it. Get your hormones in check, girl, this was supposed to be a good-bye kiss—temporarily at least—not a good-bye fuck. I stepped back, shaking my head.

"I love you," he said.

"I know."

"So how long is this 'step back' supposed to last?"

"No idea."

He nodded. "You'll call me?"

"I will."

He grimaced again, then he let out a big sigh and cleared his throat, clearly trying to keep it together.

"Good night, Jonathan."

"Good night, Kate."

I went into the house. My parents were out to dinner with friends so the house was quiet, thankfully. I leaned against the front door and listened to Jonathan drive away. And I cried. A lot. Ugly cry.

I went up to my room (still crying) and changed into my comfy clothes and crawled into bed without bothering to take off my makeup. The smeared mascara seemed in keeping with my pity party. I knew I needed some space from Jonathan to get everything straightened out in my head and it was *my* call. So why do I feel like my heart is breaking all over again? Because that good-bye felt real, not temporary.

I don't want to be alone. I probably *should* want to be alone, but that would mean I was mature and introspective, and let's be real, this is only Kate 2.0. That may come in a later upgrade. I want Adam. Not to complicate everything, but just to hold me and kiss my forehead. And tell me to shut up.

I looked at my phone. Two texts. Logek wanted the lowdown on my date with Jonathan. And Dave wanted to remind me (again) to have a terrible time. That text drew another inadvertent smile.

Nothing from Adam. Of course. It got complicated and he walked. Just like he said he would. And he's right—he never hid who he was, never denied his intentions, nothing. I should text him to tell him that. Weak excuse.

Save me from myself, Dave. *Wish granted.*

In less than a minute Dave texted back. *Terrible?*

Oh, good, more tears. I was worried I'd run out. *Basically. I'm sorry, beautiful. You okay?*

Not really.

And then nothing. No reply. Really, Dave?

Finally he replied with, *At the front door.* That's right. He lives out here. I forgot.

Guess I need to start giving him more credit than I do. I headed downstairs (after a quick stop in the bathroom to wipe off smeared mascara).

I opened the door and Dave was standing there in a T-shirt and sweats, looking all genuine and sympathetic, and I started crying again.

"Oh, beautiful," he said, coming in and closing the door behind him. He pulled me to him and held my cheek against his chest. I was barefoot so he seemed particularly tall since I'm usually in high heels. And five-feet-nine girls don't feel little very often. He stood there with one arm around me and the other rubbing my back gently until I stopped crying.

I stepped back, wiping my face again. Thankfully the majority of my eye makeup was lost during the first battle. Not much left to make a mess this go-round.

"Sorry," I said.

"Don't be."

Quiet for a minute, then he said, "Want to watch a movie?"

That sounded like a pretty decent idea. I nodded.

I headed to the living room and he followed close behind. I walked over and looked at my parents' DVD titles on the rack next to the big-screen TV. I named off a few options that included *Sex and the City, Sleepless in Seattle,* and *Gone with the Wind.* When I turned around and looked at him where he was sitting on the sofa, I got about the expression I'd anticipated. He looked ready to run for the door . . . or perform an exorcism.

I smiled. "Just kidding," I said. He looked relieved. I named off a few action movies. He picked one of my titles and we sat down on the couch quietly as the movie began. We'd already hugged so it was sort of a given that there would be cuddling now. He sat back in the corner of my parents' overstuffed L-shaped sofa. I crawled up next to him and he did the rest. I stopped short of winding up right next to him so he grabbed my arms and pulled me toward him so that I was practically on his lap. Once I was close enough, he wrapped my arms around his sides and held me against his chest. I couldn't see the movie so well, but let's be real— not really the objective here.

He rubbed my hair, my back, and planted the occasional kiss on my head. All very sweet. I pulled back to look at him.

"What have you done with Dave?"

He smiled. "He is our hostage on the mother ship. I'm here in his place to investigate Earth women."

Now I smiled. "Sounds scandalous."

"If I'm lucky." And he kissed me. Nothing too aggressive, but I guess I brought it on myself by staring up endearingly into his face. Can't do that with a man without repercussions.

* *Subject to the following terms and conditions*

He was sweet, though. Didn't go for tongue, just a lot of soft lips against mine, then against my cheek, my nose, my forehead.

When he seemed finished, I rested my face back against his chest before he took it any further. He let out one big breath and then relaxed along with me into watching the movie.

About ten minutes had passed when he gripped my chin and turned my face up to him. He'd been thinking and he had that crease between his eyebrows. "What prompted the 'What have you done with Dave?' comment?"

"I guess that night you drove me home. The predator. Everything about you. What happened to that guy?"

"He's right here."

"But since that night—you've been sweet, thoughtful, almost overly attentive. That's not the Dave from that night."

"It's that same guy . . . but he's getting kind of hung up on you."

Oh. Well if that isn't just a kick in the nuts. If I had any. I sat up and faced him on the sofa.

"Dave, you don't know me that well."

"I feel like I do."

What do I say? Shit. Nothing is coming to mind. I like Dave. But this pretty much screws up my one uncomplicated option. I wonder if that is how Adam felt about me?

"You're going to start burning out brain cells if you keep thinking that hard," he said, trailing a finger down my cheek. "Why is this a bad thing?"

So many reasons. I'm in love with Jonathan. I have a wicked crush on Adam. And you. What do I feel about you?

Totally undefined. And there is the unending possibility that you are totally playing me.

"I told you—just us hanging out. Not me trying to figure out how to get into your pants," he said. "I just want to spend time with you."

"Dave. Be serious."

"Oh, I'm one hundred percent serious." Yep. That's what it seems like. Then again, my decision-making skills have been pretty lacking lately.

"Why me? You are a gorgeous TV personality. There are literally hundreds of women that would love to go out with you. Without even leaving the city!"

"But not you? Why not you? Why aren't you one of those hundred women?"

I shook my head.

"Is it Adam? Your ex? What?"

"It's everything, Dave. I'm not over my ex and it took a lot for me to tell him I needed some space tonight rather than just running back to him as soon as he asked. And Adam . . ." Hmm. More complicated. "I'm not sure what that was, but I don't think he and I are even friends anymore."

"I doubt that," he said, with a certain amount of derision.

"And, I hope you'll understand when I say, I just don't trust you. I don't trust that this is sincere."

He shrugged, not looking overly concerned by that declaration. "You will."

"You didn't answer me. Why me?"

He looked at me intently. "I like the way you make me feel."

---

* Subject to the following terms and conditions

"Really? You feel good right now? 'Cause you look a little hurt."

"Well this *precise* moment sucks a little since you see my feelings for you as a negative. But I like being with you. You're beautiful. You're smart. You're an attorney. You're sort of the whole package."

Oddly, that makes more sense to me . . . that he'd be looking for a package. That because I look good on paper, I must be a good match.

"Have you ever had normal relationships?" I asked.

"I had girlfriends in high school. And a few in college."

"But nothing serious?"

"What qualifies as serious? I wasn't sleeping with anyone else. Does that count?"

"I guess. Anything long-term?"

"I dated a girl in college for five months one time."

"Impressive."

"Thanks."

"Ever been in love?"

"I thought I was in high school. But teenagers always think they're in love."

"So when did you start focusing on signed women?"

He smiled, and I saw my first flicker of Dave's evil twin that I met that first night. "When I realized that all women were clingy, needy, manipulative, or insane."

"Ouch."

"Not you, beautiful. That's why I like you."

"Well, I think I may qualify as a little needy tonight."

He shrugged. "You were upset. You didn't ask me to come be a shoulder to cry on—I volunteered."

"Appreciate it. So, give me an example of these girls."

"Just one? I have a dozen. I dated one woman when I was about twenty-five. I only went out with her like two or three times and I caught her going through my phone to see if I'd been talking to other girls. Another I went out with a handful of times and she just wanted to embed herself in my life. She wanted to talk all the time, spend all our free time together. I practically had to get a restraining order to shake that one." I was shaking my head listening to him. Man, the crazy ones really make the rest of us look bad. Settle down, ladies. Obsession never works.

"A few years ago I met a girl that seemed really cool. She wasn't clingy or suffocating. But it was all bullshit. Just a game to try to rope me in. She was trying to ingratiate herself with my parents . . . befriend my sister, my friends. Then I found out that she'd actually contacted some of my female friends without me knowing and told them that she expected them to keep their distance since I was in a relationship with her. Which, by the way, I never considered us in an actual relationship."

"That is insane behavior."

"Right?"

"But it's also unusual behavior, Dave."

"Not from my experience."

"That's a shame."

"After that last one, I wasn't willing to deal with any more shit."

"So you started dating signed women."

He nodded.

"It doesn't bother you that you're cheating?"

"I didn't sign a contract."

That was Adam's response, too, I think.

"So I got to the point where I hated dating and hated women. But I love sex." He shrugged and gave me a wicked grin—all bad Dave. It was actually comforting to see that side so that I could reconcile that Dave from the first night with the guy he's been since then. He went on. "And wrong or right, forbidden sex is good sex."

"Nice scruples."

"Whatever. I own it. And I was pretty sure I was turning into a complete misogynist. Until I met you."

"You may be giving me too much credit."

"I don't think so. Or you're just good at hiding your crazy."

I frowned at him and he laughed.

Time to change the subject again. "Are your parents to-gether?"

"Yep. They re-upped a couple of times until my sister turned eighteen and then they stopped with the contract bullshit."

"So when the last contract expired, nothing changed?"

He shook his head. "They wanted my sister and me to have the security of the contract, but they always said they didn't need it. That must be true because I don't think they've been under contract for at least the last ten years or so."

"Are you close to your family?"

He nodded. "Like you?"

My turn to nod. "Only child, though."

"My sister is going to love you." I'm trying to make conversation and he keeps interjecting these little romantic nuggets. That are ruining everything.

"How old are you?"

"I'm thirty-one." He raised his eyebrows. "How old are you?"

"Thirty-four. I'm robbing the cradle."

"Hopefully."

More frowning on my part. More laughing on his.

"Why the dirty looks?" he asked.

"Because. Stop. Stop with all the cute, flirty crap."

"It's not crap. It's sincere."

"Then stop with the sincerity."

"I can't help it. You bring it out in me."

I made an exasperated grunt sound and looked up at the ceiling.

He grabbed me around my waist and pulled me onto his lap and kept his arms wrapped around me tightly—likely anticipating that I would squirm away if I could. I was sitting sideways across his lap so our faces were very close.

"New bet," he whispered in a husky voice.

I raised my eyebrows.

He continued in the same hushed, half-whisper voice. "The original bet was that I could get you into bed, no strings attached. But now I want strings." My heart was beating really hard and he was holding me tight enough that I wondered if he could feel it. "So—new bet. I make you fall in love with me."

Oh, my. I had butterflies that were not confined to my stomach. They were all over my skin, it seemed, because I

* Subject to the following terms and conditions

was tingling everywhere. I swallowed the lump in my throat. "And what is my part of the bet?"

"You let me." And he kissed me with all the heat he held back earlier. He put a hand to the back of my head and pressed my mouth to his. His tongue came into my mouth aggressively and rubbed against mine. His other hand loosened its grip around me and went to my waist, slipping under my T-shirt.

The feeling of his hand on my bare skin made me shiver as his hand slid upward toward its target. When he reached my breast, he cupped it tightly and kissed me even more feverishly. I was breathing heavy. Uh-oh. Kate was about to leave the building. What if I'm wrong? What if this is part of his plan to get me into bed? What if . . . I forgot my question. He had a hold of my nipple and was squeezing it lightly.

He pulled his lips away from mine a little. "Let me kiss you again," he whispered. Hmm. Given the kiss he just ended, I don't think he was asking to kiss my lips. "Can I kiss you?" he asked quietly. Apparently he was going to wait for the go-ahead. I nodded. The moment I did, he yanked my shirt up, exposing my breasts, and immediately latched onto one. He covered a lot more than my nipple with his mouth and sucked hard. I think I squealed. Actually squealed.

He pulled me against him and moved his mouth to my other one and continued licking and sucking. He pushed me onto my back and released my tight nipple from his mouth. He started a descent down my stomach, kissing his way down.

I reached down and put my fingers under his chin, lifting his face to me. "I'm not having sex with you, Dave."

"I'm not trying to have sex with you," he said, planting a couple more kisses on my stomach. "This is strictly for you. Okay?"

I tried not to nod, but I mentioned that I haven't seen any action for a month, right? After I gave the slightest nod, he pulled my stretch pants down slowly until I was completely exposed. And exposed was how I felt. Naked and slightly embarrassed. And completely effing horny. And, as I mentioned before, with me, horny usually carries the day.

He looked up at me from between my legs. "You are so beautiful."

Good timing. Made me feel slightly less awkward that someone new . . . for the first time in years . . . was seeing me so up close and personal. I could feel him run his fingers against me before slipping them inside. Once he did, I gasped and arched my back.

He chuckled. "Beautiful, I am just getting started."

He proceeded to show me what that meant, and over my heavy breathing and moaning, I heard the garage door open. Oh my god. My parents. I jumped off of the couch like it was on fire. I pulled my yoga pants back into place and pulled my T-shirt down. I smoothed my hair and fanned my face. I'm sure I had an awesome sex flush going. Whore. Dave was smiling casually. He looked down in his lap so that I would notice the enormous tent he'd pitched in his sweats. This keeps getting better and better.

"Sit there. Movie." He obediently sat back in the corner of the sofa and even pulled one of the throw pillows across his lap to hide his erection. He did stare into my eyes while he slid the first two fingers of one of his hands into his mouth, sucking them. Tasting me. So unfair. I glared at him in response. I crawled across the couch and sat down next to him and immediately engrossed myself in the Bruce Willis movie we'd watched about two minutes of since we turned it on.

He did the same. He whispered, "Just like being in high school again."

"Yep. Lucky me."

My parents came in through the door from the garage, all smiling and cheery. They both looked surprised that I had yet another strange man for them to meet. Time to tell them I'm becoming a call girl, I guess.

I smiled. Casual. We were just watching a movie. Harmless. We were so not about to commit many indiscretions on your leather sofa. Not me. Dave and I stood up and walked around the couch to where they were standing by the kitchen. I don't know if Dave's erection was gone, but I'm trying out this denial thing so I'm going to go with "what erection?" Yeah—that works.

"Mom. Dad. This is my friend, Dave. Dave, my parents, Deanna and Jeff."

"So nice to meet you, Dave," Mom said, shaking his hand. Dad followed her lead while Mom snuck a glance at me. What was that look? Surprise? Disapproval? Approval, maybe? Dave was pretty cute.

"Great to meet you both," Dave said. "Wow, Kate really looks like you," he said to my mother.

"Yeah, we get that a lot," she said, tucking her hair behind her ear. "So how do you two know each other?"

"Through a friend," Dave said.

Mom looked back at me, eyebrows raised.

"Adam. You met him."

"Of course," she said. No woman could forget meeting Adam.

"My date with Jonathan didn't go so well so Dave just came over to watch a movie with me. Help me take my mind off it." Read into that as you will, Mother.

"Oh," she said. "Well, you can tell me about it later. We'll let you two get back to your movie."

Mom looked like she wanted to laugh and Dad looked suspicious. Yep. I was seventeen again.

"Nice meeting you, Dave," Dad said.

"Great meeting you. I'm sure I'll see you guys again soon." Nice, Dave. Couldn't try a little harder for the "casual" thing I was going for?

Smiles all around and my parents headed toward their room on the other end of the house.

Dave and I faced off. "See you soon?"

He grinned. Cheshire cat grin.

"My parents are going to start thinking I'm a hooker if they keep meeting strange guys around here."

"Then stop bringing strange guys around."

Touché, Dave. Touché.

CHAPTER 14

I was startled awake the next morning when my mom dropped down onto the bed next to me. She scooched back toward the wall so that she could sit up against the headboard. And then she waited for me to roll over and face her.

"Good morning, sunshine," she said, once I had rolled over.

"Good morning."

"So what's new?"

I laughed. "Isn't it obvious? I'm working on a beefcake calendar and I've just lined up July and August."

"I suspected as much."

I moved a little closer to her and laid my head in her lap. She immediately went All Mom and started stroking my hair. Definitely one of the perks of being a thirty-four-year-old living with her parents.

"So?" she asked. To be translated as "Are you going to tell me what's up or are you going to keep giving me smart-ass answers?"

I sighed. "I'm losing it, Mom. Honestly. My life has never been this confusing."

"What's confusing you?"

I rolled my eyes up to look at her. "Boys."

She laughed. "Boys are dumb. I told you that when you were in the fifth grade."

"You were right. I just can't figure out how I ended up with man trouble. Me! I was always the settle-down, one-man woman. Now I don't know what I'm doing."

"Well why don't you tell me what you're doing and I'll see if I can break it down for you."

She twiddled a strand of my hair and listened while I gave her my feelings about Jonathan wanting me back and even offering to sign a new contract. Then I followed it with an abbreviated version of my Adam conundrum (not like I'm going to tell her about his penchant for unavailable women—moms can be kind of judgmental when it comes to the people in their children's lives). I finished by telling her about how Dave seemed like an easy distraction that was becoming less simple by the day.

Her fiddling my hair between her fingers was so relaxing, part of me just wanted to go back to sleep. It must have shown because she took my tendril of hair and tickled my nose with it.

"Hmm. You're right," she said. "That is a frickin' mess."

"I know!"

"So two guys who are trying to get you and one guy who walked when things got complicated."

"Thanks for the summary, Mom."

"Confusion aside, well done. Those are three very handsome men."

"No kidding. Since when have I ever been a magnet for beautiful men?"

"Since always," she said, gripping my chin. "You just never saw yourself for how special you are."

"You have to say that. You're my mom."

"Good point. Well, I thought I was going to be able to give you some advice, but I got nothin'."

I frowned.

"I will tell you one thing," she said. "Listening to you . . . I think you have a little more than a crush on Adam and I would guess that is part of the reason you didn't take Jonathan back."

"That was sort of Logek's take as well. But it's irrelevant how I feel."

"It's always relevant. You just don't get to control the situation."

"And now I feel like Dave is weaseling his way into . . ." I tapped my fingers to my chest. "But is that by default? Because I need space from Jonathan and can't have Adam? Or am I genuinely developing feelings for him?"

"No idea, cupcake. But that is only one of your million-dollar questions. I think you just need to give it time. You may get over your issues with Jonathan and decide to take

him back. Adam may show up ready for some complica-
tions. Dave may turn out to be an asshole."

I laughed and looked up at Mom. "Nice."

"Just pointing out that it is all too early to tell. Just . . .
enjoy being single for a while. Try to enjoy your new job.
You don't have to make any decisions *right now*."

"See? And you said you didn't have any advice for me."

"Advice you might listen to?"

"Well, don't get crazy. And speaking of all of this crap,
Dave has booked me for the day."

"The day?"

"Yes. Run. Lunch. Movie. Dinner."

"That's dedication."

"Well, if nothing else, the next eight hours should be very
telling."

*

Dave and I took off for our run, heading out for the trails
that wind around the lake by my house. We both had our
iPods on so it wasn't as though we attempted to converse
much. The trails are pretty hilly and by the third mile I was
sucking air. Because he's tall, Dave has a really long stride.
Mine is long. His is longer. Plus, I get the impression he's a
much more hard-core runner than I am. Point being, I'm
pretty sure he was holding back so that he didn't leave me
in the dust. I'd been running faster than my usual pace (hence
the reason I stopped and bent over at the waist to catch my
breath) and I could still tell he was waiting on me.

He stopped when I did and drank water from his squeeze bottle.

"Sorry," I said, between breaths.

"Take your time. I'm not in a hurry. I've got you all day," he said, grinning.

"If you don't kill me first."

"How far do you usually go?"

"Four miles. Six if I'm feeling ambitious."

He checked his phone for the GPS. "We're at three. How far is it back to your house?"

"About a mile and a half."

"Perfect."

Yeah. Perfect. Okay. Suck it up, whiner. You can do this. I took off again at a slightly less brisk pace and he fell in alongside me.

By the time we finished the loop and were standing in my driveway, I checked my own GPS on my phone and realized I just did that four and a half at my fastest pace ever. Little victories.

He stood in front of me, barely winded. And annoying.

"That was fun. Go shower. Back in an hour?"

I nodded. "That should be enough."

He leaned in and kissed my (very) sweaty cheek and got back in his truck and left.

Well, I don't want to kill him yet. Time for the bonus round.

By the time I was out of the shower, all clean and pretty again, he was back at the door. His hair still looked slightly damp from the shower and he was in jeans and a T-shirt, just like I was. See? No great expectations here.

"Ready?"

"Yep." I grabbed my purse and followed him out to his truck.

"You mind going downtown? All the best lunch spots are out there."

"That sounds great. Actually, if you are cool with it, I was sort of wondering if we could skip the movie and go look at a couple of rentals for me?" I finished with a cheesy grin and puppy-dog eyes.

"Like I could say no to that. Although I do like you living near me."

"The commute is giving me road rage."

He laughed and we headed into the city. I made a few calls from the printouts I had for the rentals I wanted to see. The first two were strikeouts. Already rented. Damn. Tight market. I was able to line up viewings on three others, however, for after lunch.

Dave was surprisingly quiet. Then again, I'd been focused on my phone calls and it's not as though he was going to talk when I was on the phone. Now that I was off, he still wasn't talking, though.

"Anything on your mind?" I asked.

He looked at me, then back at the road. "Maybe we should give this a shot."

"Give what a shot?"

"Us. Like, without all the games. Just like two normal people."

I laughed (trying to keep it light). "Sweetie, we are not normal."

He looked over at me again. Not light. Damn.

"Okay," I said respectfully. "I'm not sure I know what you mean." Or I'm hoping I'm wrong.

"If you met me and you didn't know my history or my aversion to relationships and all that, this would be going differently."

I frowned. "How so?"

"Because. You would see me as a potential . . ."

"Potential?"

"Boyfriend. Partner. Whatever. But now, I have this stigma attached to me and it keeps you from taking me seriously."

Inner sigh. Once again, Dave, thanks for complicating the hell out of everything. "I take you seriously."

"But you don't. Be honest. Have you, even once, considered being in an actual relationship with me?"

Nope. Now I see where he was going. He's not wrong. Yes, that's sort of a double negative. It's a side effect of being a lawyer. No one ever actually says "you're right"—just "you're not wrong." My law degree stripped me of the proper grammar I'd learned while getting my English degree.

"No," I said. "It never occurred to me that you would ever suddenly become someone who would want one."

"And that's the problem. That's why this is all going differently, because of my history and what you know about me."

I shrugged. I honestly did not know where to go with this.

"I want to drop the stigma and just have us spend time together like two normal people." When I didn't say anything, he kept talking—probably assuming I was missing his meaning. "Forget what you know about me. Pretend we just met and none of that baggage came up. Let's give it a shot."

"How do we 'give it a shot'?"

"Stop seeing other people. Spend time together. See where it goes."

And my mouth dropped open. Couldn't be helped. I believe "flabbergasted" would be the word.

"Dave, that sounds an awful lot like a relationship."

He looked at me. Didn't nod. Didn't say anything. He knew damn well what it sounded like.

I opened my eyes wide. "You've known me for like a week, Dave!"

"So? My dad said he fell in love with my mom on their first date." Please laugh. Please look like you're joking. Nope. No such luck. He was appearing quite sincere. Shit, shit, shit.

Breathe, girl. "I can't believe that you could go from being a cynical woman hater one minute, to wanting a girl-friend the next. How is that possible?"

"I don't know. It's crazy. But that's what happened. I want you and I don't want to share you."

The possessiveness in that statement made me a little uncomfortable, but I just tucked it away somewhere in the back of my brain. "I don't want to belong to anyone. I'm still reeling from the end of my contract. I'm sorry, I just can't even think about being in a relationship right now."

He nodded, but didn't look happy. We arrived at the park-ing garage near the restaurant he'd picked out. I got out of the truck and he walked over to me, grabbed my hand, and led the way.

His was acting proprietary and a little moody and I didn't really know how to react to it, so I bumped him with my shoulder. Hard.

* Subject to the following terms and conditions

He looked at me, eyebrows raised. "Careful, little girl, or you might get a spanking."

There we go. I seem to have resurrected the old Dave—which I have to say, I could handle so much better than puppy-love Dave. I laughed and did it again.

"Behave or I'll throw you over my shoulder and give you that spanking you seem to be begging for."

Yikes. We'd moved from puppy love to porn. That statement was so dirty that I just stared at him. He gave me a quick peck on my nose. This is proving to be an interesting day.

After we ate lunch, we headed to the midtown area to look at the first rental on my list. This was a particularly cute part of midtown—mostly houses from the 1920s, many converted into duplexes like the one Logek lived in. In fact, the first one is only about eight blocks from her (which is what put it at the top of the list. Well—that and the fact that it's about five minutes from my office).

We pulled to the curb and got out, looking at the little blue house that had seen better days. A middle-aged man walked toward us. Must be Jerry.

"Are you Kate?" he asked. Bingo.

"Yes. Thanks so much for showing me the place."

"No problem. Let's go in."

We followed him up a flight of steps and into the apartment. Okay. Not a duplex—a fourplex. A little, teensy, tiny fourplex. So this isn't really an apartment—more of a studio. The kitchen and living room were combined and an alcove is basically what qualified as the bedroom. I'm thinking no. It's a little awkward when the guy meets me out here and I know sixty seconds after I walk in that I don't want it, so I did a slow, contemplative sweep of the place (which took about fifteen seconds) and headed back toward the door.

"It's really cute, but it's smaller than I anticipated."

"It's small, but you'll find it's hard to find stuff in midtown if this is where you want to be."

Jerry had a point.

"I really appreciate your time."

He nodded and we followed him down the stairs, did the cursory wave, and got back in the truck.

I sighed. "One down, two to go."

"Yeah—the rent on that seemed a little high for a walk-in closet," Dave said.

The next one was still close to work, a little farther from Logek, but still cute enough.

A sixtysomething woman was standing on the porch. She had dark hair, heavily sprinkled with gray, and she was about my height. Sandy, I presume.

I walked up to her, smiling. "You must be Sandy?"

"Kate," she said, shaking my hand. She had a lovely smile. I hope I look that good at her age.

We followed her inside. Score. Duplex. These are old houses, so nothing is going to be huge, but I'm definitely looking for bigger than a breadbox.

There was a very cute living room with a picture window complete with a deep window seat and dark hardwood flooring. The kitchen was beyond and was a bright mix of old and new. It had the style of a 1950s kitchen, but the appliances all looked new. There was an old wooden staircase that went to the second floor. It creaked as I walked up the steps, but even that held some charm for me. What can I say—I like old houses. There was a large bedroom and a bathroom on that level and that was it. I'm sure the layout mirrored the other side of the duplex since you couldn't escape the feeling that they had just cut a house in half and put in a wall.

"I really like it," I said, wandering around downstairs some more.

"It's my favorite. I have a couple of other rentals here in the city, but this one has the most personality," she said, smiling. She was so pretty. "What do you do, Kate?"

"I'm an attorney."

"Oh. That must be interesting." Nope. But I nodded anyway.

"And is this your . . . partner?" she asked, looking at Dave.

"No, just a friend who is helping me find a place to live."

Dave smiled and shook her hand. TV Dave. And it worked on her—she seemed charmed to meet him, which was his goal.

"Oh—are you signed?" she asked me, but then she seemed to realize that that was a fairly personal question to ask so she quickly amended with, "I mean—are you looking for a place for just yourself?"

I smiled. "Just me."

"Well, for a single girl, this is a good place to be. The man that lives next door is a police officer, so you'd have a little extra peace of mind."

"Well, I'm in love. Can I fill out an application?"

"I have one right here," she said, handing me an envelope.

I pulled out the paper and a pen and started filling it in against the banister.

"So no children?" Sandy asked.

I laughed. "Nope. I'm on my own."

"I'm sorry. I'm nosy. My son constantly tells me that I pry too much."

"Oh," I said, looking up from the paper momentarily. "How old is your son?"

"Thirty-four."

"Oh. Do you have any grandchildren?"

"No. I'm not sure my son will ever settle down enough to have any. And he's more interested in his career. He's in advertising with Samson and Tule."

What. The. Hell. It can't be. It just can't. I stopped writing and looked up at her. "I worked there briefly. Who is your son?"

Don't say it. Don't say it. "Adam Lucas. Do you know him?"

"Actually, I do. He's sort of a friend of mine. Actually, he's a friend of Dave's as well."

Sandy seemed thrilled by this news. "Oh my gosh. What a small world!"

Isn't it, though? I looked down at the paperwork. Hell with it. I love this place. I'm not going to sacrifice it because it has some weird affiliations. I signed the bottom and handed the form back to her. She waved it, saying, "Oh, this isn't really necessary since you're a friend of Adam's."

It made sense now—why I thought she was so lovely . . . Adam looks just like her. And that son of a bitch is definitely lovely. Even her eyes were the same color as his.

* Subject to the following terms and conditions

"So when did you want to move in?" she asked.

"Would next weekend be okay? I can bring the check the day I get the keys? Or I can drop it off ahead of time? Whichever way you'd prefer."

"Oh, the day you get the keys will be fine." Wow. She clearly adored her son because by virtue of being his friend, she seemed to now trust me implicitly. Hmm. He certainly didn't get his guarded, cynical nature from her. "I can meet you here about nine a.m.? I'll bring you the key for the shed around back, too, and we can do a quick walk-through."

"Sounds wonderful. Thank you so much, Sandy."

We all wandered back out onto the porch. She was all smiles.

"Well, I will see you next Saturday, Kate."

"Perfect. Thanks again."

Dave and I got into his truck and watched Sandy drive away in her cute, little, blue Mercedes. Yep. Adam's mom.

"That was weird," Dave said.

"I know. What are the odds?"

"Well, odds in general? Or *your* odds?"

I laughed. He had a point. I whipped out the last sheet of paper and called to cancel my last viewing. No answer so I left a very apologetic voice mail.

Dave laughed. "What?" I asked.

"You. You're like a little kid, so excited."

I definitely was smiling ear to ear. I bounced up and down a few times. "I have my own place again!"

"Not as convenient for me, but I'll make it work," he said with a wink. He was apparently over his sulking from earlier.

He started to pull away, but I stopped him. "Wait!" I

hopped back out real quick and snapped a picture with my phone. "There," I said, climbing back in. "Had to have a photo." And I was back to the cheesy-grin thing. Okay. Job . . . check. My own place . . . check. I might turn into a grown-up yet.

I texted the picture to Logek. *My new place :) I move in next weekend!*

A minute later she texted back. *LOVE! How close?*

About 2 miles from you.

Perfect :)

Adam's mother is my new landlady!

No. Way. Okay. It's destiny. You're clearly meant to sign with him and have his babies.

Lol. Well, I'm currently on a date with Dave so it might be rude to start planning my future with someone else ;)

Good point. Okay. I need more details later.

Promise.

I looked over at Dave. "Sorry—just had to text the picture to Logek real quick."

He shrugged. "No problem." Dave took us back onto the freeway and headed back out to the suburbs. We were heading in the direction of my house, so I was wondering if dinner was off and he was taking me home. I didn't say anything, though. His call. He drove past my neighborhood. Curiouser and curiouser.

He turned into an area populated with homes that had the same flavor as my parents' street, just smaller versions. He pressed a button and pulled into the garage of a very nice, suburban-style home (that would probably fit three of my little apartments).

"Very nice," I said.

"Thanks. I like it."

I climbed out and followed him into the house. It looked a little like a model home—not somewhere you would expect to find a single man. The floors were wood, the kitchen counters granite, the furniture expensive.

I looked around, and then looked at him.

"My mother and my sister," he said. "I'm not much for decorating."

"They did a beautiful job. How long have you been here?"

"Little over a year."

I wandered around a little, pretending to check out the house, but I was actually trying to figure out why we were here and what I was going to do about it. Things have a way of getting out of hand when we're alone. And we all know how my resolve holds up once I'm the least bit turned on. This had bad news written all over it.

Dave walked up behind me and wrapped his arms around me tightly. "I figured we could make dinner here," he said quietly next to my ear. Warm breath on ear—not good. Okay. Control the situation. I stepped out of his arms and turned to face him.

"Dave . . ." I started.

"Uh-oh," he said with an exaggerated sigh and walked over to the sofa and flopped down on it. I went over and sat down next to him.

"What, Kate? What now?" he asked, sounding fairly perturbed.

My face hardened a little at his tone. "Don't get pissy with me. I need this to slow down." He just looked at me. Okay. "I like you, but I just feel like this thing is out of my control."

"What's wrong with that?"

"Everything. I'm not ready for this. For anything, really. I mean, I have a brand-new job, a brand-new place, and I'm recently single."

"And a brand-new man?" he said, giving me a flirty smile.

"God. You're like a force of nature, Dave. I just feel like I'm getting caught in your undertow."

"I can think of more flattering ways to put that."

I laughed. "I just don't understand why you're in such a hurry."

"Because I know what I want."

"And you are used to getting it. And you are not used to waiting."

"Your point?"

"You're acting like a spoiled kid who gets whatever he wants. Guess what, sweetie, it doesn't apply to *people*."

"Says who?"

I glared at him. "Fine. It doesn't apply to *me*."

His expression softened and the wave of arrogance receded. "I know that, beautiful. But if you aren't willing to go for what you want, you're never going to get it. I'm a 'go for it' kind of guy."

I sighed.

He scooted over next to me on the sofa and wrapped his arm around my shoulder and pulled me close to him.

"Okay," I said. "But if you don't want me to just start pushing you away, you need to slow down. You're overwhelming me."

"I'll try," he whispered, kissing the side of my head. Then my forehead. Then my cheek.

"And," I said, pulling away, "I'm not ready to sleep with you. I don't know you that well." *Although I have let you see* all *my lady parts.*

He leaned in closer and started trailing kisses down my neck. "Got it," he said. "No sex. How about if I just make you come?"

Well, sure. That sounds like a perfectly reasonable suggestion to me. No harm, no foul. Kate will be flooded with poor decision-making in five . . . four . . . three . . . two . . .

"Dave. I think this needs to slow down, too. 'Cause, let's be real, once we hit a certain point, there will be no stopping."

He rolled his eyes up toward me and kissed my neck. "And what point is that?"

Holy shit. This is ridiculous. I bet Dave Sex would be really good. But there is something causing panic in my brain right now making me want to stop this.

Adam.

The answer to my million-dollar question. Suddenly I had a flash of that hurt expression I got from him the night Dave drove me home, and it was apparently the bucket of ice water I needed. *At least this time.*

I pushed Dave back. "Easy, killer."

He sat back against the couch and looked at me. "We could go take a cold shower," he said.

"Yeah, Dave. That will solve all our problems."

"It's only you that sees them as problems."

"For now I do." I smiled. "If you stop being a dick, maybe I'll stop seeing them that way."

He laughed and looked affronted. "Fine. But if I don't get to rip your clothes off, I'm gonna need a drink."

You and me both.

CHAPTER *15*

I put on my spiffy navy suit that my parents bought me for law school graduation the next morning since I was going to court. On my own. For a client I'd never met on a file I'd looked over for two days. Makes perfect sense.

As I drove into the city in stop-and-go rush-hour traffic, I thought about my upcoming move and felt a wave of excitement similar to when I went off to college and lived on my own for the first time.

I had the Britton file in my black leather satchel, which was sitting on my passenger seat since I wasn't going to the office before heading to court. I kept playing our client's argument in my head so that I could answer confidently whatever questions the judge might pose.

I took the freeway exit that led downtown and headed

toward the courthouse. I heard a noise in the back of the car—something ominous and vaguely familiar. No, no, no, no, no. I pulled over to the curb as quickly as possible and got out of the car and walked around to the passenger side. The rear tire was completely flat and the rim was resting on the pavement. I looked at my watch. 7:50 a.m. Court starts at 8:30 a.m. And I literally just stared at the damn tire for a minute like I could convince it to *not* screw me over like this.

Dave would come, but he was evening sports guy, meaning he wouldn't be out this way till around lunchtime. Jonathan's office was too far away. Daddy? Take too long to get here. I love my life. Yes. That was sarcasm.

Well, you wanted an excuse to call him, I told myself, dialing Adam's number.

"Ms. Shaw," he said, answering on the first ring.

Tingles. Okay, cut to the chase. "Busy?"

"Always."

"I'm having a damsel-in-distress moment. Care to play White Knight?"

"Not my usual role," he said. I could hear the smile in his voice.

"I am stranded on the side of Fourteenth Street with a flat tire. I have to be in court in . . . shit . . . thirty-five minutes," I said, consulting my watch again. "I don't *technically* know how to change a tire, and I'm wearing my nine-hundred-dollar law school graduation present from my parents."

Loud sigh. "No time for triple A. What cross street?"

"K?"

"Be there in five minutes."

Yay! Let's be real. This euphoria was only about 30 percent

due to the fact that I might actually make it to court in time for my hearing and about 70 percent was that Adam was willing to come to my rescue. We hadn't talked for almost a week, which I guess isn't that long, except that we'd talked— at least a little—nearly every day since we met.

I was only about three blocks from Samson & Tule so I figured he'd probably walk rather than take the time to go to the parking garage to get his car and fight the downtown traffic, so I was watching the sidewalk waiting for him to round the corner. When he did . . . he basically took my breath away. He smiled at me when he saw me, sweet, slightly ridiculing, but undeniably warm. He continued his quick stride toward me, (thankfully) hurrying. When he neared me, he started unbuttoning his shirt, first at the cuffs and then down the front. Like my own little happy Monday morning sidewalk striptease.

He stopped in front of me, slipped his shirt off so that he was just wearing a snug white undershirt. Dude. This is the best flat tire, *ever*. He gave me a quick once-over before focusing on my eyes.

"Nice graduation gift."

"Thank you."

Then he opened my trunk and started changing the tire. I stood back out of the way and watched the show. For such a snazzy dresser with perfect hair, he was surprisingly handy with tools. He had the lug nuts off and was squatted down by the side of my car sliding the wheel off the pins. It belatedly occurred to me that my entire suit probably cost about the same as his pants . . . which were not smudge proof. A dry cleaner can get axle grease out of wool trousers, right?

He had the new tire on and was dropping the flat in the trunk. I reached into my glove box and grabbed a handful of Starbucks napkins (yes, I'm a frickin' Boy Scout when it comes to preparedness).

He took the napkins and wiped his hands as best he could and then took a couple quick brushes across his pants where he'd picked up the smudges. He looked up at me and I bit my lip and mouthed "sorry."

"Don't worry about it, Kate." He took his shirt back from me and slipped it on. He glanced at his watch. "You better run."

Screw the time. Not really, though. Damn. I only had fifteen minutes to get to court. "Can I at least drop you back at the office?"

"You don't have time. Lunch?"

Hell, yes. I nodded.

"Text me when you're out of court."

I smiled. Without overthinking it, I threw my arms around his neck and hugged him. I let go and bolted for my car.

"You're my hero," I said, smiling, as I got into my car.

He watched me with a little smile and put his hands into his pockets. Okay, girlie, he's cute, but you need to haul ass.

Apparently my good-girl karma was in effect because I managed to hit all green lights and was parking in the garage and heading for court within nine minutes. I got to the front door and buzzed through my attorney line where I got to cut in front of everyone. When I'd cleared security, I pulled my phone out of my pocket and pulled the battery out and returned it to my pocket. I reached Department 4 before the doors had even been unlocked. Yes! Best. Morning. Ever.

I scanned the dozen or so people gathered around waiting for the doors to be unlocked. How to find Rochelle? I
pulled out my file and flipped through the correspondence.
Dr. Dickhead's attorney was a man by the name of Simpson.
I looked up from my file and scanned the crowd. Somehow
I figured she and I would be looking for each other and so
we'd magically find one another. There was a slightly balding man with a file in his hands. Attorney. Breaking out that
keen intuition now. Look out. He looked up and did a quick
scan like I had done. Our eyes met and he walked over to me.

"Any chance you are Mr. Simpson?" I asked.

"That's me. Call me Doug. You don't look like Tony Manetti."

"Thank you," I said. That earned me a chuckle. "I'm an
associate with the firm, covering the hearing for Mr. Manetti."
I extended my hand and we shook. "Kate Shaw."

"Is your client here?"

"No idea, actually. I've never met her," I admitted. "And
the . . . doctor? Is he here?"

"I talked to him half an hour ago and he said he would
be early, but I don't see him. And I don't see Ms. Britton,
either."

"Okay. So what exactly is the protocol if both clients are
no-shows?"

"Judge Stanford gets pissy and blames us."

"Fabulous. Never met him. Looking forward to it."

Doug laughed again. The doors unlocked and everyone
began filing into the courtroom. Doug gave me the universal,
"oh, well" look, accompanied by a shoulder shrug, and I followed him inside. I checked the calendar and we were

number two. Doug and I sat next to each other . . . because I guess that's what opposing counsel does when both clients are AWOL.

The first item on the calendar was continued. When Judge Stanford called our matter, Doug and I approached the table. Doug looked at me and held out his hand telling me to go ahead and explain. Gee. Thanks, Doug. I've been in signing law for a whole week. Sure. I'll field this.

"Kate Shaw for Ms. Britton."

"Doug Simpson for Dr. Pope."

Hmm. Dickhead was a Pope. "Your honor," I began. "It appears that our clients are running late. Would it be possible to trail our matter?"

"Ms. . . . ?"

"Shaw, your honor."

"Okay. You've got fifteen minutes to track them down and get them in here. Next matter on the calendar is Hanson v. Whittaker." And apparently we were dismissed.

Doug and I quickly headed out of the courtroom and down the stairs. I pulled out my file to find Rochelle's number and, after dropping my phone battery back into my phone, tried to call her. Voice mail. Doug was doing the same I assume and he shrugged as he hung up his phone.

"I'd wander around, but I don't know what she looks like."

"I'll walk with you," he said, as we made a slow sweep of the first floor of the courthouse. And came up empty-handed.

I made a quick call to the office and got Mags.

"Mags. Rochelle Britton is MIA. She hasn't called the office, has she?"

"Shit. No, she hasn't. Is her ex about to screw her over?"

"Unlikely. He's missing, too."

"Hmm. I'll check with Tony and call you back if he's heard from her."

"Thanks. Text me, though—I'm going to pull the battery out of my phone," I said.

She laughed. "Oh, yeah. I heard about your phone going off in court."

"From who?"

"The lady at Starbucks."

I laughed (because she had to be joking) and hung up the phone. And, yes, pulled out the battery again before putting it into my pocket.

I may have to revise that whole "best morning ever" thing.

"Kate, I'm going to check outside. See if there is still a line to get in or anything."

"Okay. I'll go with you." Not like I can *look* for her in here. This whole representing people you've never met thing is bullshit.

I followed Doug outside. Unfortunately, no line still waiting to get in. He turned to face me, frowning. We were at a loss. He looked like he was going to say something when his eyes suddenly focused on something over my shoulder.

"Fuck," he said. Well, that can't be good.

I turned around to see what he was looking at. There was a woman with a double stroller, an old man jogging, and a couple making out against the wall of the courthouse. I'm gonna go with the third option on this.

I raised my eyebrows at Doug. "Rochelle and the doc?"

He nodded. Rochelle was against the wall with her arms wrapped around Dr. Dickhead and his hands roamed all over her while they kissed. To be clear, this wasn't just inappropriate PDA. This was ridiculous. Like teenagers-in-the-back-of-a-car ridiculous.

Doug was apparently just going to stand there and light up a cigarette so I walked over to them.

I did the obligatory throat clearing. "Rochelle Britton?"

Awesome. Even that didn't stop them immediately. They finished the deep-throat exercise they were working on before she lazily turned her face to me. "Yes?"

"I'm Kate Shaw."

She just looked at me with an ever so slightly annoyed expression.

"Your attorney."

"Oh," she said, seeming a little embarrassed. Finally. She straightened her skirt and actually rebuttoned the top button of her blouse. She smiled at me and that smile said it all. She was screwed. Literally and figuratively. Her eyes were glowing, her cheeks were flushed, and her brain was on sabbatical.

The doctor turned toward me as well and took Rochelle's hand tightly between his. "Rochelle and I are going to sign again."

Of course you are. Dr. Dickhead was okay-looking—nothing to make a girl lose her head. But he clearly gets plenty of action so I must be missing something. Ick.

The doctor looked past me. "Doug. Rochelle and I are getting signed again. I need you to draft up the contract."

"Fine, Rich, but the judge is pissed that you guys didn't show."

Dr. Rich shrugged, clearly feeling that wasn't his problem anymore. "We don't need a child support hearing if we're signed." That's romantic. So sincere. So sleazy.

I looked at Doug. "I'll go back and let the judge know we need to be dropped from the calendar."

"I'd appreciate that. Are you the one I should send Rochelle's contract to for review?"

"Yeah, that'd be great." I handed him one of my crisp new business cards that said "Attorney" under my name. Still weird that it isn't a misprint. I walked toward Rochelle. "Could I have a minute?"

Rich didn't seem like he was going to let her hand go at first, but Rochelle followed me a few steps away, sliding her hand out of his grasp.

"So sorry we didn't give you the heads-up . . . it was just so last minute," she said, grinning like an idiot. God, I sound jaded.

"I can see that. I'll have them drop the child support hearing from the calendar. Mr. Simpson is going to draft your new contract. I would advise you have us review it *before* signing anything. I've asked Mr. Simpson to send it to me once it's drafted."

She looked like I was being needlessly worrisome. "Oh, definitely. Once he sends it to you, please look it over and let me know what you think."

I think Dr. Dickhead has no intention of keeping it in his pants—that's what I think. "I will. Don't sign anything," I said firmly, and probably uselessly. I'd be shocked if she didn't sign the second it was put in front of her whether I'd okayed it or not. Damn.

I said good-bye and headed back inside to the courtroom.

As I entered the room, a couple of attorneys and their clients were leaving the table and walking back through the gate. And, since he was in between calling cases, Eagle Eye Judge Stanford spotted me immediately.

"Ms. Shaw."

I walked through the gate and stood at the table. Alone. Feeling like I was standing in front of the firing squad.

"Where is your client?" He looked toward the back of the room. "And have we now lost Mr. Simpson as well?"

"Your honor, I apologize. If we could just have the matter dropped from the calendar."

"Why?"

Why? Really? Shouldn't he just say fine and move on to the next case?

"It seems that the parties are going to sign again."

"If that is the case, why wasn't it dropped from the calendar before today?"

"This is a very recent development."

"How recent?"

"About five minutes ago outside of the courthouse?"

Judge Stanford actually smiled. "Thank you, Ms. Shaw. The matter is dropped from the calendar."

"Thank you, your honor."

And I turned and headed for the door, trying not to sprint.

Once I was back in the office, I stopped by Mags's cubicle and rested my arms on the top of one of the walls of her cubby. She was in red today. Red-red. *Scarlet Letter* red. Lipstick, sweater, four-inch heels. Red. God, I envied her . . . balls.

"What?" she asked, eyes lit up with whatever tidbit I had to share.

"Found Rochelle Britton. Making out with her ex *against* the courthouse wall. Outside wall, that is."

Mags erupted into laughter. "Oh my god. That is fantastic."

"Yeah . . . apparently they are going to sign again."

"And they decided this when?"

"I'm guessing about ten minutes before court started when he put his hand on her ass."

We were laughing when Uncle Tony's loud voice cut through our fun.

"Kate!"

I rolled my eyes at Mags before turning and heading into Tony's office. Seriously. Is he always going to yell for me like a dog?

"Tony," I said, walking into his office.

"Mags said Rochelle was a no-show."

"Turns out she was there. She was just hooking up with Dickhead outside of the courthouse." I figured if I used his actual name, Tony might not know who I was talking about.

Tony chuckled. "Idiot. And they say it's only men that think with their dicks."

Thanks for that visual, Tony. "Anyway," I said, trying to sidestep his comment. "They are planning on signing another contract. The other attorney, Doug Simpson, said he would send me the contract for review after he'd drafted it. Then I told Rochelle to not sign anything till I'd reviewed it. Pretty sure she won't wait for me to approve it, though."

"You're probably right about that, darling. But, fuck it.

We make a lot more money off of breaches than off of reviewing contracts."

Harsh. Valid, but harsh.

Tony continued. "Isn't he the asshole that was fucking anything that came along?"

Ew. "The neighbor, the babysitter, the kindergarten teacher."

"Yeah, I'm sure he's sincere now about being faithful."

I nodded agreement.

"Well, perfect. Rochelle Britton is officially your problem now. When he sends the contract, review it, ask questions, give feedback. Then when Dickhead starts screwing all the women in town, you can handle his breach for Rochelle. Again. You gotta love a business where you make money off the same people for the exact same work over and over again." Yep. Everything I love about signing law.

"Alrighty," I said. Time to slink back to my office and mentally steam clean my brain of Tony's colorful imagery.

I sat down and started going through my e-mail, while simultaneously putting my battery back into my phone.

"Kate!" Tony bellowed. You are *freaking* kidding me, right?

I walked back next door and raised my eyebrows.

"You didn't tell me what you thought of Judge Stanford."

"He didn't seem particularly pervy. Besides, all I did was ask him to drop the matter from the calendar so not a whole lot of interaction."

"Not yet," Tony chuckled.

Time to nip this shit in the bud. I walked over to his desk and picked his phone up off the cradle and held the handset in front of him. "I'm extension six-seven-five." I smiled and hung up the phone. Okay, maybe I only had the balls to do it since I was his niece, but, whatever, it needed to happen.

He frowned at me. Time to skedaddle my butt out of here. How long do I have to be here before I can request a different office? I sat back down at my desk and texted Adam.

Thanks for your help this morning.

You're welcome.

Lunch?

Yeah. Want to meet in the middle? There's a little sandwich place called Dad's on 12th.

Love that place. Noon?

Perfect. See you soon.

I did some work on a couple of briefs I was writing for other attorneys and tried not to look at the clock. At about 11:45, I grabbed my purse and headed for the door. I did a quick stop by Mags's desk again.

"Meeting the 'complication' for lunch," I said, widening my eyes.

"Well, on behalf of women everywhere, I would just like to say . . . fuck him already. The rest of us need to live vicariously through you."

I laughed. "I'll take that under advisement."

I got to Dad's about five minutes to noon. The sandwich shop is little more than a counter to order from and a couple of tables on the sidewalk out front. The storefront is painted in bright colors and looks like Dad may have painted it himself. But the sandwiches were totally amazing.

"Kate."

Adam. I faced him. Looking at him, I could tell he had a lot going on upstairs. I guess the question was whether he was going to feel like we needed to talk stuff out—or if he just wanted to pretend the awkwardness hadn't ever happened. Either way, I smiled at him. I was happy to see him—pointless to try to hide it.

I reached out and hugged him and he hugged me back, one good meaningful squeeze. "Thanks again for helping me out this morning."

"My pleasure. Have you ordered yet?"

"Not yet."

We wandered inside and ordered, and once we had a little plastic number to rest on our table, we headed back outside to snag the only remaining open table. We sat down and regarded each other quietly. Hmm. Not quite awkward. Yet.

He looked at the plastic tablecloth and smoothed it with his hand. "I've missed you."

Easy, girl. "I've missed you, too."

He looked back into my face. Apparently he hasn't decided if we're going down the whole avoidance road or not. I couldn't help but be a little touched that it was important enough to him to tie him up like this. Screw it. I'm not an avoidance kind of girl.

"Okay," I said, with a deep breath. "I know who you are, Adam. I really do. And I have no ridiculous ideas that I'm going to change you and I don't want to." Okay—not entirely true on that one. "But, it's not just me who's struggling with us defining this 'friendship' thing. But I miss you when I don't get to talk to you. Even though we seem to keep screwing it up, I'd like to keep trying to be friends." There. Ninety percent honest. Eighty-five percent. Seventy to eighty percent.

Some undefined emotion went across his face. I don't think that's where he saw this going. "I have never known anyone like you, Kate."

"Is that good or bad?"

"It depends on which day you ask me."

I smiled. "Fair enough."

"So, friends. We just need to stop making it so damn complicated."

I nodded. He has more to say, but I don't think he's going to share.

"So, I understand you met my mother." Nope, no baring his soul.

"I did. She's lovely."

"That's pretty much what she said about you."

I maybe blushed a tad.

"She said you were with a blond guy. Dave, I'm guessing."

I didn't confirm it. No need.

"But she also told me that you said you two were just friends."

Now I nodded. Might as well help the situation along.

"Which gave her an opening to encourage me to pursue you." He finished, eyebrows raised, irony in his voice.

I laughed. "Uh-oh. She doesn't know you're a hopeless case?"

A waiter came out and set sandwiches in front of us and picked up our plastic number from the table. Instead of responding, Adam picked up his sandwich and started eating, making it clear he was ignoring my question.

When we'd just about finished our lunch, Adam wiped his perfect lips with a napkin. "So my mother enlisted me to help you move this Saturday."

"That's nice of her."

"Is Dave going to be there?"

"I don't know."

"Well, don't take this the wrong way, but I don't feel like spending my morning watching him hanging all over you."

"Is it him in particular?"

"Of course. Otherwise that would imply that I was being irrationally jealous."

"So you just don't like Dave."

"I like Dave. Just not in the context of 'you and Dave.'"

"Interesting. So is that your subtle way of asking me to warn you if Dave is going to be there so that you can come up with an excuse to avoid helping?"

"You know me so well."

"I will let you know if he insists on helping."

"Thanks." He looked down at his empty plate. "So how's that bet going?"

Oh, right. I forgot I'd told him about that. "Oh. Um." Awkward. "We just sort of dropped the whole bet thing."

Adam looked at me with wide, green eyes. "Really? He stopped trying to sleep with you?"

"Well, I guess he's still hoping for that . . . but he *claims* he wants a relationship with me."

"Wow. That was fast."

"He's probably full of shit. You know that."

"I certainly don't trust him, no."

"Exactly. It's probably just part of his game to get me into bed."

And that was the reassurance Adam was looking for, that I hadn't slept with Dave yet. He didn't say it, but I could tell a little weight was lifted.

"You are spending a lot of time together, though."

"Some. It may be less, now. When he brought up the whole relationship thing yesterday, I shot it down, so he may be upset with me. I don't really know."

"He actually said he wanted you to be his girlfriend?"

"He didn't use the word 'girlfriend,' but he did say he didn't want us to see other people. Which is ridiculous. We barely know each other."

"I've never known him to have a girlfriend. He must be quite taken with you."

I shrugged. "Felt a little more possessive than genuine."

He tipped his head to the side a little. "What is it about you?"

"Logek says I'm contract killer catnip," I said, winking at him.

He laughed. "Certainly my drug of choice," he mumbled, looking at his watch. "I've got a meeting at one thirty so I've got to run."

We stood. "Thanks for having lunch with me," I said.

He pulled me into a tight hug. When he let me go he said, "Okay, let's see if we can avoid sabotaging things this time."

"I'll try to stop being so incredibly irresistible, but I'll need you to do the same."

"I'll do my best," he said with a chuckle. Yeah . . . I'm thinking that isn't going to be possible for him. Damn.

*

As soon as I was back in my office, Mags came in and sat on my desk. Today her hair was in some sort of retro-looking back-brushed style. She was in her typical micromini so she crossed her legs (somewhat) demurely.

"So?" she asked, with her eyebrows moving up and down.

"Yes?"

She sighed. "Quickie at lunchtime?"

"Yes, Mags. We just went for it in the back of my car."

She laughed. "I would. Any more sneaky alleyway kissing?"

"Not today. *Friends* generally try to avoid making out."

"Friends, my ass."

"It's currently the only option on the menu."

She frowned and hopped off my desk. "Luckily you keep spare men lying around," she said with a grin as she walked out of my office.

I laughed loud enough that I knew she could hear me at her desk. Spares indeed.

I got back to work on a complaint I was writing (aka plagiarizing). The only part I actually had to write from scratch was the Statement of Facts. The rest of the document was basically cannibalized from other complaints for the same breach.

"Hey, slugger."

I looked up to see Brad standing in my doorway smiling at me.

"Hey." I was genuinely happy to see him.

He stuffed his hands in his pants pockets and strolled toward my desk. His oversized glasses gave him a nerdy quality that was sort of endearing. He wasn't bad-looking—kind of average—but the glasses sort of set the tone for his appearance. He studied me when he got closer.

"Wow. Looks good," he said, referring to my eye.

"Yeah. It's not gone, but I can hide it pretty well."

He nodded. "So what do they have you working on?"

"I went to my first child support hearing today."

"Nice."

"Yeah—the client didn't show because she was outside hooking up with her ex."

He laughed. "Williams?"

"Britton."

"Oh. Williams is one of our other clients who we represent *every* time her partner breaches. Same guy has breached on her three times."

"Tragic. That woman needs therapy."

"She has the mistaken impression that it's part of my job description. I keep telling her there are therapists that would charge less than I do, but that doesn't seem to stop her from calling me once a week to cry for an hour on the phone."

"All the reasons I wanted to go into signing law."

"Don't kid yourself—all clients treat their attorneys like their shrink, no matter what type of law you are in." Probably an accurate statement. He turned to leave. "My office is straight across from yours right there," he said, pointing across the office. "Let me know if you need any help."

"Thanks, Brad. I appreciate it."

A little after five o'clock, I was shutting down my computer and getting ready to head out the door. I checked my phone and I'd missed two texts—one from Logek and one from Dave. Logek was telling me that Derek wanted to take her to dinner (in conjunction with paying off his breach of contract) and she included the little surprised-face emoji. Interesting.

Dave just texted *Thinking of you*. Which is sweet. And for some reason, it gives me anxiety. Maybe because I feel like I could end up in a relationship with him whether I want to or not just by his sheer force of will. Which is probably absurd, but my stress level doesn't know that. Does that text warrant a reply? Not like I can say "me, too." Not honestly, anyway.

:)

Nailed it. Although, I suppose it's possible to read into that. Damn emoticons.

I was picking up my things from my desk and getting my keys out of my purse when I realized someone was standing in my doorway.

Jared Mann was there, staring (naturally), in a crisp black suit, holding his briefcase in one hand.

"Hi," I said, smiling.

"Hi." He looked tired. "How did the child support hearing go?"

"Our client decided to hook up with her ex five minutes before the hearing."

He laughed. "I hate it when that happens."

"Tony didn't seem too put off by it."

"It's the capitalist in him."

I laughed. "Nice to be comfortable profiting off of other's misery."

"Well, someone's going to."

"Good point."

"Leaving?" he asked. "I'll walk you out."

"Thanks," I said, picking up my things and following him out the door. Read nothing into this, Kate. That's an order.

We rode the elevator down in silence, but he was watching me . . . because that is his thing.

We exited the building and headed for the parking garage. He was a step ahead of me, but seemed to be heading toward my car. And stopped in front of it. Not sure how he knew which car was mine. People always seem to know more about me than I expect.

"This is me," I said, with what I hoped wasn't an overly uncomfortable smile.

He looked at me, but didn't respond immediately.

"Have a good night," he said finally.

I smiled and slipped into my car hoping to avoid any further awkwardness. There's always tomorrow for that.

*

The next morning I was trying to finish a complaint I was drafting when my phone rang. I picked up the phone, saying, "This is Kate."

"So how are you with depositions?"

It was Tony. He used the phone instead of shouting for me! Victory!

"Virginal," I said.

He laughed. "Okay. You know the drill. Find some to sit in on. I want you to take one next week."

"You got it. Who's the client?"

"Trainor." And he chuckled. "You're going to love this guy."

Ominous.

I left my desk and headed for Brad's office in search of a depo to sit in on. He looked up when I stopped in his doorway.

"Hey, slugger."

"Hi. Any chance you have any depos coming up?"

"I'm not taking any, but I've got a client being deposed tomorrow. Opposing counsel sucks, though, so you'll want to chalk it up to 'what not to do.' It'll be educational, though."

"Got it."

"And you can see how we defend our client during their depo."

"That'll work."

"When are you doing one?"

"Next week. Trainor."

Brad laughed. "I thought Tony *liked* you."

"That doesn't sound promising."

"Jim Trainor is . . . well, you'll see. You are deposing his ex?"

Excellent question. "Tony rarely gives me more than one-sentence orders and this one did not include the name of the deponent."

"Fun. Well, when you get more details, we can go over it ahead of time."

"Thank you," I said.

*

The next day I followed Brad into the conference room where his client was waiting with a cup of coffee.

"Kate, this is Mike. Mike, this is Kate. She's a new associate with the firm and she's going to sit in on the deposition today, okay?"

"Absolutely," Mike said, with an unidentifiable drawl. "Nice to meet you." Mike was about thirty, wearing Levis and a plaid shirt, giving off a good-ol'-boy vibe, despite looking distinctly uncomfortable.

"You, too."

Next, a lanky man in a suit with a bald head and a beard (funny how hair migrates like that) entered the conference room. Brad shook the man's hand and then introduced us.

His name was Sam Bowerman and, based on Brad's commentary yesterday, he sucks. But he seems nice enough.

We all sat at the conference room table, along with the court reporter. Sam started the deposition with all the standard preliminaries: don't guess, don't nod, speak clearly for the court reporter, etc.

As Sam started asking all the basic questions about Mike's background, Mike fidgeted and looked nervous. And cleared his throat before every answer. That is going to get old fast.

"When did you first meet Susannah Myer?" Sam asked.

Mike cleared his throat. "About . . . four years ago. At a bar."

"And then you started dating?"

(Throat clearing.) "Yes."

"How long did you date before deciding to sign the contract?"

(Throat thing.) "About two weeks."

"So when you told her you wanted to sign, did you mention you didn't want children?"

Mike paused. No throat clearing? False alarm. He cleared his throat. "Actually, Sue brought up us signing, not me."

"Okay."

"But when she did, I did say I wasn't sure I wanted kids."

"So when you brought up signing . . ."

Brad interjected. "Objection. Misstates testimony." No kidding.

"Fine. When you *discussed* signing, what was her response to your statement about children?"

"I don't remember."

"But did she agree to the no kids thing?" Is he serious?

"I told you. I don't remember what her response was."

"So you don't even remember if she agreed?"

Mike was looking flustered. Brad interjected. "I think he's answered that question twice already."

"Did Susannah ever tell you she wanted children?"

"Objection. Vague as to time," Brad said.

Sam sighed like he was getting annoyed with the objections. Well, stop asking stupid questions, Sam.

"At any time *before you signed*, did Susannah tell you she wanted kids?" Sam asked.

"Not that I recall."

"You don't remember?"

"No."

"At any time *after you signed*, do you *remember* her telling you she wanted kids?" Getting a little snide there, Sam.

"Yes. About a year ago she started talking about it, but it wasn't something . . ." Mike stopped when Brad put a hand on his arm. Just the facts, Mike. Not sure an attorney is supposed to corral their client like Brad was, but Sam didn't fight it.

"Okay. About a year ago. And what was your response?"

"That I'd been up front with her before we signed about not being sure I wanted kids."

"So when you said no to her request . . ."

"Objection," Brad said. "Misstates witness's testimony."

"I didn't say no—I just reminded her that I had said up front I didn't think I wanted any," Mike blurted out, his face turning red. Brad put his hand on Mike's forearm again— basically telling him to shut up.

"Fine," Sam said with an eye roll. "Then when she brought it up and you told her you didn't want kids, what did she say?"

"Objection. That is not what he said. Again." Brad was beginning to look fairly annoyed as well.

Louder sigh from Sam. "Objection noted. You can answer."

"No," Brad said. "He can't."

"Your objection is noted, Brad."

"Rephrase the question, Sam."

I was tempted to go get my boxing gloves.

"What did you say to Susannah when she said last year that she wanted kids?"

Mike looked at Brad nervously, no doubt waiting to see if

he would object again. When Brad remained silent, Mike cleared his throat (of course). "I reminded her that before we signed, I told her I didn't think I wanted to have kids."

"And what was her response to that?"

"That she'd hoped that I'd changed my mind over the years."

"And had you?"

"Not really. I mean . . . I don't know."

"No or you don't know?"

"I told her I wasn't sure."

"But when she realized you didn't want kids, what was her reaction?"

Mike's face scrunched up. "That's not the way it went."

Brad cut him off. "Objection. Misstates testimony. Again."

Okay. Sam does suck. He's doing his best to manipulate the testimony and get Mike to say what he wants him to say. Which, yeah, I guess is a tactic, but it's a sleazy one.

"What was her response when you *said you weren't sure?*"

"Just that she wanted them. And that was the end of the conversation."

"Is there any provision in your contract concerning children?"

"I don't think so."

"Don't you think that the absence of such a provision leaves it open to interpretation?"

Mike started talking, but Brad interrupted. "Objection. Calls for a legal conclusion."

"Objection noted," Sam said blandly. "You can answer."

---

* Subject to the following terms and conditions

"Don't answer that," Brad said to Mike. "You are asking him to make assumptions about contract law that he would have no understanding of."

"This is a deposition, Brad. That's not a proper objection and you know it. And it's his contract. He can give his interpretation of its drafting."

"You are asking for the legal theory on contract interpretation. That has nothing to do with its drafting."

Sam looked at Mike. "Did you draft the contract?"

"No. Susannah got it somewhere."

"So you didn't have any input as to the provisions included in it?"

"No. I mean, we used a generic contract and didn't make any edits."

"Susannah didn't make any edits?"

Brad chimed in. "Objection. Calls for speculation."

"Did you *see* Susannah make any changes to the contract?"

"No."

"Did she tell you she made any changes to it?"

"No."

"Okay, so how did you react when Susannah told you she was pregnant?"

"I wasn't happy."

"Because you didn't want children?"

"Because she told me it wasn't mine."

Damn! It all came together. It was Professor Plum in the library with the candlestick. Sam was trying to make his client seem like a desperate woman who wanted children so much that when her mean ol' partner refused her, she was forced to go outside her contract to have them.

Sam knew he'd stepped in a doggy pile on that one and looked like he was searching for a way to turn back time. He flipped through his notes for a minute before turning back to Mike.

"If the child *had* been yours, would you have been happy?"

"Objection. Calls for speculation. You are asking him to give a hypothetical reaction to a highly emotional situation. He can't possibly know how he would have reacted in those circumstances." Get 'em, Brad.

Sam didn't look friendly anymore. "I have no more questions."

I don't blame you, Sam. Brad was right. This was very educational.

*

Late that night I was continuing my slow progression of getting the last of my things back in their boxes so that I would be ready for my move on Saturday. True, I never unpacked a ton of stuff, but you certainly do spread out some over the weeks. I pulled up the picture of my perfect little apartment on my phone and felt a thrill of excitement all over again. My phone suddenly buzzed in my hand and scared the crap out of me so I dropped it on the floor. Guess I need to work on those nerves of steel.

I knelt on the floor and bent down looking under the bed. How the hell did it get that far under there? I lay down on my back and reached my arm under the bed until I had my fingers around it.

Lying on the ground still, I looked at my phone and pulled up the text message. Adam. I smiled. I'm alone—not like I need to pretend.

Excited for Saturday?

Nah.

Sure. Not mentally decorating your place or anything?

That would be silly. I'm a grown woman.

Of course Kate.

:)

Lol. So?

So?

Am I helping you move?

Oh. I hadn't even mentioned that to Dave. Probably because I knew if I did he'd insist on helping. And moving in. And planning out the rest of my life.

Haven't mentioned it to Dave.

How has he not brought it up?

Dunno. I suppose he may feel like helping me move is a forgone conclusion.

But you hate that ;)

Indeed.

Well, I'm available to help. I'm not sure my mom will let me out of it even if Dave is there and I try to bail out.

Sweet of her.

Don't kid yourself. She has sinister motives.

Right. Her ill-advised matchmaking.

Very ill-advised.

Thanks a lot.

It's not you, Kate. It's me.

Thank you for that very clichéd breakup line.

Good thing we aren't breaking up.

I smiled and got off the floor and into bed. And left it on that note.

CHAPTER *16*

The next two days blew by. There is definitely something to be said for keeping busy, because each day is kind of a blur from the moment I boot up my computer in the morning, and suddenly it's Friday afternoon. I stopped by Mags's desk on my way out.

"I think my friend Logek and I are going out tonight. Wanna come?" I asked.

She smiled. "Yep. Where to?"

"Not sure yet. Suggestions?"

"Ummm . . . Ravenwood has live music on Friday nights."

"I love that place. Okay, let me run it by Logek. I'll text you. Figure around eight?"

"Sounds good."

I texted Logek on my way to the parking garage that I was on my way to her place. By the time I got to my car, I'd also gotten texts from Adam and Dave, both asking what I was up to. Cue the Death Star music.

I texted them both back the same thing. *Going out with some friends.*

From Dave, *Let me know if you feel the need for a late-night booty call ;)*

From Adam, *Where?*

Probably Ravenwood.

Maybe I'll see you later.

And for tonight's entertainment . . . we have Kate drooling over her unattainable man crush who is determined to constantly dangle himself in front of her nose. Cruel.

I got to Logek's and walked in after my typical single knock.

"Hey!" she said, giving me a quick hug.

"You're in a good mood," I observed.

"Uh-huh," she said, grinning.

"Any particular reason?"

"High on life, Kitty Kat."

"I invited my friend Mags from work."

"Jersey Shore?"

"Yeah. You'll love her."

"Cool. Where are we going?"

"She mentioned that Ravenwood has live music on Fridays . . ."

"Sold. We haven't been there in a while."

I went into her room and opened up my duffel bag so that

I could change my clothes. I slipped off my suit and shimmied into my jeans. I held up two sassy, cleavage-bearing shirts to Logek.

"Ooh . . . red. Slut."

"Is that a vote for the red one? Or just commentary on the fact that I own a red shirt?"

"A vote. And commentary."

"Thanks."

Once I was dressed, Logek insisted on doubling up on my eyeliner and convinced me tonight was a lipstick kinda night. What can I say? The girl could sell ice to Eskimos. So . . . cleavage—check. Too much makeup—check. Bright red lips—check. Definitely time to go out in public.

I texted Mags. *Ravenwood. We're going to take a cab. Do you want to meet us there or come to Logek's and go with us? She lives a few miles away . . . W and 20th . . .*

I might be a little late so I'll meet you there about 9?

Sounds good. See you soon.

"Mags is going to meet us there about nine," I said to Logek.

"K. I called a cab," she said, setting a cocktail on the kitchen counter in front of me. Because you need to warm up before you go out drinking. And here it was free. For me, anyway.

I sipped the gin and tonic she made me. "So what exactly did Derek say?"

She made a shocked face. "Oh my god! Can you believe that? So he actually called, probably because he figured I'd hear about his inheritance—and was super friendly and sweet and actually said he missed me."

"Charming. What was her name again?"

"Exactly. So I asked how Hannah was and he said she was the biggest mistake he ever made, and on and on . . . how could I have ever let someone like you go, blah blah blah. It was a very strange conversation."

"Sounds like. So what did you tell him?"

She rattled the ice in her glass like she was stalling. "I . . . sort of said I would have dinner with him." She said it all whiny and apologetic—appropriately so.

"Logek."

"I know!"

Derek was gorgeous. *Gorgeous,* gorgeous. Model material. Not Adam gorgeous (in my opinion, at least). Come to think of it . . . he was sort of *her* Adam. A beautiful, unattainable heartbreaker. The difference is that she landed *her* Adam . . . and he broke her heart. I'm sure there is a lesson in there for me somewhere. Nah.

"What about Daniel?" I asked.

"We aren't exclusive. And it's just dinner. Totally harmless. Come on—I'm not going to get drawn in by him again. Been there, done that, have the therapy bills to prove it."

"Why do you sound like you're asking for my permission?"

"Because you're my conscience and if you disapprove, it probably means I'm doing something wrong." She pouted.

I laughed. "I really don't think I'm equipped to be anybody's conscience these days."

"Good point. So then I'll just follow you down your reckless path of poor decision-making and hope for the best."

I gaped at her.

She slapped my thigh. "Totally kidding."

"Reckless?"

"Hmm. Untamed, for a change. You are usually so cautious. So controlled. It's nice to see you let loose a little."

I scrunched up my face at her because I couldn't think of a response to that. "When are you having dinner with Derek?"

"Tuesday."

"Good. Weeknights are safer. And don't shave your legs."

"Kate, we were signed for two years. He's felt leg stubble. Pretty sure that will be insufficient to stop me if I'm so moved. Not that I will be."

"Well, you haven't seen him in a few years. Maybe he's completely let himself go. And he could be balding."

"No such luck. After I talked to him, I stalked his Facebook page. Bastard looks better than ever."

"Damn."

"I know. So unfair."

"Does Daniel know you two aren't exclusive?"

"I've tried to drop enough hints that he hasn't brought up the subject. So . . . I think so?"

"Fair enough."

Logek's phone buzzed and she looked at the screen. "Cab's here."

We finished our drinks and headed out the door. We climbed into the back of the yellow cab and Logek engaged in her usual long-lost-friend banter with the cab driver who didn't seem to have an entirely firm grasp on the English language, but did his best to keep up with Logek anyway. When we pulled up outside Ravenwood, he slipped his card to Logek and told her to call him when we needed a ride home.

Ravenwood was more of a bar than a club, thankfully, so there wasn't a line to get in and it tended to weed out the twentysomething, need-to-be-seen crowd. It wasn't too busy yet so we headed to the end of the bar closest to the stage where the band was setting up.

Once we had drinks in hand, Logek and I stepped away from the crowded bar.

"Talked to Jonathan at all?" she asked.

"Not since I told him I needed a time-out."

She nodded, but didn't comment. "Dave is smothering me."

"Poor baby," she said, with a laugh. "Why is that a problem?"

"Because there's the chance he's a manipulative asshole who is so determined to get me into bed that he's pretending to be crazy about me."

"And if he's not a manipulative asshole?"

"Then he's . . . I don't know. It's weird. I don't feel in control of that situation."

"Not always a bad thing."

"I know. You think I'm a control freak."

" 'Cause you are."

"But it's not . . . swept-off-my-feet out of control . . . it's more like caught-in-quicksand out of control."

"I don't follow."

"I feel like I could end up signed to Dave and have two children before I've even figured out if I like him."

"Well, that could be problematic."

"Exactly." I sighed to let her know I needed a little serious Logek time and not just banter. "I don't want a relationship. I don't have any idea what I'm doing. So how is it that Dave has me on the verge of being his girlfriend?"

"You don't sound on the verge."

"I guess I'm not. But . . . he's overwhelming. And in some ways, I do really like him."

"But?"

"But that is outweighed by the ways I feel I don't know him. And the ways I feel he's . . . oppressive."

"I can honestly say I don't think I've ever been in a relationship I would call oppressive."

"Me, either. And I'd like to keep it that way."

Logek clinked my glass, but I could tell she was having trouble mustering up any real sympathy for my situation. Yeah. Poor Kate has this gorgeous sportscaster wanting to rope her into a committed relationship. Oh, the humanity.

"Hi, Kate," I heard from a deep voice behind me. I might have gotten flustered if I hadn't seen Logek's face when it happened. She smiled—but it was more a glow. Derek.

I turned around and there was Derek. I hadn't seen him in a couple of years. Logek was right. He looked fantastic. He's about six feet or six feet one, somewhere in there. He has blond hair, but now it trailed down to his broad shoulders. Okay, picture those covers of romance novels. Now picture the good ones with the guys who don't look like Fabio. It was like that. And so not my thing, but so clearly hers. Shit. She was in deep for all her talk of being in control. I haven't seen Logek light up like that in a while.

"Derek." We shook hands.

"Long time."

"Couple of years. How are you?" I asked.

"Great, actually. Figuring things out finally, I think."

Crap.

"What are you doing these days?"

"About six months ago, a local studio did a show for my photography, so that was amazing. Even sold a couple things," he said, with a modest shrug of his shoulders.

"Good for you," I said (genuine this time), "you have an amazing eye."

"Thank you. I appreciate that. So, Logek tells me you're a lawyer now?"

"True story. Though, how it happened, I have no idea."

Derek's best quality was that he lifted people up, made you feel like more, made you feel . . . like a superhero, sort of. Like what you'd accomplished was not so different from Batman saving Gotham. So, yeah. You liked talking to him. But when you sign with him, apparently he realizes that he needs to lift up a few other women, too, which can severely diminish your superhero persona (as I had to witness first-hand).

"That's amazing. I don't know how you did it. And she said you passed the bar the first time. I hear that's a feat in itself."

I smiled. Yeah. That was pretty cool.

Derek turned and focused on Logek again. He was sort of lit up as well. Inner sigh. If he wasn't a dick who broke her heart before, you'd think they were the perfect couple. They were ridiculously beautiful. They adored each other. But. Always the "but." Unfortunately, I felt like this was becoming an inevitability. This was happening. And Daniel would be heartbroken to be thrown over for her ex, and if (when) Derek broke her heart again, she'd realize how great Daniel was. Well, we can always hope for the best, right? Novel concept.

"So, Derek," I said, drawing his attention back from Logek, "I didn't expect to see you tonight." And, yes, I may have shot Logek an accusatory glance.

"Logek and I were going to do dinner on Tuesday, but she mentioned that you guys were going out tonight. Is it okay that I stopped by?"

No. "Of course."

He smiled and then leaned in next to Logek to order a drink from the bartender. I raised my eyebrows at her. She shrugged, then grinned.

"Speaking of dirty bitches inviting forbidden fruit out to the bar . . ." she said to me quietly.

"Were we?"

"That's how I interpreted it," she said, tipping her chin past my shoulder.

I turned and Adam was crossing the room toward me. And I had all the physical symptoms of the flu. Fever. Chills. Delirium.

When he reached me, I got another friendly hug that I never wanted to end. He reached in and gave Logek a quick hug, too.

When Derek turned back to us from the bar, Logek made introductions. "Derek, this is Adam. Adam, Derek."

They shook hands.

"So, how did you manage to steal this one away from her man?" Derek asked. Perfect. This evening just did a 180.

Adam looked down at me. Then he frowned. He had no idea how to respond to that, apparently.

"He didn't," I said. Kate—saving the day. "Adam is just a friend. And Jonathan dumped me." I grinned at him in the awkward silence. "And now you're all up to speed."

"I'm sorry. I had no idea," Derek said, with all that likable sincerity.

"Well," Adam said. "He dumped her and realized he was a total fuck-up about twenty-four hours later and has been trying to get her back ever since."

"Oh," Derek said, with a slight smile. "That does make more sense."

I looked up at Adam gratefully. He nudged me with his elbow in reply. And it hit me. I didn't just want him, like I'd been telling myself. I liked him. *Liked* him, liked him. I could fall for him. I could love him if I wasn't careful. Love him as much as Jonathan. I took a deep breath and looked back at Logek, and I'd swear she'd followed my train of thought based on the look of pity on her face. Shake it off, girl.

"So what kind of law do you practice, Kate?" Derek asked.

And Derek is now my best friend. Thanks for the redirect. "I'm doing signing law."

"That must be interesting," he said, adding the lilt of a question.

"I hate it, but I needed a job, so here I am."

He laughed. "Oh. Why do you hate it?"

"Because it's mostly handling breaches and everyone is bitter and miserable and there are no winners, only losers."

"Oh," he said thoughtfully. "I guess I could see that. You don't help people write their contracts, then?"

"Not really. So many people use form contacts these days. We have one attorney in the firm that drafts contracts. The rest of us deal with breaches. I guess that tells you something, huh? One attorney drafting contracts and twenty handling breaches."

"Ouch. I guess so."

"I mean, I will be reviewing a new contract—my first one."

"Well, isn't that a positive?" he asked.

"It would be if the woman signing hadn't already been screwed over by this guy before and we all know we're going to be handling her breach in another year."

Oops. Derek looked down at his feet and I got wide eyes from Logek. I didn't mean to provide commentary on their relationship . . . it just happened. Shit.

"That's just one specific couple," I said. Backpedal, baby. I could feel my face growing warmer. At some point, might I actually learn to think before I speak?

Adam must have caught the whiff of awkwardness in the air because he suddenly jumped in with, "Kate actually got punched in the face on her first day with the firm."

Derek looked back up, eyebrows raised, sufficiently diverted.

"Yeah," I said. "Ninety-pound Hispanic gay guy took a swing at his cheating partner and I was in the way."

Derek laughed loudly and Adam rubbed a hand up and down my back. He knew he'd saved me.

"I'm gonna get some Scotch," Adam said. "Anybody want anything?"

We shook our heads (or our glasses) and he bellied up to the bar.

Derek and Logek had locked eyes again and I was feeling like a third wheel. My phone vibrated. Mags! Please be Mags.

I looked at my phone. Jonathan. I hadn't heard from him at all since our dinner last week when I told him I needed space.

I was flipping through the channels and stumbled across an old Twilight Zone *marathon and the episode with that creepy talking doll was on and I thought of you. Not because you're creepy, but because that was your favorite episode ;)*

So cute. I did love that episode. We love that show and they seem to always be playing the old episodes on some random channel.

Talky Tina, I replied.

That's the one :)

I felt a tap on my shoulder and spun around. Mags was standing in front of me, big smile, big hair, little dress.

"I'm so glad you're here!" I said sincerely. I turned to Logek. "Logek, this is Mags."

Mags leaned in and gave her a quick hug. Cute and unexpected.

"So good to meet you," Logek said, grinning. "Kate talks about you constantly. She says you're a ray of sunshine in a dungeon."

Mags laughed. "I wouldn't exactly call it a dungeon. They stopped chaining us to our desks."

"Hey, Mags," Adam said, working his way back from the bar.

"Adam," she said all cool and calm. Why can't I be that cool and calm when I talk to him?

Derek looked at her with appreciation (or maybe fascination—hard to say).

"Derek," he said, extending his hand to her.

"Mags," she said. "Seriously, Kate," Mags said, looking at me again. "Do you grow these men in a lab or something? Real people don't look like this."

We all laughed. God bless Mags.

"Actually, yes. Just put your order in with me and we'll do the rest," I said.

"I'll have to give it some thought," she said. She glanced around. "Where's the rest of your man candy?" Dave. She was asking about Dave. And I believe, to an extent, trying to annoy Adam.

"Just us, tonight," I said. My drink was magically empty, so I held it up and headed toward the bar. Yes. Another drink. Bad decisions. Maybe I can manage another regrettable kiss with Adam. Ugh. The definition of a double-edged sword. So good. So bad.

I set my empty glass on the bar and waited for the bartender to get to me. Mags scooted in next to me.

"So. Adam is here."

"Yep."

"Interesting how he's always around, don't you think?"

"Just felt like getting out, I suppose."

"Of course." And she stared at me.

"What?"

"Don't 'what' me, missy."

"Mags," I said, with a heavy sigh. "Nothing has changed with him. He is exactly the same."

"But you aren't."

I pouted and shook my head. I gave my whole body a shake. "So!" I said brightly. "Do you have a beau?"

She laughed. "A beau?"

"Uh-huh."

"Currently, no. I dated a guy from the office for a couple of years, but we just broke up a few weeks ago."

My eyes sprung open. "A guy from the office?"

She nodded.

"Who?" I asked, putting hands on her upper arms. Oh, yes, she was going to tell me.

"Between you and me?"

That didn't even dignify a response so I just gave her a sneer.

"Brad."

"Brad. Brad? Glasses Brad?"

She made a little crooked smile and nodded.

"I know Brad! Brad gave me boxing gloves."

She laughed. "I know."

"I like Brad. What happened?"

She tipped her head back and forth like she was thinking of an answer. "Just . . . he was great. But a little tame. He's kind of a homebody. I'm sure in a few years when I start to mellow, I'll realize leaving him was the worst mistake ever."

* Subject to the following terms and conditions

"Well, you have to be happy. That's important. Life is too short."

"I was happy. Some of the time."

The bartender appeared in front of us and we ordered. Once we had our drinks in hand, we headed back to the group.

It was obvious Adam and Derek had been doing the typical "What do you do for a living?" exchange.

"Have you done anything I might have seen?" Adam asked him.

"Most of my stuff is more gallery-type photography, but I did do fashion photography for a while."

Adam was nodding. He passed Derek a crisp, white business card. "If you want, send me some of your samples. We only have a few photographers we use for campaigns, and we're always looking to add some diversity. Some of our clients are looking for more of that gallery-art look."

Derek took the card. "That would be amazing. Thank you."

Adam looked at me. "So what time do you expect to be out to your new place in the morning?"

"Your mom is meeting me there at nine . . . so nine," I finished, smiling.

"Your mom?" Mags asked.

"Yep. His mom is my new landlord."

She chuckled. "Small world."

"Any other company?" he asked.

I shrugged.

He frowned at me just a little, keeping it subtle. Eagle Eye Mags, however, misses very little.

"Not excited to spend the morning watching Dave hang on your girl?"

Okay. I realize I'm like a five-year-old when I drink and every little thought just spills right out. But I'm pretty sure Mags is sober, making her the grand-prize winner in the prob-ably-shouldn't-blurt-this-out-but-what-the-hell department.

He just laughed. "I am rather particular when it comes to Kate."

"I noticed," she said. "Although, 'particular' wasn't the word I would have used."

Mags and Adam looked at each other quietly, as though they were communicating telepathically. I was a little worried this much scrutiny of his behavior toward me might make him try harder to keep his distance. That would suck. I kinda liked him best when he was contradicting himself.

"Would you two like to be alone?" I asked them.

Mags laughed and gave Adam a pat on the arm. "You're a good man, Charlie Brown."

Adam shook his head, smiling. Yeah. None of us knew what to make of her, but she certainly keeps things lively.

"I'm going to run to the bathroom," I said. "Be right back."

After hitting the little girls' room, I headed back toward the group still gathered near the bar.

Adam was AWOL and Logek and Derek looked like they were solving world hunger or something. Not really the kind of conversation you want to interrupt.

"Where did Adam go?" I asked Mags.

She shrugged. "I assumed he was following you like he seems to do most of the time."

I laughed. "If only." I glanced around the bar, but didn't see him anywhere. "So, tell me more gossip about Jared Mann. Why did you say he was cruel?"

"Because he has fired two secretaries in the time that I've been there and he's made every one of his secretaries cry."

"Really?"

"Yeah. Don't let his Dr. Jekyll fool you. You'll meet Mr. Hyde. Well, you're an attorney, so it most likely won't be *directed* at you, but you'll see him lay into someone else."

"Something to look forward to."

"I don't know much about his personal life. I'm not even sure he has one. I think he works most of the time."

"Well, he said he's not signed, but that most signing attorneys aren't. Does he actually like girls?"

Mags laughed. "Yeah. Pretty sure he does. Didn't you say he stares at you all the time?"

"Yeah, but not like that. More like it's a bad habit and he doesn't realize he's doing it."

"Oh, I think he realizes *everything* he's doing."

An interesting-looking guy of about thirty tapped Mags on her shoulder, smiling. Interesting-looking in that he was wearing heavy-rimmed glasses and reminded me a little of Brad.

She smiled at him as he made his awkward introduction. He asked if he could buy her a drink and she took a long pause and nodded.

She winked at me and headed to the bar with the guy. I glanced over at Logek and she and Derek were still engrossed in conversation. I started feeling self-conscious standing there by myself with no one to talk to. Yes, I'm a thirty-four-

year-old woman. I should get over it. It's on my to-do list. I
scanned around again, looking for Adam. Then I found him.

He was a ways down the bar talking to a woman. A beautiful woman. She was petite with dark hair that fell to the
middle of her back. She laughed as she talked to him, touching her fingertips to her chest. Please. He's not that funny.

Adam smiled that Adam smile and leaned down closer to
her. I knew that move. I'd been on the receiving end of that
move. And it made me want to throw up. I couldn't look
away. I watched them like I was watching a car wreck—
horrible, grotesque, and captivating.

She put her hand on his upper arm and I could see the
token on her bracelet. Contract killer. How could you forget, Kate? That's who he is. You've deluded yourself that he's
someone else, but he never lied about who he was. Tears
burned behind my eyes as he smiled down at her and snaked
his arm around her tiny waist.

I am the stupidest woman alive. I have a great guy I could
be with. A guy who wants to be with me. Someone who
makes me happy. Not someone that makes me feel this
way—this terrible. Pull it together, Kate. Deep breaths. Don't
lose your shit. Don't, don't, don't. My phone buzzed. Yes.
Check your phone. Look away. Don't cry. He only wanted to
be your friend. He was clear. You're the one who turned it into
something else. Shit. A tear ran down my cheek. I knew all
of these things. Practically. But my insides had clearly been
feeling differently.

I read the text. *Wishing I could see you.*

Time to get your head straight, Kate. Time to get the hell

out of La-La Land and back into the real world. Where there are real men who want you—not imaginary ones.

Ready to leave.

Need a ride? I could come get you.

Yes.

I passed Logek and pointed toward the door. She frowned and I shook my head. She walked up to me quickly, cutting off my exit.

I took a deep breath and smiled. "I'm fine. I've got to get up early and get my dad's truck loaded and be out here by nine."

She just looked at me, expressionless.

"And Adam is in contract killer mode and I can't stick around to watch."

"Oh," she said. "Well, let's go."

"No. You stay. Definitely. I have a ride coming."

"You sure? You look so sad."

Shit. So much harder not to cry when someone calls attention to it. I shook my head, eyes open wide, doing my best impersonation of the girl who didn't want to go into the bathroom and have a wicked meltdown.

"Okay. I'll see you in the morning," she said, rubbing her hands up and down my arms.

I nodded.

"At your new place," she said brightly, trying to make me smile. I faked it for her. Yay. New place.

She hugged me and headed back to where Derek stood, watching us. He smiled and waved. I waved back and turned back toward the door.

I looked toward the dance floor and Mags was dirty

dancing with the same guy, having a good time. I'll just text her later. Another tear rolled down my cheek.

Shit! Why am I getting this upset? I knew I didn't have him. That I'd never have him. I guess I didn't know everything I thought I did. Or maybe my head and my heart weren't communicating much these days. I headed toward the door. Apparently a little too fast because I caught my heel on the stupid rug in front of the door and stumbled, causing the bouncer to reach out and save my dumb ass before I wound up on the ground face-first.

"Whoa. You okay?"

I nodded, but he was looking at me closely, undoubtedly assuming I was wasted. Nope. Just feeling like a waste.

"You need a cab?" he asked. His subtle way of making sure I wasn't driving.

"I have a ride coming. Thanks," I said, giving him a hasty smile and heading for the door. Not even going to turn around to see if anyone else caught that spectacle. Let's just assume they did. 'Cause that's how my luck rolls these days.

"Kate." The voice was deep and more tears spilled out of my eyes. Perfect. He'll think I've lost my frickin' mind. Your strictly platonic "friend" is getting it on with another woman and you fall apart? Pretty sure that violates some of the rules.

I brushed away the tears as subtly as I could and tried to pat my cheeks dry in case he saw me. I acted like I didn't hear him and kept walking.

I walked outside to the sidewalk and Adam wrapped his hand around my upper arm firmly.

"Kate."

Okay. I probably look normal. Maybe. He turned me around to face him.

I raised my eyebrows like I didn't know why he was stopping me.

"What's the matter, Kate?"

I shrugged, not trusting my voice. Calm, girl. "Nothing. Just have to be up early so I felt like going home."

"I can drive you."

"I have a ride coming."

He frowned. "Kate."

"Adam."

He shook his head.

"It's fine. I'm just tired."

"Bullshit. You were practically sprinting out of there."

Oh, good. I would have hated for him to miss the show. My turn to just shake my head.

He wrapped his hands around my upper arms and pulled me closer to him. "Tell me what to do, Kate."

"Nothing."

"Nothing?" The streetlight was illuminating his face and his green eyes glowed.

"Nothing to do."

And we stared at each other. His hands still holding me close.

"Kate, I can't have a friendship that's as restrictive as a relationship."

"I realize that."

"So tell me what to do."

Love me.

His shoulders slumped a little as though he could read my

mind. He sighed and leaned down and rested his forehead against mine.

"I don't know what to do with you, Kate," he whispered.

I glanced over my shoulder. "My ride is here," I said, pulling back from him. He immediately loosened his grip and let go, stuffing his hands into the pockets of his jeans.

"Kate," he said quietly.

"Good night, Adam," I said. And I turned away and walked to the curb, to where my ride had stopped in front of me. I looked at my reflection in the window as I reached for the door handle and took a deep breath. I could see Adam's blurry silhouette in the reflection behind me, standing still, watching me leave.

Time to let go of the nonsense, Kate. Time to move on.

To Be Continued . . .

ABOUT THE AUTHOR

ERIN LYON is a practicing attorney who spends her free time writing fiction about lawyers. *I Love You Subject to the Following Terms and Conditions* is her debut novel.

www.erinlyon.net